# THE DUST OF DAWN

## ELOISE J. KNAPP

THE DUST OF DAWN
The Dust Series, Book 1

Editing by Jonathan Lambert and Aaron Sikes. Cover art and formatting by EK Cover Design

www.EloiseJKnapp.com

This one is dedicated to you.

You, the person who still loves the feel and smell of a paperback. You love dead trees, huh?

You, the person who won this on my fan page or bought it at a convention. I guess I successfully tricked you into thinking I was a great storyteller.

You, Grandma—my only family member who has read every one of my books. And still tells all her friends how proud she is of me even though I write about zombies and guns and the end of the world most of the time.

You, unsuspecting person I know in real life who thought, "oh she seems nice, yeah I'll read her book and support her, how cool" then never look at me the same way in the hallway again. Assuming you read this book at all. Let's see if you make it past chapter 3. If you do, let me know.

You, 11 year old version of myself who hated reading and writing and spelled "humorous" "humeress" on a spelling test in a fit of drama, provoking a laugh from your aunt who said, "you can do better." Laura, I hope I've done better. I wrote 7 books. Does that count? I still have a problem with run-on sentences though. We should work on that.

You, the 27 year old version of myself who thought you had no more stories to tell. You still do.

# JACK

"I wish you would've come out here, Jack. We wanted to see you."

"Before we all die?" Jack regretted it the moment he said it. He was nearing forty and still causing his stepmother grief. He imagined her cringing, crow's feet deepening around her eyes, the phone pressed against her papery cheek. "I'm sorry, Leanne."

"It's fine. I just wanted to call you one last time."

"I know."

In a matter of hours, Jack and everyone else on Earth would be dead. But before that, he would kill the man who murdered his daughter and that's all that mattered to him.

The truth still surprised him each time he lingered on it. It was only a year ago that NASA had announced the discovery of an extinction-level comet hurtling towards Earth. They spotted it near Jupiter and said it would reach them in about a year. In the very same press conference they said Zabat's Comet would safely pass by Earth. It was supposed to be beautiful when it appeared, visible by most of the northern hemisphere.

About eight months later, the news broke that the comet had changed course. The public went into total shock. When Jack watched the president's address, he thought he had to be hallucinating. Most of the president's words blurred together in a sugarcoated haze. But—like everyone else watching—Jack had heard what the man was really saying.

Zabat's Comet was going to hit Earth in three months. Everyone was going to die.

On the rare occasions Jack ventured to the bar, he had heard people talking about their end of the world plans, their regrets, how fast they'd die. Would the impact kill them, or the aftermath? Then reality settled in and nobody brought it up, almost as though if they didn't say the words out loud, maybe it would change things. That maybe they'd survive. That their superstition and wishful thinking would cause another solar flare to nudge the comet out of its trajectory towards Earth. Or that it would magically disappear. Leanne, his stepmother, was one of these.

"Honey, where are you?"

"Just driving," Jack lied. He slowed down his pickup as he scanned the ravaged city for an intact street sign. The thick, oily scent of smoke and destruction was giving him a headache. He closed the air vents.

"I don't think that's a good idea," she said. "You know it isn't safe out there."

She was right. It *wasn't* safe. It didn't take long for the country to collapse into chaos once everyone knew they had three months to live. Once the food shortages and looting started, feelings turned primal and violent. It only took a month before the "every man for himself" mentality took hold.

After another address from the president and harsh enforcement of martial law, the chaos stabilized to tolerable levels. Of course, it couldn't last. How could it? The closer the comet got, the quicker civilization unraveled. Jack knew many people who packed their camping gear and left so they could avoid it all.

Not him. Not when he had unfinished business.

The medium-sized town of Monroe, Washington was what he expected. Roads were blocked with abandoned cars. Recent fires had raged through the strip mall to his right. A few suites were still smoldering. The smoke was thick here; Jack almost couldn't see the sky. Just ashy fog overhead with the occasional glimpse of clouds. Every store was picked clean, from jewelry to electronics to groceries.

People saw the opportunity to have everything they'd ever wanted, and they took it. Jack was just surprised it had taken three months to overthrow civilization as he knew it; he would have bet on two.

"Did you hear me? It isn't safe out there."

"I know. I needed to clear my mind."

"Tell me you've at least been eating?"

"I've gotten enough, yeah," Jack said.

In protest of the lie, Jack's stomach rumbled. He hadn't eaten a decent meal for a week. Jerky, nuts, and whatever canned goods he had left made up most of his diet and left much to be desired. Grocery stores in his city had stopped being restocked months ago. Scavenging was difficult and carried too much risk. He never kept much food around his apartment anyway. He'd been carefully rationing what he had left. Just enough to get him to Doomsday.

"You sound just like your father," Leanne said absently.

He shook his head and leaned forward, ignoring the stomach pain. Idling in the street wasn't safe. He entered an intersection and looked for a street sign. He found one, bent over a wrecked yellow Corvette, the sign itself stuck in the hood of the car. The beautiful sports car was missing all its tires, and a grotesque penis wearing a bowler hat had been spray painted on its side.

Leanne was now talking about Jack's father's favorite casserole, but Jack cut her off. It was time for him to go. "I have to hang up now. Thank you for raising me after mom died, Leanne."

"I love you, sweetie. You know you've always been a true

son to me. Are you sure you can't drive out? There's time. We've got the generator running. We're going to watch a movie and—"

"I love you, too." Jack hung up. He tossed his phone on the passenger side floor, already feeling guilty about cutting her off.

Growing up, Jack called Leanne names and fought with his dad endlessly as a teenager. He never understood how his father could get over his first wife so quickly. After his dad died, Jack had patched things up with Leanne. She was the only family he had. Maybe he should have driven out.

Movement caught his attention. On the sidewalk to his right, a man was pulling a woman by her hair, kicking and screaming, out of the frozen yogurt shop. Her naked flesh caught on shattered glass as he dragged her, leaving a bloody trail. He walked with confidence, like it was just another day. For him, maybe it was.

Jack clenched his jaw and pressed the gas pedal, turning his gaze away. He reminded himself everyone was going to die soon. Saving that woman from another few hours of suffering was pointless. It wasn't his problem.

He had only one problem—and he was about to solve it.

Before the end came, Jack was going to get revenge. With no one to stop him, no one to talk him down, and no repercussions, killing Stewart Grange was the only thing that made sense. It was the one piece of light left in this dark world, and he *would* have it.

Jack imagined for the thousandth time what it would feel like to point the gun at Stewart's head and pull the trigger. The flood of sweet relief and vindication. When the comet hit, he would die in peace knowing he killed the man who'd snuffed out his daughter's life. That's why he had called Leanne. He wanted to tell her what he was going to do, but as soon as she answered the phone he couldn't bring himself to do it.

Jack turned left, off the main highway that split the town in half. His pickup lurched over steep speed bumps as he entered an apartment complex which consisted of low-income housing painted a garish shade of yellow. He found building C. The windows on the first story were covered with plywood. The same talented artist had spray painted more monstrous phalli, these with smiley faces. Below one of the windows, a dead body lay bloated. Two crows picked at its flesh.

Jack retrieved his well-cared for Glock 40 from the passenger seat and tucked it into the holster at his hip. A bottle of whiskey rolled away from his grasping hand, but eventually he managed to snatch it up from the floor and finish it off. The liquid burned his throat as it went down and warmed him from the inside. He took a deep breath and exited his truck, not bothering to lock it.

Outside, the smoke made him cough. His eyes stung. He brought the collar of his jacket over his mouth and dashed to the entrance of the apartment, which gaped open into blackness. Without the white noise of his truck's engine, he heard the sounds of a city gone to hell in its last hours of life. Screaming, near and far. Some were screams of pain, some crazed, and some perhaps of ecstasy.

One building over, a group of figures approached. They carried baseball bats and crowbars, smashing up cars. Purple bandanas covered their mouths and noses. Jack had seen these kinds of gangs before, in his own town. They mowed down anything they saw.

Jack darted inside. It was an old building with no elevator. Not like he could've used it anyway: the power was out in all of Monroe from what he'd seen coming in.

There were feces and urine stains on the staircase,

along with discarded food wrappers and an abundance of used needles. Jack choked from the smell as he placed his steps carefully. Despite his best efforts, he slipped once and banged his knee hard against the steps.

He reached the second story and came upon the body of an old Hispanic woman wrapped in a patchwork blanket. At first he thought she was dead, but then he saw faint movement in her chest. Her eyes fluttered open as he stepped by her.

"Tienes comida? Por favor, ayúdame."

Jack shook his head. He didn't know what she said but it didn't matter. "I can't help you."

Her lips quivered. She pulled the blanket tighter around herself.

Jack kept walking. He'd steeled himself against the world ten years ago when Stewart Grange took Katie away from him and the The Ex—*Colleen*—left him. She didn't grieve their daughter as much as he did. She turned to God and away from Jack. Hell, she remarried barely a year after they split. To him it felt like she wanted to forget about Katie entirely.

And to top it off, Grange got off with an easy, short sentence due to the incompetence of the police and the lawyers. The murderer had walked free and Jack receded into his own prison. He had shunned his friends and eventually stopped going to work.

Jack ascended another two flights of stairs and found 4C. The door was closed. He tested the handle and found it unlocked. Withdrawing the Glock, he paused to take a deep breath.

The apartment opened up into one living space that was bathed in muted light from two windows. There was a single couch against a wall. To his right was a bathroom, to the left a bedroom. Jack barely registered the sparse furnishing. The man kneeling in the center of the room was the reason he was there.

Only he wasn't what Jack expected. Ten years ago, Stewart Grange had been a scrawny meth addict. His teeth were rotten, some missing, and his thin body was covered in sores. When they showed photos of his trailer where he kept Katie, it was full of junk and grime. Kiddie porn, crack pipes, and massive heaps of fast food containers. There was no remorse on his face during the trials, just outrage that they were accusing him of the murder when he swore it was an unnamed, unidentifiable accomplice who had done the deed.

Now Stewart prayed to a simple wooden cross mounted on the wall in front of him. He'd gained twenty pounds and wore a frumpy gray sweater and stained khaki pants. His feet were bare, the heels cracked and dark brown. Just as Jack entered the room, Stewart finished a Hail Mary and looked up from his rosary beads. He'd had his teeth fixed at some point, though they'd gotten yellow and dark around the gum line since.

He still had tattoos creeping up his neck that hinted at what his life had been before.

"I prayed you would come," Stewart said.

Jack's heart skipped a beat. He lifted the gun and kept it pointed at Stewart's head as he reached behind himself to close and lock the door.

"What did you say?"

"For years I've prayed for forgiveness for what I did to your daughter. To all the children I hurt by looking at those bad pictures. Then when God sent the comet to carry out His judgment, I prayed I'd see you again so I could tell you." Stewart smiled gently. "To tell you I am sorry for what I did. I know I'll pay for my crimes in the next life. I ask for your forgiveness."

For a split second Jack's conviction faltered. Like a shimmering mirage, he saw the possibility of an outcome where both of them left this apartment alive. As quick as it came, it was gone. Jack gripped the gun and took a step closer to Stewart.

"Forgive you?" Jack felt tears welling as he remembered the autopsy report. His stomach was in knots. "You want *me* to forgive *you*? How in the fuck could I do that?"

Stewart turned his gaze to the cross. "Because that is what He wants us to do. Only through forgiveness can we truly have peace."

"You're fucking insane. You know where my peace is going to come from? Putting a bullet between your eyes."

"I didn't kill her," Stewart answered, almost reflexively, his peaceful tone turning defensive. "The torture and the murder wasn't me. I won't apologize for that because I didn't do it. I only wanted to keep her and look at her. Her skin was so dark. She looked like a baby jaguar. So beautiful."

"You shut the fuck up about my daughter! That bullshit story about some other guy being the murderer may have worked on the jury, but it won't work on me."

"I was a victim in the judicial system. The evidence that would prove me innocent *or* guilty was mishandled and tainted. I still served time for what I did wrong. I'm paid up according to man's law."

"Jesus, shut up! I know your story. I know every fucking word of it. It won't help you now."

A thick silence grew between them. Jack's heart thundered in his chest.

Stewart blinked slowly and then broke the silence. "Have you ever killed a man before, Jack?"

"I've never had a good reason to until you." Jack's body was overloading on adrenaline. It pulsated in his veins, making his body feel tingly and his eyes twitch. "My whole life was ruined because of you. This is my last chance to get justice for myself and Katie."

Stewart shook his head. He was still kneeling on the stained carpet. His shoulders were relaxed and his face blank, almost serene. It made Jack want to beat his head in. He'd come here to find a meth-addled child killer. Not this religious nut who called for forgiveness, who admitted what he had done was wrong.

"This isn't what you want to hear, Jack, but though I hurt your daughter in my own way, you destroyed your own life. At church I've seen people experience tremendous loss. They turn to their fellowship and to God for comfort. They do not self-destruct. That's on you."

A flash of anger swelled inside Jack. He closed the distance between him and Stewart and kicked the man in the side. Stewart yelped and fell over, clutching his ribs. Jack kicked him again and this time heard something crack.

Stewart deserved to die; that had been Jack's mantra for years now. He called on it now to carry him through.

"This whole thing is a joke. You haven't found Jesus. I know what kind of person you are."

"You know that killing me isn't right."

"Maybe it isn't," Jack admitted. "But I don't believe in an afterlife. I regret this, I won't have to live with it for very long."

Jack remembered his daughter's small body, gray and lifeless in the morgue. When he had touched her face it was rubbery and cold.

The gun was heavy in his hand. He walked in front of Stewart and brought it up to the man's forehead. Let the muzzle press into his flesh.

"You don't want to do this, Jack. I know you don't." His quivering voice betrayed the calm look on his face. "I can prove to you I didn't kill Katie. Look in th—"

Jack pulled the trigger.

Stewart's body sprawled on the ground like was making a snow angel. A halo of blood soaked the carpet around his head. Jack stared at him and waited. Justice was supposed to feel good. He was supposed to enjoy peace for these last few hours on earth. While he did feel a strong sense of relief, a rotten, dark dread lurked just behind it, swallowing up all the good.

If anyone deserved to die, it was Stewart. But standing there, right then, watching blood spread across the carpet, drove home the truth. Jack was a murderer now, too. He had just shot someone point-blank in the head.

His stomach convulsed. Jack dashed to the sink where he spewed the whiskey he'd been drinking all day. His body shook so hard he had to set the gun down and grip the counter for support.

A drink would calm his nerves.

After wiping his mouth and smoothing back his hair, he set the gun on the counter and began searching for alcohol. He opened kitchen drawers and cupboards. He searched the fridge, the pantry. He found a few cans of soup and a box of wafer cookies. Jack moved to the bedroom, where he tore out every article of clothing just because it felt good. Nothing. Jack returned to the living room. He ignored Stewart's body as he checked the couch.

Then he noticed a narrow drawer on the coffee table. A wad of duct tape made a makeshift handle. Looked like a good hiding spot. Jack gave it a tug, and the drawer slid open.

There was a heavy manila envelope resting on top of a stack of *700 Club* DVDs. He picked it up with one hand and dumped out the contents. Case files cascaded onto the table and floor. He'd seen them before during the trial. He skimmed the printouts of articles from the web.

Jack snatched one up. It was about a murder in southern Washington, near Olympia.

Stewart had been in prison for four months when it happened.

The details were familiar. A girl kept in a small cage, molested, abused, then killed. Bile rose up in Jack's throat again. He dropped the article and found another. It was dated two years after Katie's death. This one was in Oregon. Stewart had taken a yellow highlighter to the articles, marking up similarities to Katie's death. Both involved cages or confined spaces and sexual assault.

Two more articles told similar stories. On separate occasions in Seattle, college sophomores were abducted and held hostage. One was held in a narrow closet, the other a foot locker. Both were raped. Unlike the girls, these women lived. They were gagged and blinded the whole time and could not identify the man who took them.

Up until the end, Stewart had held true to his innocence. What if he hadn't killed Katie? What if there *really had been* another guy?

Jack set the last article down and sat on the couch. He looked out the window, through the hazy smoke, to the parking lot below. The gang from earlier had surrounded his truck and were slashing its tires and breaking the windows. A second gang came and picked a fight with them. The battle raged furiously for twenty minutes until both sides ran away.

Suddenly, the apartment began to shake. It was barely noticeable at first, but it grew until the building wobbled and the walls cracked. It was time. Jack took a deep breath and closed his eyes. Guilty or innocent, it didn't matter now. Nothing did. He was ready to die.

# LARA

Lara lit another candle and set it on the toilet lid. She surveyed the bathroom. It looked romantic. A bottle of Zinfandel was open, a glass already poured beside the bathtub. Since there was no power, she'd had to boil every pot of water with her camp stove and fireplace before putting it in the tub. At least the water still worked.

Her favorite book of Tennyson poems—the very same copy she had in college—waited beside the wine. It was a beautifully composed scene in which to spend the last moments of her life. With no windows, she wouldn't see what was coming. The wine would help her relax. Maybe she would even fall asleep before the comet hit. And the poems brought her immense joy. It was a good way to go.

She felt a tightness start above her heart and work its way into her throat. The props in the scene she created weren't adequate substitutes for being with people she loved. Her siblings lived across the country and had families of their own to spend their last days with. They'd invited her to come out and stay with them, but the freeways were clogged and the threats associated with driving were too numerous, especially for a woman on her own. Flying was out of the question. Even if she made it to the airport, the inflation on airfare was well beyond what she could afford. There were simply too many people trying to get everywhere all at once to see their loved ones or cross off one last item on their bucket lists. Of course, all of that hinged on pilots even showing up to work.

At least she had the chance to talk to her brothers and sisters before the phones went out. Those conversations had been some of the most honest and vulnerable she'd ever experienced. They talked about Dad, about growing up. Dreams they never achieved and unexpected ones they did. Things they despised each other for, or little moments of gratitude they never expressed. At the end of the world, the bonds between them had grown stronger than they'd been in years.

Her hand drifted to the purple and green bruises on her arms. Reconnecting with her brothers and sisters wasn't the only achievement she'd made in the face of doomsday. The house was missing its other inhabitant: her husband.

She grabbed the wine and took a swig straight from the bottle. The glass was fogged from the steamy bath water, making it slick against her fingers.

Harry was gone for good, and she accepted that with pride and absolution. Had he still been there, he would've just kept taking out his anger about the comet, about everything, on her. It's what her dad would've done, too. She'd made countless promises to herself over the years not to let men like that into her life. Those promises had been met with failure. But not anymore.

Lara squeezed her eyes shut, hard enough to see a static pattern of colors on her eyelids. The memory of what had driven her to cast Harry out of her life once and for all had haunted her for weeks. They had decided to drive to Hedone. Some of their neighbors had gone, and Harry had been curious. And wasn't she, an open minded woman, also interested in seeing such a sight? She'd never said no to Harry before, and in the face of certain death, she'd decided she was curious, too. She agreed to go.

Hedone was a twenty-mile drive southwest of their home in Monroe in a lake-side town called Kirkland.

Thousands of people had flocked to the impromptu party city to indulge in non-stop drugs, sex, and music. Lara had been mildly impressed by the choice of nickname, Hedone, after the Greek goddess of pleasure. It was supposed to be a safe, pleasure-fueled place to spend your last months. Maybe it had been that way once, but by the time they decided to check it out, Hedone was horrifying. Lara saw things she wished she could erase from her mind forever. Harry had insisted they go into the town hall, following a steady stream of people. There had been an orgy inside, a sea of damp flesh, slapping and grinding. Cries of ecstasy and pain intermingled to a point where there was no differentiation. While the majority of the participants had been exuberantly consensual, she wasn't sure about all of them.

A middle-aged man with a cross tattooed on his chest had pulled Lara to the ground and tried to get her clothes off. He was frenzied, his eyes wild, pupils dilated. She clawed at him until he released her, but she'd sustained a black eye and a deep scratch on her neck in the process.

After Lara had gotten to her feet and stepped away, awareness spread across the man's face. "I'm…I'm so sorry! I thought you wanted it rough. A lot of these chicks do."

She hadn't known what to say. Neither had he. He'd frowned and offered up his hands in a gesture of apology, then slipped away into the crowd.

Harry had been watching two girls joyously flog each other, oblivious to Lara's ordeal as he rubbed his crotch with a fevered, distant look in his eyes.

The drive back had been quiet. It gave Lara plenty of time to think about how she wanted to spend her last moments. If it couldn't be with her family, it sure as hell wouldn't be with a man she despised.

When they got home, she told him to leave and never

come back. Harry didn't put up a fight. He'd wanted to go back to Hedone anyway.

How easy it had been to get him out of her life. She was a *therapist* and it took her until the end of the world to follow her own advice. How pitiful.

Lara shook away the memory of Hedone and tried to focus on the present. She closed the bathroom door and stripped off her clothes. She stepped into the lavender-scented bath and hissed as the warm water engulfed her. Steam soothed her tired eyes.

The day of reckoning had arrived. Before the electricity had gone out, she synced her watch with the doomsday timer all the news channels ran. In exactly one hour, a comet three miles across was going to smash into Seattle. When it hit, it would obliterate everything within a six hundred mile radius. It would cause tsunamis. The ash it would generate would block out the sun across the planet. Eventually, almost all living organisms would die.

Three miles. When she'd first heard the number, it hadn't seemed like a lot. That was the loop she jogged on weekends at the lake, or the distance to walk to the strip mall to get a sub. But when it was hurtling towards Earth at insane speeds, it carried the force of dozens of nuclear bombs.

She dunked her head under for a moment and then came up. Water trailed down her face. A tired, forlorn smile found its way to her lips.

Lara took comfort in knowing there was no escape. For her, for Harry, for anyone. If there'd been some shred of hope that a few might survive, in a hidden bunker or a remote corner of the world, she would've been depressed. But since the whole earth was doomed, she decided to let it be what it was.

She sipped at her Zinfandel, opened her book, and

began to read. She savored the words more than ever, the last she'd ever read. Her bathwater went cold, but she stayed. Her body pruned and her head felt big and fuzzy from the wine.

Then the shaking began. Water sloshed in the tub. Her wine glass toppled over and shattered on the tile. Lara heard a series of thunderous booms outside. Gently at first, then they picked up in speed to every few seconds. The TV had said pieces of debris would hit the earth before the main impact. She imagined them leveling her neighbors' houses. Maybe one was headed for her.

Lara took deep breaths. When the comet hit, her death would be virtually instant. There would be no pain.

The rumbling reached a crescendo and then....

She opened her eyes. Silence. Then, faintly, the soft pattering of what sounded like rain. She got out of the bath and wrapped a towel around herself. She opened the bathroom door, stepped into the hallway, and looked up.

The skylight was covered in yellow dust.

# DAN

Dan lay on the bed, staring at Chrissy's flat tits. He wished Bianca was still around. She had the biggest rack ever, and he was almost certain that they were real. Not like that mattered too much to him. Real tits or not—if a chick was hot and stacked, she was hot and stacked. At least Chrissy had a pretty face. She had long blond hair—definitely not natural, since her carpet didn't match her drapes—and a decent ass.

Trading Bianca for the six rocks of meth had been worth it. He and Chrissy had been high for days. At first they thought they'd have enough to get them to the last day. They wanted to be rolling and fucking as the comet came down and drove them straight into hell. But self-control was something Dan didn't have, and they'd used most of it already. He was so strung out he couldn't get it up and Chrissy didn't seem interested anyway.

He was feeling shitty. Dan rolled off the bed. His foot came down on Chrissy's calf but she barely made a sound. He ground his heel into it, harder and harder, until finally she whimpered and curled up into a ball. Satisfied, he got up and wandered into the kitchen.

A trace of irritation made him clench his jaw. Why bother looking? There was no food. When they came to Hedone they had a few bags of chips and some canned fruit. It seemed like a lot when they put it in the motel kitchenette, but they ate everything in two days. The closer they got to the last day, the less eating mattered anyway. When they left the motel to wander the city looking for fun, there was plenty of drugs but no food. Nothing to drink. People were beginning to crash from weeks of nonstop partying.

Dan remembered how he went into a 7-11 convenience store early on. No food on the shelves, but he did find a guy jacking off to a *People* magazine in the empty candy aisle. That shit was desperate. There was a fucking *Cosmo* two shelves away. The guy had a bulging duffel bag beside him.

"You got any food?" Dan had asked. His hand was on the 9mm in his waistband.

The guy had grunted and continued handling himself. "Nope."

"What's in the bag then?"

"My wife."

The whole thing left him spooked. That weirdo had been dead fucking serious. Dan had taken the girls and went to the motel to chill until the last day.

When *was* the last day? He'd lost track of time a while ago. He searched his brain for any landmarks in his memory. When he went to the town hall to trade Bianca for drugs, someone had said there was a week until the comet hit. He tapped his fingers on the fridge as he counted the days. It looked like today was the day. Probably.

He turned on the faucet. The pipes groaned. A trickle of water came out but was gone before he managed to get his mouth to it to suck up the few precious drops. He kicked the cupboard and leaned against the counter.

Dan was satisfied with his accomplishments during the last few months of total shitfaced abandon. His parole officer, and law enforcement in general, were gone. People like him could get away with anything. Stealing, fights in bars that went too far. He had walked into a high end watch store, broke a display case, and took a Rolex. The salesperson tilted his head, looked from the case to Dan, then took two for himself and walked out of the store. It was hilarious and left Dan in a good mood for the rest of the day.

Then came Hedone. He wasn't sure what the name meant, but it sounded bitchin'. Dan had heard about it from a guy he was buying some weed from. Hedone had devoted itself to a non-stop End of Days party. It sounded like heaven on earth. Dan hijacked a car and went there the same day.

It was everything he'd dreamed of. Every girl he found was ready and willing to fuck him for nothing, and they didn't care where he wanted to stick it. At one point, he'd wandered into the town hall and had three chicks on him at once. Whatever drug you could dream of was available for the right price. That's when Dan started keeping a harem of girls—and some guys, too—to trade. Like a well-trained dog breeder, he knew how to pick his bitches.

Then shit got a little rough at Hedone and they split back to the motel on the outskirts of town. It wasn't all fun and games anymore. It kinda reminded him of prison or high school. Not all the fresh meat came willingly. The price of everything—booze, drugs, chicks, food—was high, and the currency was other people.

Unfortunately, he'd run out of girls fast. Bianca was his last good bargaining chip. Chrissy was just too flat and sickly looking. No one ever wanted her. Her sister had been better, but she was dead.

The thought of Diane made him look at the bathroom; that's what the smell was. He'd almost forgotten they had stashed her body in the tub. Diane OD'd, that stupid bitch. Took more than her share of the smack, when they had it, and killed herself.

Dan smirked. Maybe he had time to trade her body to someone at town hall.

He paused and remembered that the last time he'd fucked a really old corpse, it was nasty. He'd never do that again. But there had to be some necros somewhere who would. Spray some fucking Febreeze on her and she'd be good to go. Or not. Maybe necros got off on the smell, too.

That plan was quickly forgotten when he checked on her. She'd fall apart if he moved her, she was so rotten and juicy.

He returned to the bed and retrieved his last rock. He prepared it with care and smoked all of it. When Chrissy smelled it, she woke up and tried to get a hit, but he kicked her away until she gave up and watched from the corner. With the split lip he'd given her and all the drool, she was totally pathetic. It made Dan feel good to make her watch. He blew smoke her way and watched as she scrambled to inhale it, like it would do her any good.

When the motel started rumbling, he dropped his pipe and ran outside to look up at the sky. It was time. Thousands of tiny, fiery meteors came from the sky. Most burned up. Some were big enough that they stayed intact. The ground shook as they hit the city around him.

Zabat's Comet broke through the clouds, hung there for a split second…and then broke the fuck apart. Slabs of rock fell and a giant, swarming cloud of dust stretched outward from it in every direction as far as Dan could see. From the center of the cloud, a sparkling, diamond-like object the size of a car plummeted towards the surface. It was shaped like an egg, with blue and white lights flashing on the tip of the thing. At least a hundred beams of light soared away from it in a perfect circle. Dan lost sight of it as it fell behind a building. Then there was nothing but the massive dust cloud.

The way the dust moved unsettled him. It looked like it was alive. The cloud pulsated, testing the air with probing tentacles of ashy yellow, and then formed multiple spiraling tunnels that crept downward until they touched the ground.

Dan pumped his fists in the air. "Holy shit! I'm high as fuck!"

He tossed his head back and howled. His dick twitched and he grinned. When he looked back, Chrissy was standing in the doorway. She stared wide-eyed at the yellow dust rushing toward them. The cloud would soon engulf the city. He grabbed her by the neck and led her back into the motel, already reaching for the zipper of his jeans.

Maybe he'd have his epic end of the world after all.

# COLLEEN

"Mom, can I have some peas?"

"More peas, puh-lease," Colleen replied.

The kids laughed at Colleen's sing-song voice. It was genuine and pure, like chimes in the breeze. Colleen wanted to cry when she heard it, but she and James agreed to avoid openly weeping in front of the kids.

They knew a comet was coming. Liana, at four years old, couldn't comprehend what that meant. Serena, her eleven-year-old stepdaughter, knew more than she let on for the sake of her sister. In a world of TV, the internet, smartphones, and other gossipy pre-teens, information had been too accessible.

At first the girls thought it was fun not having to go to school. They could play all day and Colleen gave them sweets whenever they wanted. There was no limit to how many times they could watch *Frozen* and *The Lego Movie*.

Colleen and James were adamant that they'd spend their last months in their home, living off food storage and spending time with their children and each other. If they hadn't gotten into disaster preparedness after the recession began, Colleen couldn't imagine how much suffering they would've undergone. Instead of spending time looking for food or hoping FEMA would help, they read books and opened a bottle of champagne they'd been saving for their upcoming anniversary. Colleen retrieved her oil paints and, after years without picking up a brush, painted. Every night, she and James made love like they had when they first met. It was beautiful.

They'd been living in a bubble.

Weeks later, a gang had rolled through their suburban neighborhood. Riding motorcycles and jacked up trucks, they went from house to house to steal, hurt, and kill. Her family hid in the loft of their small workshop in the backyard and weren't harmed. The gang did rough up their house and take what wasn't locked up tight in the basement.

When it was over, Colleen did everything she could to keep the girls away from the window until someone—or she and James—could do something. But they still saw Mr. Williams and his wife strung up in their front yard with the words *die niggers* scrawled in red spray paint across their garage.

Colleen was sickened by it, yet immensely grateful the gang hadn't found her family. They were the only other black family on the block. Her family could've been the ones lynched outside their house.

It was then Colleen realized how dangerous it was outside of their home, and so they never set foot outside. They boarded their windows and doors like everyone else and kept quiet. They were prisoners in their own homes. The kids were afraid. So were Colleen and James. With their windows boarded, the house was painfully dark. They hauled the dining room table upstairs and took their meals in the den where there was at least sunlight.

"Really, mom, can I have peas?"

Startled, Colleen stared at Liana who still held up her plastic *Star Wars* plate. The light hit the left side of her face, almost hiding the patchwork of burn scars on her right. The burns were a result of an accident when Liana was a baby. Colleen's breath caught in her throat. How terrified and lost she had felt when Liana toddled over to the wood burning stove and fell.

Colleen had been spacy all day. Today was the last day. She'd been marking off the boxes on her calendar. They had their favorite meal of peas, mashed potatoes, and roast beef which Colleen had canned herself the previous year. She used up the last of their vegetable oil to sear the meat, replacing the grayish hue with crackling brown.

"Of course, my little Wockie!" Colleen lifted the bowl of warm peas and spooned some onto Liana's plate. "Is that good?"

"It's Wookie, mom. Jeez," Liana corrected. Colleen knew it was Wookie, but also knew Liana liked to prove her Star Wars knowledge. It made her feel grown up.

Colleen smiled. "Oh, you're right. More peas?"

"No, that's all. Daddy, are you saying grace?"

James was focused on Serena. They shared the same wild, curly black hair. Their faces were similar too, all soft and round, except Serena's nose which had her mother's sharpness. Colleen felt her throat tighten up. There was love in this family. There was care. They had survived this long, safe from the hands of the corrupted marauders, and now they would have the chance to die together.

Serena shot a look of embarrassment and preteen disgust at James. "Ugh, dad, why are you staring at me? You're being weird."

"You want to say grace?" James asked his daughter.

She frowned. "You always say it."

"Maybe today we can try something different? Just for fun. Tomorrow …." James coughed and blinked slowly once. He used one finger to push his glasses up his nose. "Tomorrow I'll say it."

Serena was suspicious. But she clasped her hands together and closed her eyes. "Dear Lord in heaven, we are thankful for our family and for this food. We are—"

Her words were cut off as the house began to shake.

"Mom! What's happening?"

"Get under the table!" James yelled.

They crammed themselves under the table. "It's okay, sweetie. Just hold my hand. I lo—"

Something hit the roof. Outside, an explosion.

Colleen clutched Liana tight in her arms, James and Serena beside her. She thought of her children's laughter as she closed her eyes and waited for the end.

# CRAIG

Dr. Craig Peters took a sip of bourbon. He bent forward to set down the glass, reconsidered, and brought it up again to finish the remaining amber liquid.

"Why not have another?" he slurred, his voice too loud. He spread his arms and looked around the empty cabin, waiting for a scolding that would never come.

Not long ago, he had been highly regarded in the world of theoretical physics, as well as in his second loves of planetary sciences and meteorology. Hell, he had been on Samuel Zabat's team when the comet was first discovered. If Sam hadn't been pulling later nights than Craig, it would've been called Peters' Comet. Craig had set aside his brief pang of jealousy and worked tirelessly with the team to figure out where the comet came from and why they hadn't seen it coming months, if not years, in advance.

Now, Craig was in the middle of a particularly rousing game of *Agricola*. On a normal day, the sight of the board with all its units and cards would've made him happy. It was such a complicated, lengthy game, and he loved that about it. Years ago, during the summer when his kids had returned from college, they had teased him ruthlessly when he went to his weekly Monday night sessions.

Despite all the teasing, Craig's daughter, Sharon, would play a game with him as long as her brother wasn't around. She secretly loved it as much as he did—and beat him a few times, too. He kept her secret and suffered his son's mocking. It was the only pure, happy thing Craig shared with Sharon, so he coveted it. He would've given anything to have a bond—even one as small as a love for a board game—with Brandon.

But dammit! Today was Doomsday, and no one was around to judge him. He glanced back at the board, his expression creasing into a frown. *Agricola* wasn't cheering him up this time. A sudden stab of fear hit him, and his eyes flitted to the wall where a clock had been.

When he went to the mountains in Northern Oregon, abandoning his empty home in California, he had left behind all timekeeping devices. He'd gone so far as to destroy the beautiful wooden clock above the fireplace when he arrived. The comet was supposed to strike at 12:35pm, and a clock would only cause him unnecessary suffering as the hour approached.

His plan had been to stay drunk and forget what day it was. Instead, he had carved a tally of days in the doorframe. He couldn't help himself. His internal clock did feel off, what with the later sunsets as spring gave way to summer, but he still knew today was The End. Within hours, he'd be dead.

He'd always thought he'd die from heart failure like his dad and grandfather. It was a tradition for men in the family. His wife Betty had done everything she could to help Craig keep his blood pressure in check and live a healthy lifestyle. Once she had died, he'd given that all up. When his annual physical reminder came in the mail, he threw it in the recycling bin. Why worry about a heart attack when a comet was going to obliterate him?

Craig was ironically proud to be the first Peters man to break the tradition.

He chewed on his lip as he poured another glass of bourbon with clumsy hands. It sloshed onto the coffee table and wetted the game pieces. Craig didn't bother dabbing it up. Glass cradled in his hand, he leaned back on the futon and closed his eyes.

Four generations of Peters had made so many good memories in the cabin. At first, spending his last days there seemed like a great idea. Two or three weeks into his stay, he realized the memories were nothing but ghosts now. The few fluttering thoughts of his children laughing and swinging on the oak tree outside, of Betty cooking dinner for them in the small kitchen, were painful to recall. He'd never been close to his kids. He watched them drift away as they grew older without the slightest clue how to show them how much he loved them.

After another gulp of bourbon, he sank deeper into the couch and deeper into his own thoughts.

Now Brandon and Sharon lived out east. They rarely returned his calls, and when they did it was brief. Craig had only met two of his four grandbabies. His kids had always politely discouraged his attempts at spending a weekend with them. They never said the exact words but he knew what they were thinking; they didn't want their kids around an alcoholic grandfather.

Then, when the comet changed course, he had tried to reach out again. He had no idea how many times he tried to call them. Once the phone lines were overloaded and failed for good, and he couldn't charge his cell, he had no choice but to stop.

Since he was banished from his family by his own children, and there was nothing and no one for him in California, the cabin and his memories were all he had.

He kicked the coffee table and sent the *Agricola* pieces flying across the wood floor. Too late, he noticed he had also knocked the bourbon bottle over. The last dregs sloshed out.

"Shit," he mumbled. He finished off his fresh glass and

dropped to his knees to pick up the pieces.

The hot tears rimming his tired eyes were unexpected. One minute he was gathering up little wooden cattle and cards, and the next he was watching fat droplets hit the ground. He curled up on the ground and brought his knees into his chest, sobbing like a child. Maybe he could just fall asleep and miss dying all together.

Months earlier, he had sent out what he liked to call "Last Hurrah" emails. He wanted to have a clear conscious at the end. He told his longtime friend Timothy Williams that he'd seen his fiancée with another man the night before the wedding. He'd kept the secret all these decades not so much out of concern for Tim but because he couldn't work up the guts to ruin their marriage.

Craig had also emailed both of his children, tried to say how sorry he was for…well, basically everything.

When he was honest with himself, he regretted all of his cathartic emails. What good would they do? It was unlikely anyone would even see them.

His old college friend Tim, for example, would undoubtedly be somewhere deep underground in a bunker with his family, the POTUS, and everyone else who mattered. There were contingency plans up the wazoo depending on the level of destruction Zabat's Comet caused, but Craig knew one way or another, they'd all die. There was no escaping the behemoth chunk of rock and ice hurtling towards them. At least Tim and his family were together. They didn't have to fight droves of insane raiders for scraps of food or worry about being murdered. But if Tim managed to check his email, he'd spend his last weeks devastated by the revelation of his first wife's affair. Doubly so if his current wife got the message about Tim's own affair a few years back.

Almost instantly after Craig sent them, he sent another

message to Tim apologizing for the confession. He'd suggested if there was an afterlife, they should get together and smoke some pot, listen to Bach, and play Dungeons and Dragons like they did in college. Forget about anything to do with wives.

Why the fuck would he do it? Why would he ruin the last few weeks of his friend's life? He knew what his kids would say. That he was a narcissistic, alcoholic life ruining expert.

Craig took a long, deep breath and tried to clear his mind. A breeze wafted in from the open windows, carrying with it the scent of pine trees, fragrant under the warm sun. Birds chirped; the intermittent drilling of woodpeckers added to the cacophony. Engines roared and…

Engines?

He pushed himself upright and stumbled six feet to the front door. Through the screen he saw two Humvees parked by his sap and pine needle covered Jeep Wrangler. Two soldiers exited the vehicles and marched up to hm.

"Dr. Craig Peters?"

He tried to swallow the lump that had formed in his throat and nearly gagged on the aftertaste of bourbon and stomach acid. "That's me," he muttered.

"Captain Berg. We have orders to transport you to Castle Rock in Washington State."

"Castle Rock? That's two hundred miles north! Whose orders?"

"My Commanding Officer. Timothy Williams."

"Jesus! *Why*?" Craig laughed hysterically in a voice that sounded like it belonged to a stranger. His hand flew to his mouth but he couldn't stop himself from chuckling. This was a joke. It had to be. He blinked and considered slapping the soldier in the face to see if he was real. Maybe he was dead already, or dreaming. "We're done. We're going to die today."

Berg's features remained stern. "We're five hours after impact, Dr. Peters. You're the only person we can locate from Zabat's team. My orders are to take you to the dust zone at ground zero."

Craig choked and stopped laughing. He stiffened his back, realizing this wasn't a dream after all. He blinked again in an effort to pull himself out of the drunk haze clouding his brain. If what Berg was saying was true, then everything had just changed.

A kaleidoscope of questions crossed Craig's mind, but all he managed to ask was, "Dust Zone?"

Impatience flickered crossed Berg's face. It made Craig wonder how many times he'd had to answer that question in the past five hours. "Yes sir, but it's hard to explain. Instead of striking the planet as predicted, Zabat's Comet released some kind of dust cloud when it hit."

"How is that possible?"

One of the soldiers stepped forward. There were dark bags under his eyes. He needed a shave. "There's this force field—"

"Private, did I ask you to weigh in on this conversation?" Berg boomed without turning to face him.

"No, sir." The young man fell back.

"Force field?" Craig *had* to be dreaming. "What in the hell is he talking about? Is this some kind of joke?"

"Private Brody here spoke out of the line. Sir, with all due respect, we need to get you to camp so you can be briefed. Everyone's got a lot of unanswered questions, which is why we need you." Berg peered into the cabin where Craig knew he'd see plenty of empty liquor bottles and the trashed board game. "You need help packing?"

"What I need is a couple hours of sleep, a scalding hot coffee, and a cold shower, but judging by the look on your face, something tells me I won't be getting any of those."

"You have time to grab a coffee, sir, if you're quick," Berg said. "But that's it. We need to move. Like you said, we've got two hundred miles to cover."

Craig rubbed his scraggly, graying beard, looking back into the cabin. Other than clothes, enough booze to last months, and a few books, he hadn't brought much. He'd left all his mementos back in California, placed exactly where they would've been when his kids were at home and Betty was alive. The thought of his home sent a painful jolt of nostalgia through him, but it was immediately replaced by a flood of relief as another thought occurred to him.

This meant his kids were alive. This was a second chance. He was going to get to the bottom of when and why it all went wrong and how it could be fixed.

"Before we go find out what this mysterious dust is, I need something in return," Craig said.

Berg gave a small nod.

"I want to know if my kids are okay. I'll give you their addresses. If you have people out there, maybe you can—"

"Done. Now can you get moving?"

He slipped into a pair of loafers that had been resting by the door and pocketed his wallet, which contained a photo of Betty and the kids. Then he hesitated.

*You're forgetting something*, a little voice reminded him. The same little voice he wished so desperately wouldn't rear its ugly head. Not until he was too far away to do anything about it. He grabbed his duffle bag from the dining room and put his last two bottles of bourbon inside, wrapping one quickly in a kitchen towel so no one would hear them clink.

Then he walked out of the cabin and into the sunshine, the little voice quiet and pleased.

"Yes, Captain. Let's go see this dust zone."

# LARA

Lara sat in her dining room and stared at the alien world outside. She wore only the damp bathrobe, and she was cold. Her lower back throbbed from sitting so long. She didn't care. All she could do was look out the window. Yellow dust hung thick in the air and was settling on every surface it could get to. It was beautiful, in a disconcerting way, and it captivated her. She'd been peering outside for almost two hours. Not a single sign of life. Just the dust, twisting and swirling. It seemed to have a life of its own as it danced in the street.

Her stomach grumbled loudly, startling her. It was raw and gnawing as it tried to devour her from the inside out. The last thing she'd eaten was a packet of airplane snack mix she found in her purse. That had been three days ago.

Still, this wasn't the worst hunger she'd ever felt.

When she was six, her father had told her and her siblings that "he wasn't in a good place." Not being in a good place meant drawing the blinds and lying on the family room couch, or drinking until he passed out. If they asked their father for help, or questioned him, he hit them. It was generally one swift, open-palmed slap to the face followed by an apologetic grimace. *Sorry I had to do that to you.* The single time they had gone to the neighbor's house for help, the children discovered how much more violence he was capable of.

Lara finally got to her feet and shuffled into the kitchen. The memories made her feel lethargic and hopeless. She fixed herself a glass of water and retrieved the sugar canister from the pantry. Six tablespoons later, she had a sweet liquid that provided some calories. It was better than nothing.

"Christ," she said aloud, taking comfort in hearing something other than ringing silence, even if it was her own voice. "I guess life really does flash by your eyes before you die. Sort of."

Despite the fatigue and pain, she fixed her attention on the fact that she was not dead. The comet had not destroyed Earth. The eerie dust outside was something to be concerned about, but she was okay—for now. While she was well hydrated, she had to find food soon.

The dust. Certainly it would be dangerous to breathe it. Fine particles of anything were unhealthy to inhale. She'd have to search the garage for the respirator she'd used while refinishing the wood floors last year. She hoped it would be enough while she looked for food. She would take as much water as she could in her backpack and start her search.

Lara wondered how far the dust went.

She tossed back the last of her sugar water and left the kitchen, confident she could carry out her plan. As she passed the dining room, movement outside caught her attention. She walked closer to the window, peering through the yellow haze on the street.

At least a dozen figures were walking down the middle of the road. They wore goggles and gas masks and carried rifles, but they were not military. She recognized them by the white crosses painted on the front of their jackets. They'd passed through her neighborhood last week. While they hadn't raided her house, they'd hit the neighbors to her left and almost all the homes across the street. Were they back to finish the job?

She crouched down out of sight, lifting her head up just

enough to watch them. They dipped into a driveway and went to the front door. A man who stood at least at 6'5" rammed his body against it until the door crashed inward. Half the gang entered the house, the dust rushing in to follow.

A nervous shudder coursed through her body from her head down her back. The comet hadn't killed her, but she was far from safe.

"There!"

She heard the faint shout and saw one of the raiders point to the side of the house. Two figures had darted out of a side door by the garage and were making a run for the road. After no more than thirty feet, they stumbled and grabbed at their exposed faces.

Lara looked harder and gasped. Something was wrong with their skin, and the more they clawed at it, the worse it became. They were far away, the haze making it hard to see detail, but she was sure she saw blood. They were tearing their skin off. The gang members watched and pointed. It seemed like they were laughing.

Lara crawled out of the dining room and went to her bedroom. The dust was dangerous. She needed to cover every inch of her skin, like the raiders did, if she was to set foot out of the house. She pulled on leggings and a long-sleeved shirt, pants, and a sweater. Her winter clothes and back pack were always in the closet by the bathroom. From the closet she took out her parka, boots, gloves, and ski goggles. The weight of the ensemble was already exhausting, but Lara forced herself to keep moving. She grabbed her ski mask and scarf.

She had already filled two water bottles, which she dropped into her pack. Her hands shook as she rifled through the Tupperware drawer, looking for something to store more water in.

The first loud thump against the front door made her heart stop. The second sent her into overdrive. She abandoned the water and finished putting on her protective clothing. The room darkened as she put her ski goggles on. She snatched a roll of duct tape from the junk drawer and wrapped it around her wrists where the gloves met clothing. She did the same on her boots.

Lara ran to the door to the garage. She scanned the room for the respirator.

If anything good could be said about her husband, it was that he was extremely organized. The mask was hanging on a peg on his tool wall. She grabbed it and pulled it over her head, then taped anywhere she felt her skin might be exposed. Both the respirator and goggles were tight against her ski mask.

She heard a crash as the front door broke. She'd planned on going out the back door, but they'd see her. The garage door was heavy, and she doubted she had enough strength to push it up manually—and even if she did the raiders were outside.

Her gaze fixed on the single narrow window above Harry's workbench.

She grabbed a metal stool and wedged it under the knob of the door leading back into the house. She went to the small window and pushed it open. The yellow dust flooded into the garage.

She tossed her pack out the window and squeezed through just as the door to the garage shuddered. Lara dashed toward the backyard of the house next door. Her neighbors had been in the middle of putting up a new fence when they'd found out about the comet and hadn't bothered finishing it. She ran through a gap in the fence, not once looking behind, and then paused on the far side of the neighboring house.

It was quiet, save for her own breathing. It reminded her of when it snowed, how the flakes seemed to dampen all sound. She walked slowly along the edge of the house and peered around it. The raiders did not appear to have seen her. Lara sighed in relief.

Momentarily safe from danger, she relaxed her shoulders and looked around for her next move. Her breath felt heavy and damp inside the mask, and her lungs burned from running. She couldn't go far without calories. She waited until the raiders left her house and then headed down the street.

She made it fifteen steps before a bullet whizzed by her face.

# JACK

Jack sat against an empty refrigerator and nursed a bottle of cherry kirsch. It was the only liquid—alcohol or otherwise—the tiny convenience store had to offer. He'd found it lying opened on its side, most of the kirsch long gone. The rest of the store was picked clean. Not a single can or condiment remained. He had chosen this place not in hopes of finding liquor, but because the windows were intact and no one would find him in here. He was safe from the dust. The kirsch was just an added bonus.

As long as he was nowhere near Stewart's body, he wasn't complaining.

Anxiety churned his stomach. He fought to keep down the syrupy drink. God, he'd *killed* someone. And to top it off, the world hadn't ended. At least not yet. When Jack faced his own inner vigilante, he knew he would've killed Stewart whether he'd seen the articles or not. Stewart had been involved in what happened to Katie. He might not have killed her, but he had admitted he'd photographed Katie inappropriately in addition to all the other voyeuristic acts he had confessed to. It had been *his* trailer where she'd been kept hostage. *His* trailer where she'd been murdered.

Yes, he had murdered Stewart. It weighed on him, but he couldn't truly regret it. He doubted any other father out there would.

What bothered him was the envelope. Jack glanced at it, bent down the middle where he had stuffed it in his jacket, now sitting beside him on the grungy tile floor.

Deep down, he knew Stewart had been on to something. Should Jack be grateful he was alive so he could find the real killer? Or angry that he had gotten the wrong guy? He had blood on his hands, and it wasn't even the right blood.

He cringed. What a cruel, sick joke the universe had played on him. Debris from the comet had damaged buildings around Stewart's apartment, but not one piece landed on Jack. He remained unharmed. When he'd run out of the apartment and seen the yellow dust coming from down the street, a wicked sandstorm engulfing the city, survival instinct had taken over and led him to the store. He wished he'd just stayed in the dust and let it kill him. He'd seen it happen to two other people already. They clawed at their throats and tore at their faces, fell, and never moved again. The dust settled on their bodies, camouflaging them.

"Walk out there right now," Jack said out loud. "Walk out there and die."

The words were empty. Jack liked the idea of killing himself more than actually doing it. And if he did do it, he'd use his gun. He hadn't been lying when he told Stewart he didn't believe in an afterlife. While he and The Ex had been active in their church, he never felt the same sense of peace it gave her. Mostly he had liked the sense of community. After Katie, a switch had flipped inside of him, and he'd realized how pointless it all was.

Jack got to his feet and stumbled around the store with no purpose. The Ex was probably rejoicing that very moment in a doomsday bunker she and her husband built, claiming the comet not hitting the earth was an act of God. She had tried telling Jack that Katie was in heaven and that even though it was painful to have her gone from the world, she was at peace and they'd someday see her again. She tried to tell him to be grateful for the time they'd gotten to spend with their daughter.

What a load of bullshit. What about all the time he *wouldn't* have with Katie? He had been robbed of the opportunity to help her with homework, to teach her to swim, to interrogate her first date, and to be there for college graduation.

He heard his stepmother's voice. "Colleen is a good woman. She deserves to move on. So do you."

The Ex didn't deserve to move on. No one did.

Jack stopped at an employee-only door. Through the dirty porthole, he saw a storage room. The metal shelves were barren save for a few cleaning products. Mounted on the wall was a huge analog clock behind a metal cage. Straight across from him was another door. When he had first arrived, he'd searched the room and found nothing. Now he heard something.

*Tap. Taptaptap.*

Gunfire. Jack ducked into the storage room and stood at the backdoor, listening. He hadn't seen or heard much activity since the dust had fallen, other than the two people that died. He couldn't go outside even if he wanted.

Shots fired again. Quick footsteps. Someone ran behind the shop.

Before the oncoming wave of claustrophobia and panic overtook him, a figure burst through the door and knocked Jack aside. A plume of the yellow dust began to flood into the room, and Jack ran into the main shop to get as far away from it as he could. He watched through the swinging door as the person shut the rear exit and engaged the bolts on the bottom and top of the door.

"Stay back!" It was a woman's voice underneath the layers of clothing and duct tape, muffled beneath a respirator. "That stuff will kill you."

"I know," Jack called. He felt compelled to tell her to leave—this was his spot and she put him in danger—but he wasn't sure he wanted to be alone anymore. The woman propped the door between them open with a bucket. Then she leaned against the back door and tilted her head.

"What are you doing?"

Instead of answering him, she held a gloved finger to her respirator, signaling for Jack to be quiet.

They waited in silence for ten minutes. Jack watched the little hand of the clock track the time. The faint cloud of dust she'd let in settled to the ground. During that interval, Jack heard voices outside. At one point someone tried to open the door but gave up quickly. Outside, the yellow dust was thick, mixed with smoke from burning buildings. Visibility was poor; he could only see ten feet from the shop. As long as they stayed away from the windows, no one would spot them inside.

As he watched, a tendril of dust snaked across the window, moving with purpose opposed to hanging in air like the rest. It seemed to disappear as he focused on it. Still, he shuddered. He couldn't describe it exactly, but the dust didn't feel *right*.

Finally, the woman spoke. "My name is Lara. I have dust all over my clothes so I'm not going to come any closer. I know we just met, but do you have any food?"

"I'm Jack." He cleared his throat and looked at the bottle of cherry kirsch still held tight in his grasp. He tried not to feel guilty. "No. Just this. I thought we were going to…well, you know. Why were those people after you?"

She shrugged. "Bad people. Raiders from Hedone, I think. I've seen them in my neighborhood before. They break into houses and steal things. Take people."

"How far away do you live?" Jack asked.

"A couple miles. I've been trying to outrun them, but I'm tired and hungry. I'm not sure how much farther I can go."

Jack noted his own clothing. He had on a pair of jeans, work boots, and a checkered flannel jacket. Underneath was a thin Felix the Cat shirt he'd been carrying around since his early twenties. He wasn't going anywhere at all, not without something to cover his skin and a mask.

"Is it breathing it or getting it on your skin that kills you?" Jack asked. "I saw people outside die from the dust, but I couldn't tell for certain."

"I have no idea. It certainly isn't something you want to find out firsthand. How long have you been in this place? Do you have anywhere else to go?" Lara slid down the door and sat on her butt.

"Not long." He had driven hours to get to Monroe. He was dead in the water. Of course, he had no intention of telling Lara that. "I don't have anywhere to go. Even if I did, how could I leave this place with that stuff out there?"

He wished Lara would take her mask off so he could read her face. Did he come off as suspicious? Was she wondering if she escaped one group of bad people just to find another?

"I know where you can find food," he found himself saying. He needed to win her trust. He had to prove to himself he was good. "There's an apartment just one block down. That's where I was when—"

Shit. His mouth snapped shut. Stewart had some food, but his body was still in the apartment. It was too late. Lara was already getting to her feet.

"When what? Tell me where this place is and I'll get it for us."

"When it happened. Did you see that thing in the sky?"

She took a step forward and stopped. "I didn't see what happened. I felt my house shake and heard explosions outside. Then I saw the dust. There's damage everywhere, but nothing major. Little shards or meteorites or whatever you call them. Nothing like what they said would happen."

"Right, that's what I saw too," Jack said.

"Listen, Jack, we're in dire circumstances here. I know that, you know that. If there's any chance you know where there's some food, and something bad happened you don't want me to know about, please set that aside. Whatever is in there besides food doesn't matter to me. I just want to eat."

No one else knew that Jack was a murderer, and somehow that made it seem less real. He couldn't let another soul find out what he'd done. If and when society rebuilt, he would go to prison. Others had done worse, especially those in Hedone, but eventually he would be found out. If Lara knew, if she discovered the body, his chance to find Katie's killer—the real killer—would be over before it began.

"I can't do that. Why don't you give me your gear and I'll get the food."

Lara shook her head. "No."

"Why not?"

"So many reasons."

"Such as?"

"First, and most importantly, these clothes will not fit you. Second, I have no guarantee that you'd come back. Third, I'm covered in dust. When you come in contact with it while you try to put them on, you could get sick." She paused. "I don't know exactly how the dust harms us, but I'm not risking anything."

Jack squeezed his eyes shut and took a swig of the cherry kirsch. He was backed into a corner and he didn't like it one bit.

"What if you found me some gear? I'll need it if I ever want to get out of here. Then I'll be mobile. You'd be doing me a favor, and then I could help you."

That seemed to strike a chord with her. Lara's head tilted down and she stared at her feet. After an eternity, she spoke. "No. You're hiding something, and I don't like that. You're withholding my best chance of finding food to manipulate me into helping you. Before all this, maybe I would've helped you. But as it stands, I just don't trust you. Goodbye."

Jack's heart sank. He racked his brain for something to say that would get her to stay. There was only one thing that might help: the truth. Before he could think better of it he said, "I killed the man in the apartment."

Lara's hand stopped on the door latch. "Why?"

"I wanted justice. He took my little girl, took everything from me." Jack took a deep breath and gestured around the shop. "I didn't want to tell you because, surprise, the world didn't explode and it's only a matter of time before things go back to normal."

She didn't respond. Jack pulled himself to his feet. His brain felt sluggish. The kirsch had hit him harder than he thought. Liquid courage, right? "Please say something."

"Thank you for telling me. The past few months have been hell for all of us. We've all done things, seen things. Keep trusting me, Jack. Tell me where the food is, and I promise I'll come back."

Jack closed his eyes and told her.

# CRAIG

Craig cradled a fresh cup of coffee in one hand and the flap of his tent in the other, his gaze focused on the mysterious dust zone. Or DZ as the soldiers called it.

The sight of the DZ, looming behind a line of maples and evergreens a hundred yards away from camp, sent a chill down his spine each time he saw it. It was the stuff of science fiction. Some kind of *force field* was containing the dust inside an invisible dome.

So far, all they knew was that the dome was roughly a hundred miles wide and five miles tall. Its center point was over downtown Seattle. The DZ covered almost all of the Pacific Northwest. How any of it was possible was an enigma. Craig's theories ranged from the warping of gravity to the channeling of some kind of exotic matter. Captain Berg had promised gear would be arriving soon with which he could run tests.

The captain had also advised his soldiers not to go near it, no matter how curious they were. Craig had to agree.

He tore himself away from staring at the DZ and entered his tent. Sitting down at his folding table, Craig took a swig of coffee—which was really more bourbon than coffee at this point—and tapped his tablet out of sleep mode. He then replayed the video of Zabat's Comet dismantling for the sixth time in the past hour. The images held a grim allure, like a guilty pleasure that he couldn't seem to quit. His heart lodged higher in his throat every time.

The video started with a shot of the man who had taken

it, Ralph Sansbury. Craig had spoken to Ralph when the soldiers brought him in after finding him speeding down the freeway on his motorcycle. Ralph put up a bit of a fight when Berg took his video camera, but the captain wasn't the kind of man who lost fights. Ralph had since been sequestered for further questioning and a medical evaluation.

Unlike most people Craig had seen in the days before he hightailed it to the mountains back in Oregon, Ralph was well groomed. Though his cheeks were gaunt from lack of food, his hair was neatly trimmed and his face shaved. Craig put him in his early twenties. In the video, he stood in the middle of an empty stretch of the I-5 freeway. Seattle was visible behind him in the distance. The bottom of the frame contained a tangle of ramps and overpasses. A handful of taller buildings rose behind the roads. Smoke flooded the skyline, drifting under muddy clouds the color of rust. Abandoned cars and luggage littered the road around Ralph.

Craig was sure one of the blurry heaps farther down the road was a corpse.

"So ends my documentary account of the end of the world. I'll try to get a glimpse of Zabat's Comet before I place all my memory cards into this box." The man held up a safety box. It was almost too heavy for him to hold. He strained to keep it in the frame. "I'll then drop this into the tube I showed you earlier."

Ralph had figured thousands of years into the future, some alien species or new generation of humans would find his documentary and the secrets of Earth's last days would be explained. He'd spent two months finding the right equipment and people to drill a shaft by the freeway— where he decided he could get the best shot of Zabat's Comet over Seattle—into which he'd drop the fireproof safe with his memory cards. He had hoped the hole was deep enough that the box would survive the damage from the comet.

Ralph was an artist. Not that Craig had anything against artists, but it explained the young man's foolhardy—and ridiculous, silly, and naive—plan.

For starters, that close to the impact spot, Ralph would've needed to triple the depth of his tunnel to even have a chance, and fill it with concrete, or at least dirt. Beyond that, how would aliens be able to find it to begin with? Unless the box sent out some kind of RFID signal, neither aliens nor humans would ever know it was there. That was assuming aliens would even understand radio waves, or what an SD card was if they *did* find the box.

"I just wanted to say, like, even though you'll see a lot of evidence of us doing shitty things to the planet and ourselves and each other, we weren't all bad." Behind the camera someone sniffled. Ralph's lip quivered. "Babe, don't cry. It'll be over quick."

The flap to Craig's tent opened, letting in blinding streams of sunlight. He tapped the pause button on the video and squinted to see who it was. One of the soldiers. Craig had seen him before. He had a sharp, hawkish nose and a sly grin that tugged at the corner of his mouth. His hair was so blonde it bordered on white, making his eyebrows and eyelashes almost nonexistent. Craig didn't remember his name but knew he needed to start making an effort to do so. The only soldier he knew by name was Captain Berg—and it occurred to him now that he didn't even know Berg's first name.

"What is it, Private…?" Craig asked.

"It's Private Brody, sir," he said. "Mr. Williams is on the line for you."

When Berg had first taken him from his cabin, they

gave him access to a tablet which he used to email Tim. Craig was still a bit drunk and knew his apology email didn't sound like an apology at all. Just more selfish rambling. He reviewed the email in his Sent folder once he was sober. Regret seemed too trivial a word to describe how he felt about it.

*About Jackie, I'm so sorry. But hey, the world wasn't destroyed, how about that? Can't wait to see this dust cloud. Sorry again.*

Wanting to postpone the conversation a little longer, Craig waved Brody away. "I'll be there in five."

"It's urgent."

Apparently there was a limit to how much of Craig's attitude the soldiers would be willing to take. Every day, links in the chain of command were being filled, and soon he wouldn't have the same amount of leeway. Yes, he'd be the lead scientist on the dust. But he'd also have to deal with the bureaucracy, and the protocol.

It was inevitable. But not yet.

"How about three minutes?"

Brody nodded. "Three, then I'm walking you over myself."

The soldier let the tent flap fall. Craig pushed his glasses up on his nose and tapped the play button on his tablet, then used his index finger to scrub through seven minutes of idle footage where Ralph talked about mankind. Dozens of tiny meteorites fell from the sky. Many burned up before impact. A few made it, knocking chunks off of skyscrapers.

Finally, the main event. Craig let the video play.

"Jesus, look at the sky!" Ralph shouted from behind the camera.

Defying every bit of scientific knowledge Craig possessed, Zabat's Comet broke through the clouds...and came to a stop. A three-mile-wide comet ten thousand feet above Seattle, simply hovering as though some giant hand had stilled it. The city was cast in shadows.

Then Zabat's Comet dismantled. That was the only word to describe it. A spider web of cracks appeared across the comet's entire surface. A soft yellow glow emanated from within. Then the lower half of the behemoth began falling away in car-sized chunks. The remaining mass burst outward. The shards were nothing more than dark blurs as they exited the frame at high speed and went God knows where.

A flash of white. A blue teardrop-shaped object was visible for a moment. Before it slipped from the shot, dozens of laser-like beams extended from its tip, forming a sphere. The rays were visible only a split second, then flashed out of sight as they spread outward in 360 degrees away from the pod.

Craig had no doubt it was some kind of space ship. He had satellites tracking where it went at that very moment.

Ralph's wasn't the only footage they had of the comet dismantling. There were drone and satellite feeds, many of them from NORAD. But Ralph's was the best eyewitness footage they had, and there was something about it that captivated Craig.

The dismantling took seconds. Craig lowered the volume in anticipation of the thunderous boom that would follow. The audio was distorted, crackling as the camera's sound system was overloaded.

"What is that?" Ralph called out, frantic. "What the fuck is that?"

A powerful gust of wind coursed up the freeway, sending debris into the air and rocking cars. It knocked the camera to the right. Ralph righted it in time and then zoomed in as close as the camera allowed. Yellow particles emerged from the comet's debris. Like tornadoes, they swirled together to form tunnels that seemed to be searching for somewhere to touch down.

"We have to go!" Ralph shouted. "Babe, we gotta go!"

The video ended, and the tablet went back to the home screen. Ralph had told Craig that he'd had to go eighty miles an hour on his bike to escape the dust cloud chasing them. When he looked in his side mirror, he said it was as if the dust hit an invisible wall.

Craig stared at the screen, his brain void of thought but full of anxiety. His mouth was dry. He went for his coffee and found the cup empty.

In his gut, he knew what Zabat's Comet had really been. Part of him wanted to crawl into a hole and die, while the other wanted to dance in joy because it meant they weren't alone in the universe. Alien life existed. It had found Earth.

But what was their intent?

"Dr. Peters?" Brody's voice outside his tent helped surface Craig from his thoughts.

Craig stood, the sparsely furnished tent suddenly spinning. His knees threatened to buckle under him. Damn. He needed more coffee, ideally with a slug of whiskey. After straightening his shirt and attempting to smooth his wild hair back, he exited his tent.

Right beside the I-5 freeway, Castle Rock, Washington was a plain town full of squat buildings and bars. When he was younger, he had stopped there a few times when he rode his bike on the Old Pacific Highway. It was at the bottom of the state, almost in Oregon. The drive from Craig's cabin hadn't taken long.

The outlying land was more scenic than the smudge of a city: sprawling fields, patches of evergreen forest, the occasional dairy farm. The military had set camp in one of those fields.

Craig followed Private Brody along a well-worn

path in the grass to the tent where they kept all their communication equipment. It was buzzing with activity, the temperature hotter than the summer day outside due to the cramped quarters. Two soldiers reviewed a map while they discussed clearing I-5 to improve mobility. Another pair debated sending out helicopters to circle the DZ. There was always at least one person searching for any kind of signal from the dust zone. So far, they had none. Whatever the dust was, it blocked radio signals and every other form of communication they'd tried.

An empty seat at a desk beside the radio equipment beckoned him. Craig sat down and adjusted the headset.

"Craig here."

"First, go to hell," Timothy Williams snapped. "If I was there, your face would be black and blue. Why wouldn't you tell me about Jackie? Even when we were having problems, you said nothing. You would've saved me a decade of suffering and lawsuits."

Craig squeezed his eyes shut and took a deep breath. He deserved everything Tim had to say. "I know. I'm sorry."

"I threw my laptop across the room when I read that first one. I could have let that go. But your second email? And the one to Deb? Jesus, Craig!" Tim sighed. "Deb won't talk to me now. You need to stop being such an asshole and *fast.*"

"I have no excuse. I'm truly sorry."

"Are you sure? No excuse?"

Craig sucked in a sharp breath. There was no playing dumb and claiming he didn't know what Tim was implying. They both knew what Craig was like when he was off the wagon. And they sure as hell knew Tim was the bigger, better man when it came to putting up with Craig's stupidity.

"Just watch it, okay?" Tim said gently. "We need to be

professional from here on out."

"Understood."

"Listen, I don't want to see any mention of our personal lives in future communication. The media will take anything and spin it." He heard the edge harden in Tim's voice.

"Yeah, sure. The media is a huge concern now that the internet is down and civilization has collapsed."

"It's only a matter of when, not if, on the media thing. The world hasn't reverted back to the stone age as much as you think it has."

"Speaking of juicy secrets, how's the bunker treating you? Are you and the President sipping scotch and playing cards?"

"I'm fine, Craig. And despite what you think, being a General doesn't grant me access to bunkers and the President," Tim said. Craig could imagine him rolling him eyes. "Moving on. I want to hear a verbal report from you, and then I need a thorough written report by end of day."

He scanned the tent for coffee with no luck. He considered asking Tim for another minute so he could grab some but then thought better of it. It was time to get serious.

"We arrived at the DZ about four hours ago. How did you assemble Captain Berg and his men so fast?"

"Despite what people think, the government and the military didn't disappear. There are many contingency plans in the works you don't know about. We should have the country back in order within weeks." Tim didn't offer anything else and Craig didn't ask, mostly because he knew he wouldn't get any answers.

"Then you know the soldiers already set up camp before we arrived, and are setting up tents now for survivors should we find any. Have you watched any of the videos I sent?"

"Tech guys say they're still downloading. I've seen some stills from NORAD. They aren't good."

"Well, I'll explain, but you won't believe me unless you see it yourself." Craig sucked in a deep breath then continued. "The spectroscopic analysis of Zabat's Comet wasn't accurate. A comet is primarily made of rocks and metals with an exterior of ice which, at the right velocity, would destroy anything it hit. This comet wasn't solid, and by our understanding, what it did was impossible. To put it simply, at the speed that thing was going there is no way it could stop itself without some internal or external force acting upon it. Furthermore, there's a fucking *force field* containing the dust. We're talking extraterrestrials and aliens here."

The radio crackled. Craig thought he had lost Tim, but then his friend finally spoke. "Don't go there. If anyone other than me asks you questions, don't use those words."

"What else should I call it? It's a force field!"

"You know what I mean, Craig. The ET and A words. Do you think when I report to the Army Chief of Staff I'm going to say 'alien'? The President doesn't want to hear any wacko theories on aliens. Not just because he hates timewasters and charlatans, but because it would cause mass hysteria if we went public with something like that."

"Hate to break it to you, but it's stupid *not* to go there. This isn't something you can hide. People will find out. You want to get ahead of public reaction," Craig said. "This comet was anomalous from the beginning. Why didn't we spot it sooner? Even if it were on, say, a two hundred-year orbit, we'd probably have some historical precedence for it. It defied momentum and inertia when it got here. If I walk out of this tent, I'll see a force field straight from a goddamn movie. Unless the government has secretly unlocked the power to create force fields, an *extraterrestrial* has. And mass hysteria? When was the last time you were topside?"

"It can always get worse," Tim said, but Craig heard the lack of conviction in his voice. "What else do you have?"

Craig tapped his fingers on the metal desk, his gaze unfocused. Bureaucracy wasn't, and never had been, easy for him. "At ten thousand feet it appears the comet inexplicably stopped, shedding its outer layer into tens of thousands of pieces. A dust cloud emerged from within. I say 'emerged' because that's the best way to describe it. It was like a swarm of bees or school of fish. It moved with a purpose when it first escaped."

"When it first escaped? Is the behavior different now?"

"Yes. Once it was...domed, contained...it stopped moving."

"How close have you gotten to it?" Tim asked.

"I can see it from the camp. We're waiting on the hazmat equipment the troops are bringing from the coast. The comet could've been carrying any manner of radiated or interstellar organic material. Joint Base Lewis-McChord, the National Guard Armory, and the US Navy are all inside the DZ. They're the ones we should be working with, but we've had no communication with them. This dust, it's... weird. Very fine yellow particles, almost like pollen. Until I get some samples, I won't know for sure what it is."

There was a brief pause. "Any other thoughts?"

"When I say the DZ is a hundred miles, I mean it is exactly a one hundred-mile dome. NORAD's satellite shots confirm it hasn't moved an inch since it formed." Craig leaned back in his chair and grinned. "Hey, Tim? When we run out of explanations that fit in our current understanding of what is and isn't possible, I'd love to be there when someone tells the POTUS we're dealing with little green men."

# COLLEEN

Colleen looked at the chunk of rock in the dining room, then at the path of destruction it had torn through their master bedroom. It blocked the entrance to the basement where all of their food storage was. She closed in on the meteor and checked to see if they could slip behind it. No luck. The splintered wood was nearly flush against the rock. It would be impossible to move. As she investigated, she noticed the side facing her kitchen was rough, while the basement-facing side was smooth. Black and glassy, it shimmered when the light hit it the right away.

A shiver cascaded from the top of her head down to her toes. It reminded her of the feeling she got around deep murky water or shadowy caves; innocent in their own right, but with the potential of harboring something sinister. Any curiosity to see what was on the meteor's hidden side was overshadowed by primal fear. She left it alone.

Some areas of the house were smoldering. Pieces of her life were charred and scattered across the lawn. Almost all of the drawings Liana and Serena had posted on the fridge were burnt to dust.

"Colleen?" James limped down the hallway carrying Liana and Serena's backpacks. There was a line of white dust smeared across his dark forehead. It creased when he furrowed his brow. Even though he was the one who'd been injured, he sounded more concerned about her.

She waved his worry away. "I'm fine. Let's go outside."

Colleen needed another minute alone. Had the rock been about fifteen feet to the right, it would've killed her entire family. A shard of wood had impaled James in the calf, making him limp. They removed it, cleaned it, and bandaged the wound. Once the blood was gone, it wasn't too bad.

James exited the house and Colleen trailed behind him slowly. When she got outside, she turned to survey her home one last time. The azaleas would never bloom again beneath the living room window. She and James had planned on redoing the exterior paint this year, too, and remodeling the attic to serve as Serena's new bedroom. Those plans were all so distant now, almost like they were memories from another life.

Colleen's neighbors' houses had fared much worse than hers. The meteor shower obliterated many homes on the block. Thick black smoke wafted into the sky from the craters. People wandered the street in a daze. Some tried to scavenge what they could from their wreckage. Other's sat on the sidewalk staring at everything and nothing all at once. No one spoke to each other or came to see if anyone needed help.

Colleen didn't understand what happened. According to the news, they lived within the affected zone. While they weren't going to get smashed into oblivion by the comet impact, a huge wave of fire was supposed to have consumed them within minutes.

Despite her relief that they were alive, a cold sense of dread had also settled in the pit of her stomach. On the horizon was a yellow cloud that moved closer and closer by the minute. It reminded her of the sandstorms she had experienced on a trip to Egypt.

Colleen had prepped the kids on how to use a gas mask. Those masks had almost broken the bank, but when James got his bonus at work they'd bought them for their disaster kits. They both reasoned that a gas mask was the kind of thing that, if you didn't have it, you'd probably need it. The girls thought they looked cool and liked to play superhero games with them on.

They had sealed the workshop off with plastic and duct tape. Their van wasn't damaged, but the road out of their neighborhood was impossible to navigate. Based on the size of the approaching cloud, they couldn't escape it on foot. Even though it reminded her of a sandstorm, the cloud was definitely not sand or smoke. The yellow hue was sickly, almost sulfuric. It stretched as far as she could see.

Colleen felt James's hand on her shoulder. He held two masks, one for each of them. The girls were crouched behind him observing a tiny fragment of meteorite embedded in the lawn. "Hon, you ready? We should head in."

"Yeah, ready." She paused and checked to see if the girls were listening. "How do you think they're doing?"

James's deep brown eyes flicked to the approaching cloud and then back to her. "Better than we are. Serena is afraid but she's being brave for Liana."

"Like you always say, kids are resilient."

"I'm usually right, too." James gave her a quick kiss on the cheek. His lips were dry against her skin.

"Guys, come on. We're going in." Colleen walked over to the girls. Her heart stopped. Dust, the same color as the approaching storm, was on Liana's hand. She jerked her daughter away from the meteor she'd been poking. "What are you doing? Don't touch that!"

"Mom, you're hurting me!" Liana tried to pull away from Colleen's grasp, one small hand reaching towards the dust. "That yellow stuff was moving, I just wanted to see!"

The tips of Liana's fingers and palm had a lightly coating of it. Colleen had a sudden vivid memory of when Liana got into a bottle of Ajax last year. The fiasco with poison control and the ER.

That memory was quickly replaced with the image of Katie, cold and stiff in her coffin. Dizziness overtook Colleen.

She put her own hands on either side of Liana's face. "Did you eat any? Did you get any in your mouth?"

Liana burst into tears and tried to fling herself out of Colleen's grasp.

"You're being stupid!" Liana whined.

"Colleen you're scaring her," James's voice came. "Let's just get her washed up, okay?"

Colleen turned to Serena. "Did you get any on you?"

"No," Serena snapped, but Colleen saw the fear in her eyes.

Steadying herself, Colleen took a breath and managed to stand. She carried Liana to the workshop, where she searched for a wound irrigation kit. Their supplies weren't as organized as she thought, and she ended up settling on sanitary wipes. She held her daughter's tiny hands in hers as she dabbed away at the dust, careful not to get any on herself. It turned darker as it grew damp. Eventually she cleaned it off completely. Liana's skin was red and irritated. To Colleen's surprise, the girl's tantrum died quickly and she seemed fine, so Colleen let her go upstairs with Serena to play in the loft. She sealed the wipes in a plastic bag and tossed them in the overflowing trashcan outside.

Neither James nor Colleen spoke. She didn't need to ask to know what he was thinking. She was overprotective and tended to overreact. James was much more easygoing, and their parenting styles sometimes clashed.

James shut the door and laid plastic over it, duct taping all the seams. The single LED lantern cast a painfully bright blue light. Workshop was perhaps too generous of a term.

It was mostly meant for storage, and with the four of them in there it felt cramped.

Once the door was sealed, he lowered himself carefully to the ground next to her, avoiding any strain on his injury. He turned to catch her gaze as he spoke. "It scares them when you get like that."

"I know," Colleen whispered. A few tears fought to escape. "I just...I saw Liana and all of the sudden I was thinking of Katie."

She didn't need to elaborate. James knew every detail of Colleen's first marriage and what happened to Katie. Even after years of counseling, when one of the girls appeared to be in danger, Colleen lost it.

"I get that. It's all okay now though."

Colleen scoffed. "Whatever came from that comet could be dangerous. We have no idea what it is or what it will do to us, and it was *on* Liana."

"The vacuum and temperature in space kills virtually all living organisms so I bet we're okay. But you're right, we don't know. I'm worried about Liana just as much as you are, but the girls read us and gauge our reactions. If we're scared, they'll lash out."

She squeezed her eyes shut, massaging her temples with her fingertips. "Yes, I might've overreacted. But I'm also concerned for their safety first and foremost. I'm their mother." Colleen finally opened her eyes and looked at him. "I'll watch myself around them, as long as you watch out *for* them. Okay?"

"Deal."

They smiled at each other and she felt the tension melt away. James caught Colleen's hand in his and pulled her against his side. He kissed the back of her hand then she snuggled in close, dropping her head on his shoulder. He smelled sweaty and faintly of burnt wood. "What do you think happened?"

Unlike Colleen, who had tried to avoid news about the comet, James devoured everything to do with it. That included eccentric conspiracies about aliens, which was one of the reasons why they never spoke about it in front of the girls. Serena was deathly afraid of aliens since her cousin let her watch *Alien*.

"Could be fallout from something it hit up north," James offered.

"But Zabat's Comet was huge. Where did it go?"

James' lips were pursed as he thought. It brought out the dimple in his chin as well as the crow's feet around his eyes that he was self-conscious about, though he'd never admit it. "A lot of scientists pointed out we don't know exactly what the comet was made of. Typically they're just rock. That's what makes them so dangerous. They're heavy and gain so much velocity when they approach the earth that they become like bombs. But maybe the center of this one was ice with an outer shell of rock. It could have just melted when it entered our atmosphere."

"Couldn't they have just sent a probe out and investigated?"

He laughed and tilted his head against hers. "This thing wasn't supposed to hit us. It was going to soar well past earth. If the solar flare hadn't pushed it towards us, we would've been fine. Plus, think of the budget. Do you see our government shelling out cash for that?"

"Good point," she said. "What about the other theory?"

"You won't like it."

Colleen rolled her eyes. "Out with it. I know you want to tell me."

"Aliens," James whispered. "It could be debris from an alien planet that was blown up. It could also be an attack. Maybe they sent it to destroy a different planet and we were unlucky when the flare pushed it towards us instead. One guy believed it could be a spaceship, but that sounds farfetched even to me."

"Mom, it's all yellow outside!" Liana called.

Colleen pulled away from James and dropped her head into her hands. "We need to explain what's happening. In our own words, clarify everything. We haven't lied to them, but we certainly haven't been honest. I don't know if Liana will understand, but Serena will."

"We're going to get through this, okay? We've made it this far."

James gave her a quick hug before climbing the ladder to get the girls.

# DAN

Dan watched the military dudes leading a group of people down the street. They all wore big plastic suits and gas masks. Over those were tactical vests, holsters, and other gear. Lots of guns, lots of cool black-ops shit or whatever. Behind them were big Humvee-type trucks with FEMA logos on the side. Dozens of people trailed behind. They wore regular clothes, and had different kinds of masks. Nonmilitary types. The yellow dust was thick, and soon the group was out of sight. Dan tapped the bedroom window with his fingertips, thinking.

Some guy had tried getting into the hotel room an hour ago. His skin looked jacked, covered in pus. He had been going from room to room trying to get in, screaming and pounding on doors. Dan watched him from the window as he stumbled around. Eventually the guy had collapsed, grabbing his throat as blood spewed from his mouth and splattered the walkway.

Dan wasn't the smartest guy around, but he guessed the dust was dangerous.

He scratched at his forearm. Fucking bugs under his skin. He figured he would've come off his high by now, but there was still some meth lingering in him. He used to try and cut the bugs out of his body, but he'd been around the block enough times that he knew better now.

Dan moved away from the window and collapsed on the bed. Beside him, Chrissy's body remained motionless. She'd been dead a while. He wasn't sure if he fucked her to death or if she'd finally starved. Either way, he was pretty hungry himself and was considering whether or not he could eat her. She was a skinny bitch, but he was sure she still had some meat on her.

What he needed to do was find another handful of chicks. This time he'd take better care of them since the world hadn't ended after all. No permanent trades. He also needed to find a bunch of food and booze. He needed to get his act together.

His stomach growled. Fuck, maybe he *was* hungry enough to eat Chrissy.

*Too many things to do.*

Shit. Maybe he should've tried to get the military's attention. They were rescuing people. They probably had food. Plus their gas masks let them walk around outside.

Double shit. For the first time, Dan realized he couldn't leave the motel room even if he wanted to. That yellow junk in the air would fuck him up. He slammed his back against the headboard in frustration. This sucked.

Isolation didn't work for him. It reminded him of prison. He'd been in juvie before, but that had basically been a vacation. It hadn't prepared him for the real deal. Dan had only been eighteen for two weeks when he'd gotten picked up for sexual assault. Happy birthday to him.

The shrink said his anxiety over being in a cell was because of his childhood, but fuck that. The one time he'd confided in someone about all that stuff, they had spun it against him and tried to figure him out. It was bullshit. He never talked to anyone about it after that, even though his lawyer said it might help reduce his sentence by providing a "compelling back story."

Just thinking of it sent Dan into a rage. He shoved Chrissy off the bed. Her body hit the ground with a loud thud. The movement sent a wave of pungent odor off her.

She'd shat and pissed herself. Hopefully the meat was still good.

He slid off the bed too and had marched to the kitchenette to grab a knife when he heard something outside. Voices. Not screaming in pain this time. Curious, he went to the window beside the hotel room's door and peeked out. Coming down the walkway were two soldiers like the ones he'd seen on the road. They had big guns and plenty of gear. Dangling on their sides were clear plastic packages that had gas masks. Be sweet to get some of that gear for himself.

"Body, 12 o'clock."

"Dead. 2B is locked, no contact."

They were looking for people. Dan looked around the motel room. It was a fucking disaster of a drug den. There were pipes and needles everywhere, even more empty cans and bottles of booze. And there were two dead bodies.

And he was buck naked.

Dan scrambled to dress himself and tried hiding as much of the mess as he could. He grabbed his handgun and tucked it in the back of his jeans, then pulled on his jacket. The soldiers would be there any second. They would have no reason to search the room if he told them it was just him.

He shut both the bathroom and bedroom doors and waited by the window. When he saw them pass, he pulled back the curtains and put on his best victim face. Big eyes, quivering lip. He had practiced it enough times to know it perfectly.

"Got a live one in here. Sir, are you okay?"

The soldier's voice came out louder than it should have, like through a speaker. Very fancy. Dan nodded and shouted, "I'm starving in here. Can you help?"

"Yes, how many are with you?"

"Just me."

"Back away from the door as far as you can. I'm going to toss in one of these. Do not touch the package with your bare hands. Cover your hands, open it up, and then put on the protective gear. We can't come in or you might get contaminated. When you're all sealed up, come on out. We're going to check the rest of the rooms. Do you understand?"

He wasn't a fucking idiot. "Yeah, I think so."

Dan waited in the bedroom until he heard the front door open and snap shut a second later. A small trace of the yellow dust was settling inside the main room when he emerged. Dan went into the bathroom and yanked the shower curtain rod down and used it to pull the package the soldier had tossed inside closer to him, away from the dust.

He tugged his sleeves over his hands and opened the package. Inside were gloves, tape, a plastic suit, and a gas mask with a giant canister on the side. He put on the silly plastic getup and covered the gaps at his wrists and ankles with tape, guessing its use. The gas mask was heavy and made him feel claustrophobic, but he reminded himself it was the only way out of this shithole.

One problem—there wasn't anywhere good to keep his gun. The suit had no pockets. For now, he'd have to leave it hidden in his waistband, under the suit.

He opened the door to the outside. Yellow dust flooded the room. It was weird out there. Everything looked like it did through those yellow work glasses he'd worn during his short-lived construction career. He ran his hand across the railing in front of him. It came away thick with the shit.

He heard the soldiers a level below him, checking doors. Dan wondered if they had found anyone else, maybe some chicks, but he cast the thought aside. He wasn't sticking with them. Food or not, hanging out with military dudes would definitely cramp his style. Now that he had the right gear, he was free to roam. He should've told the soldiers he had people in there with him so they would give him extra suits. Oh well.

He cracked his neck and moved in the opposite direction of the soldiers, not sparing a single glance back at his motel room.

# LARA

Lara couldn't look away from the body lying on the carpet. The giant pool of blood around the dead man's head was slick and dark.

Three years ago Lara had worked with a patient who had accidentally killed her own little brother. At the age of six, she took her two-year-old brother out of his crib to play with her at the creek near their house. It was her favorite spot, and she wanted to share it with him. Distracted by picking huckleberries, she left him unattended. The little boy had rolled into the creek and drowned. As she worked with her patient, now a grown woman, through her anxiety and guilt, Lara helped her realize she couldn't hold her six year-old self accountable for what happened. It had been an accident. It was okay to feel remorse, but to make herself suffer every day was unnecessary.

Lara hoped that was the kind of situation Jack had gotten himself into. When he'd said he killed a man, she had assumed it was somehow an accident. But looking at the perfect bullet hole in the corpse's forehead, she knew that it hadn't been the case.

She'd promised Jack she would bring him food and help him find gear, and she planned to uphold that promise. But once she'd fulfilled her end of the deal, she was going to continue on her own. Lara wasn't sure where she'd go yet, but of one thing she was certain: she could not trust a murderer.

Her heart heavy and mind set, she forced herself to

turn away from the body and search the kitchen.

The few cans of soup and wafer cookies looked like heaven. Lara had always hated cold canned food with a passion. It tasted like the metal can it came from. Yet when she looked at it now, she couldn't wait to dig in. She had enough forethought to grab a can opener and utensils from the drawers. Once the food was stored in her pack, she began her journey back to the shop, hoping the return would be as easy as the arrival.

On the way to the apartment, she hadn't encountered anyone alive, but there were dozens of dead bodies littering the sidewalk and road. Lara had found herself looking at each corpse even though they made her feel sick. Their skin was oozing. Yellow, leaking pustules were on every inch of exposed flesh. Their eyes were filled with blood. The dust soaked into it all and made a gummy paste. On her way back, she was mostly able to ignore the bodies. She took note of the rest of her surroundings as well as she could with the poor visibility, noting the condition of the roads, the buildings. She mentally cataloged the varying colors of smoke. Black smoke from buildings mixed with the yellow dust to create a muted swirl of colors. Countless tiny meteorites had left dents in the road and buildings, but larger debris had created giant craters. Those were the ones to look out for when walking through the dust. All it would take was one moment of carelessness and she'd get caught on exposed rebar and piping.

Lara shuddered at the thought of being impaled on a pipe. What a terrible way to go. She forced her mind to refocus on the task at hand. She'd been in Monroe before. There was a family-owned hardware store about three more blocks north from the apartment. She and Harry had gone there a few times while they were remodeling their house. It probably hadn't been looted for supplies yet; in the weeks leading up to the event, no one had been interested in building anything.

As she walked, she felt a growing sense of unease. There could be someone thirty feet ahead, or just behind her, and she wouldn't know because of the thick, swirling dust. Between her ski mask and hood, many sounds were lost. She brushed a thin layer of dust off the visor of her mask.

What she needed was a weapon.

A multi-car pileup blocked most of the road in front of the shop. She worked around it, her eyes straining to see through the dust. When she finally reached the hardware shop, her heart sank. The windows were shattered, the door caved in by a neon green Volkswagen bug. To make things even worse, the building had been on fire at one point. Black marks licked upward from the windows onto the brick above. She picked up a chunk of concrete from the damage the Volkswagen caused and used it to knock out the remaining glass on a window sill. The front of the shop appeared to be in bad shape, but there might still be salvage inside. She pushed her pack through the window and crawled after it. Flashlights and miscellaneous tools had melted in their packaging. The single cash register stand was charred.

It was dark inside. She wished one of those flashlights had survived. She moved deeper into the store. Unlike the grocery stores, this place hadn't been picked clean. She was disturbed to see that the wall that would contain spools of chain and rope was completely empty. Gardening tools were in ample supply, as were power tools.

The store was small, just four narrow aisles across, and Lara decided to go up and down each one in case she found anything else of use. The automotive aisle was almost untouched and she grabbed an assortment of wrenches and screwdrivers. They could be useful for their intended purposes, but the screwdrivers would also make good lightweight weapons. She kept one in her front jacket pocket and stored the rest in her bag.

The last row was the painting aisle. She started at the head of the aisle, her eyes now better adjusted to the dim light, and took her time searching the shelves from top to bottom.

When she found the white 3M coveralls on the lowest shelf, she felt her spirit lift. The only size left was XL, but they were exactly what she wanted. Best of all, there were six packages and they weighed almost nothing. She smiled as she stuffed them into her bag. Not only could she upgrade her own protection, but if she found more people she could help them, too.

The last and most important item she needed was a respirator. Lara was ecstatic when she found four of them hanging in plastic clamshell packages. They were too bulky to all fit in her pack, so she went back to the cleaning product area she'd seen earlier and grabbed a box of heavy duty garbage bags. She spotted a box of latex gloves and took those too, glad she'd come back for the bags.

A noise from the darkness startled her. Her heart rate skyrocketed as her mind went into overdrive. The noise sounded like it had come from a different room, but that could have been a result of her gear blocking the sound. Maybe a door rattling? Or something tipping over?

She waited for an eternity. Her nerves were frazzled. For all she knew, it was nothing. She returned to the respirators and put all of them in a garbage bag. She also took five pairs of safety goggles, which sealed against the skin like swim goggles. They were small and fit easily in the bag with everything else.

"Is someone out there?"

Lara jumped. *That* was unmistakable. Female and

young. The voice sounded scared.

She hesitated to respond. There was no shortage of desperate people in this city. But maybe the girl was like her, a good person, just looking for help. "Hello?" Lara called out. "I'm here."

The shop was silent. Then, "I'm stuck in the office back here. My mom is hurt. She got dust on her."

Lara felt a pang of maternal concern. Her decision was made. She wasn't going to leave a young person in need. She had masks and extra coveralls.

"I'm coming. Just hang on."

The back of the store was almost pitch black, and Lara stood at the edge of the darkness waiting for her eyes to adjust and her heart to stop pounding. After minutes of waiting, she realized her vision was as good as it was going to get—and her primal fear of the dark wasn't likely to go away. She took a step closer and brought her hands up to feel the path in front of her. After six steps she bumped into a case of some kind. The contents rattled. The hollow jangling sounded like plastic pipes.

She took a deep breath, one that felt damp and stagnant in her mask, and kept moving forward. Her hands hit a jumble of items hanging on pegs. She groped and squeezed the packages, knocking some to the ground.

"You're close," the girl called out. "Keep coming!"

Lara followed the voice and bumped into a wall. She felt along it until her hands dipped into a door frame. Her hands grazed a bar going across the door. She prepared to push it open.

"Listen, you need to get as far back from the door as you can. The dust is going to come in when I do, okay?"

"We're ready."

As fast as she could, Lara pushed open the door, slid to the side, and closed it behind her. The manager's office was lit by a dying flashlight propped up against the wall. The weak beam also illuminated the three people waiting for her inside the room. There was something about the sneers on their faces that set off an alarm inside her.

Sitting on the desk wasn't a child but a woman with long ratted brown hair. She wore a flimsy spaghetti-strap dress and knee high boots. Two men stood against the wall opposite her. One of them raised his hand, and it was then Lara saw the handgun.

"You got any more masks?" the woman asked. Her voice was childlike, but Lara couldn't believe she'd mistaken it for an actual child's. "We've been stuck here for hours."

Lara's grip on her plastic bag tightened. She had salvaged the masks to help people, but not *these* people. "I say we take hers," the bigger of the two men suggested. "One of us can go find more."

The woman snorted. "You wouldn't come back for me, you selfish fuck. Dylan can go find more, you're staying here."

"Bitch, I'm the one w—"

Lara used that second of distraction to move. A gunshot rang out, and the tile near her foot shattered. She froze. The door, barely an eighth of an inch open, gently closed.

"Don't. Even. Try," the gun-wielding man said from between clenched teeth. "Move away from the door. Slow."

Lara obeyed. The farther from the door she moved, the lower her hopes sank. She should've risked making a run for it.

The woman slid off the desk, wobbling on her thin legs. "So, whaddya you got in there?"

"Just things from the store."

"Yeah? Why don't you show us?"

Lara swallowed the lump in her throat. The man with the gun was closest to the door, blocking her escape.

Opposite him was the larger man, leaning against the wall with his arms folded. His body looked at ease, but his eyes were locked on to Lara.

As her gaze returned to the thin woman, a single idea popped into her head. It was risky. But what did she have to lose? These people wouldn't just take her gear. They'd take Lara's life, too.

"Here," she said as she set down the garbage bag. She leaned over more than necessary to plop it on the ground and stealthily retrieved the screwdriver from her pocket. No one seemed to notice. "I have gloves, coveralls, even masks."

The woman drew closer, apparently pleased that Lara was cooperating. Once she was close enough, Lara lashed out and grabbed her by a skinny arm. She swung the woman around and squeezed her tightly against the front of her dust-covered body. As weak and starved as Lara was, this woman was in even worse shape. Lara felt a pang of guilt but pushed it aside. The second she pressed the tip of the screwdriver to the woman's throat, she stopped struggling.

It all happened in seconds. Both men took a step closer, and Lara pressed the tool into the woman's bony neck.

"Back off!"

They listened.

"Kay, it's gonna be all right," Dylan, the one with the gun, said. "Just don't move, honey."

Kay whimpered. "It hurts. She got dust on me."

"The bitch is dead already," the other man said. "Shoot them both and take the gear. Think with your brain, not your pencil dick for one second. Kay's pussy ain't good enough for us to fight over."

"Shut the fuck up, Jer!"

"Hey!" Lara shouted. "Get away from the door. Go to the other side of the desk."

Neither listened. A fight that had been brewing between them long before Lara had arrived was erupting. Neither Kay nor Lara mattered anymore.

"Give me the gun, Dylan. She only gave it to you because she knows she has you whipped. Hand it over."

Lara watched, stunned, as he pulled the trigger. A split second later a huge chunk of Jer's head was splattered on the wall. Dylan turned the gun onto Lara. "Let her go. Now."

Lara squeezed Kay tighter. "I will. But only once I'm out that door. I don't want to hurt anyone. Pick up my bag and put it by the door, then go to the other side of the desk."

"Can't." Dylan shook his head. His hands were shaking, too. "We need that stuff. I'll say it one more time. Let Kay go."

Suddenly the woman went limp. Lara couldn't keep her upright, and Kay slid from her arms. The skin on her shoulders, arms, and backs of her legs were covered in blood and pus.

Dylan dove for Kay but halfway through the motion opted to shoot Lara instead. The bullet went wide and thudded into the wall just behind her. Lara lowered her center of gravity and rammed him with her shoulder, knocking him off balance. She lunged for the door but felt something tug her foot. She fell face forward on the ground, kicking wildly as she went.

Her boot connected with something soft and crunchy all at once. She flipped onto her back and saw blood pouring from Dylan's mouth from where her foot made contact. Still, he held firmly onto Lara's feet. The gun was nowhere in sight.

Lara mustered up another burst of strength and kicked. She got him square in the chest. His grip on her feet released. She kicked again. Dylan slammed against the desk and slumped into a seated position. She scrambled to her feet and was about to go for the door when she realized she still needed her bag. She darted over to Kay's motionless body and snatched up the supplies before rushing to the door. She shoved it open and thick waves of dust flowed into the room.

She was already stumbling towards the light at the front of the store when Dylan began to scream.

Then Lara was gone, climbing out the window and running as fast as she could away from the hardware store. In minutes she arrived at the alley behind the shop. She was covered in dust from head to toe, some areas damp and congealed with blood. Every crevice in her clothing was filled with it. The contamination from the dust was a huge issue that she wasn't sure how to handle yet. Eventually she'd have to take the clothes off—if nothing else, she'd had to pee for hours—and when she did, her body would be exposed.

She thought of Kay's pus-covered, bloody skin.

She had killed those people. Maybe not directly, but she had been responsible for their deaths. The adrenaline in her body made her shake. Tears flooded her eyes. They would've killed her. They'd have taken all her gear and left her to die—or worse.

Lara was a survivor. She had to give herself credit for that.

And in that moment, she understood the difference between her and Jack. It was one thing to kill in self-defense, as Lara had. Jack and the people she'd just encountered killed when they didn't have to.

She returned to the store where she'd left Jack, quickly opening and shutting the door to reduce how much dust entered. She stood still as she waited for it to settle. Jack was exactly where she'd left him, that bottle of cherry kirsch still clutched in his hand. He studied her, and she was glad she had her mask to cover her face. Lara was easy to read, and if her face was exposed he'd see the tears and quivering lip.

"I got food, plastic coveralls, and masks," she announced, trying to keep her voice steady. Her pack was heavy. She was relieved to shrug it off. "We can take two cans of soup each. I'm not sure how to split the cookies. Maybe if I toss them to you, you can take one half but keep my half in the package?"

"Are you okay? I heard gunshots. And you've got blood on you."

"Yes. I'm fine. It isn't…the blood isn't mine. I stopped at a hardware store up the street. There were people in there."

"And?"

"They had a gun pointed at me. They wanted my stuff."

Jack got to his feet and set his empty bottle on the shelf next to him. "I'm glad you made it."

She pulled out a respirator, pair of coveralls, and the latex gloves, then tossed them as hard as she could. They slid on the checkered linoleum towards him. As soon as she could, she needed to find a place to strip out of her makeshift protection and put on one of the plastic suits, too. Jack retrieved the items and opened the packages. He pulled on the gloves first, slid the box back to her, then started on the suit.

"Jack, I think we should go our separate ways from here. You have everything you need."

"Oh." He finished zipping up his plastic suit and stopped to look at her. There was something incredibly silly about him in the oversized plastic pajamas. "Are you sure?"

Just as Lara was about to respond, six figures emerged from the dust behind them and shattered the store windows.

# COLLEEN

Colleen felt a pang of heartbreak when she looked at her daughters while they slept. Serena hadn't taken the truth very well. She was old enough to be hostile. Even though she already knew about Zabat's Comet, she let out her pent up aggression on how they hadn't told her the truth right away. She took it personally, as she did most things since she'd turned eleven. That was far too early to be acting like a teenager.

"You think I'm so stupid, don't you?" she repeated each time James or Colleen apologized.

And Liana…

Liana's reaction wasn't what Colleen expected. At all. At the very least, Colleen expected her to take a cue from Serena and cry or yell. Instead, the little girl nodded and said, "Okay," with no interest, fear, or betrayal. Colleen would've preferred Liana to lash out. Through the hundreds of explanations Colleen could come up with, her mind kept returning to the yellow dust.

Colleen was sure it was making Liana sick. Liana's hand was growing worse where the dust had touched it. The skin was irritated with a scattering of tiny blisters. On top of each blister was a bright greenish-blue scab, perfectly round and a little smaller than a pinhead. That color alone sent blinding panic through Colleen. She'd never seen that hue in a wound before, and growing up on a farm she had seen a *lot* of injuries. Liana said it didn't hurt in the same, flat tone she'd used during their big talk.

Restless yet fatigued, Colleen climbed down the ladder to leave her kids alone. It had to be almost morning, but with the lantern as their only source of light on the first story, time already felt skewed.

"How are they doing?" James asked.

Colleen shrugged. "Fine, I guess. Liana says her burn scars itch, but they look normal to me. They're sleeping now."

"Maybe we shouldn't have told them. We could've skipped the part about the earth being destroyed, at least. Especially since doomsday didn't happen." James ran a hand through his dark hair as he set aside the novel he'd been reading.

"It was the right thing to do. I'm more worried about what we're going to do now."

They lapsed into silence. Colleen picked at her nails. Hygiene had been an issue for weeks before the comet, once the water stopped working. Her scalp and skin itched terribly. What she'd do for a shower.

"If we went outside, we'd have no idea where to go," James said. "Imagine walking for miles in that dust. Not knowing if you're getting farther away from it or going deeper in. What if this is what the whole planet is like? I think we should stay here."

"If the whole planet is like this, we're going to die anyway. We'll starve here eventually if we don't go."

"Jesus, Colleen."

She pulled her knees up to her chest and rested her head against them. She let her awareness drift to her toes then work its way up her body to the tip of her head. It helped ground her. She'd learned the technique years ago when dealing with panic attacks after Katie's death. Sometimes, thoughts like that flooded her. There was a tiny piece of darkness inside her mind that made itself known on occasion. If there was a time for it to rear its ugly head, it was now.

Now, when their kids hated them. When they were cooped up in a tiny workshop. When Liana was afflicted with some freakish rash and they didn't know what to do. When they had no idea what the future held.

"I'm sorry," she said, hoping her sincere tone matched how she felt. "Not doing well right now."

James nodded. He seemed like he was going to speak again when his mouth snapped shut. He sat up straight and looked past Colleen. "Did you hear that?"

"Hear what?"

All she heard was her heartbeat, which had picked up in reaction to James. Then, faintly, she heard someone yelling outside. The sound was distorted. It took Colleen a moment before she realized the voice was being amplified, perhaps through a megaphone or some kind of speaker. It was distant and not drawing any closer.

"I think they said FEMA, Colleen."

She pressed her ear against the door. The plastic felt cool and good against her skin. She picked up words, but not full sentences. Something about a FEMA refugee camp.

"We need to get out there," she said. She stood and began rifling through giant rubber tubs for what she needed. "Where are the hazmat suits?"

"They're over here. But I'm going, not you. You need to stay here with the girls."

Colleen tore the lid off the tub. Inside were sealed plastic packages of bright yellow hazmat suits. She opened one and pulled it on. Her hands slid into the attached gloves and her shoes went right into the booties. She zipped it up.

"What's going on?" Liana's voice was clear and unafraid. Colleen saw the top of her face peeking over the edge of the loft.

"I'm going outside for a second. Stay up there, okay?"

Liana disappeared without a word.

Colleen turned to James, her gas mask clenched tightly in her hands. "Serena listens to you, Liana looks up to Serena. We both know that. Plus you can't run with your leg like that. Get them to put on their suits and gas masks. I'll try to reach whoever is out there. Whatever happens, you need to have them ready to leave."

James frowned, but Colleen knew she had already won. James always gave in to rational decisions in the end. "I'm on it."

She gave him a peck on the lips then pulled on her gas mask. James helped her with the hood that went over her hazmat suit, then set a flashlight in her hand. She peeled the plastic away from the door and stepped under it, creating a pocket between the sealed off shed and the door to outside.

Behind her, James taped off edges that might allow dust to enter the room. He tapped her shoulder from the other side. "You're good!"

Colleen unlatched the workshop door and slipped out as fast as she could.

The world outside was a muted shade of yellow. Since they'd entered the workshop, the dust seemed to have settled a bit. In the distance she saw the sun rising. It sent beams of light through the dancing yellow motes. It was unbearably still. Not a single living thing was outside. Even the trees and grass looked alien now.

Somewhere in the distance she heard the low rumble of engines. Colleen began jogging in the sound's direction. The hazmat suit was clunky and made moving quickly difficult. If James hadn't been injured, he might've been better for the job after all. He'd been training for a marathon before the comet, and he'd kept up his daily run even when it seemed like the world was going to end.

She had to move faster or she wasn't going to catch up with them. Colleen reached the street and started running, but before she'd gone more than a few yards, her body flew forward and hit the ground.

She'd tripped over a disfigured body. It was covered with dust, almost indistinguishable in the dim light. She'd knocked it onto its back when she tripped, revealing a body so rotten and covered in pus it was hard to tell if it was a man or woman. More of the greenish-blue blisters. Eyes bulged from caved sockets, foggy across the iris and pupil. A sheet of skin from the face had peeled away and was still stuck to the pavement. Colleen swallowed back a wave of nausea and got to her feet.

The whites of the corpse's eyes were fluorescent blue.

Behind her, the megaphone sounded again.

She put the corpse and its horrible eyes out of her mind and pressed forward. The suit trapped her body heat and made her sweat profusely. It was hard to take the deep breaths she needed while wearing the gas mask.

Then she saw them; thick wheel marks on the ground with dozens of footprints following. She increased her pace as much as she could and finally reached the convoy. Where they were stopped in the middle of the road.

"Freeze!"

She halted. Four figures in suits similar to hers placed themselves between her and the vehicles. They were wielding rifles. There had to be another twenty people beside three Humvees. There could've been more, but the dust limited her vision. About half the people she saw were crowded together wearing mismatched gear. Some didn't even have a proper hazmat suit on. Instead, they had plastic garbage bags taped at the seams wrapped around their bodies.

Colleen wasn't sure whether she should be reassured

or not. If these people were really from FEMA, why hadn't they given better protection to these people? What if they weren't from the government? The thought hadn't crossed her mind before, but it should have. At the mere thought of organized help, she'd forgotten herself.

Her hands hung in the air. The men approached her until they were feet away. "Are you armed?"

She wiggled the flashlight in her right hand. "This is all I have. My family needs help, we heard you calling out."

The man nodded. The motion was barely visible through the heavy folds of plastic around his head. "My name is Corporal Thompson, ma'am. We're helping survivors get to a FEMA camp. Where's your family?"

"In a house nearby." Colleen still wasn't ready to trust them with a specific location.

"As you can see, we're stalled," the private said. "Humvees sucked up too much of this dust. We're going on foot from here, but you're welcome to come along."

She took the conversation as an okay to lower her arms. "Where exactly is the FEMA camp? And how long has it been there?"

Another soldier spoke up. It was a woman. "It's been at the Renton high school for months, but no one used it. Why fuckin' bother? Then we stopped getting orders and stayed there ourselves. When the dust came, communication went out completely. Nothin' but static. We waited for orders, but there weren't any. So now we're picking up survivors. The place has air purifiers, generators, supplies. We can hold about four hundred comfortably."

Colleen's instinct was to trust them. She *did* remember hearing about the high school being converted to a camp, but there hadn't been any reason for them to go. Everything they needed was in their home.

The last of the refugees climbed out of the Humvees.

The group began a slow march down the road.

The first man, Thompson, spoke again. "We can give you some suits and one of us can help you get your family, but we need to be fast. We encountered multiple hostile groups on the way here."

That she didn't doubt. "Thank you. We all have suits and masks. I might need help carrying my youngest, though. My husband has an injured leg."

"We've got a doctor that can help out," Thompson said. "Belman, go with them."

"Yes, Corporal," the woman said.

Colleen began a fast walk back to her house. The soldier's hazmat suit was much less bulky than hers, and she moved alongside Colleen effortlessly. They made good time back to the workshop. She knocked on the door and called out to James.

"I've got the girls ready," he responded. "Opening the door now!"

James had taped Serena's suit to fit her better. It looked a little silly, but at least she was completely mobile. Liana was in James' arms. He'd tried to modify her suit to fit, but it was eight times too big. He'd taped the gas mask around the hood to create a seal. It worked, but Liana couldn't walk and Colleen knew James couldn't carry their four year old with his leg like that.

"I'll take first shift carrying Liana," Colleen said as she reached out for her daughter. The plastic-clad toddler was slippery in her hands and it took a bit of shifting before she had her positioned well. "This is Private Belman. She's going to take us to a FEMA camp at the high school."

"That's almost five miles away," James said. "Bet you're glad you saved those crutches."

She imagined his grin from behind his mask and took comfort in it. When she had broken her foot two years earlier, she insisted on keeping the crutches in case they ever needed them. He had teased her, saying she was a hoarder. The crutches made their way to the back of the coat closet, forgotten until now.

"Aren't *you* glad I did," she said and laughed.

It was like someone turned a light switch on and dispelled all the dark misery that accumulated in the shed. There was tangible hope before them. His optimism in the face of his wound made her proud.

She and her family began walking with Belman in the lead. They moved slowly, and Colleen worried they wouldn't catch up with the rest of the convoy any time soon. As they walked, Colleen searched her neighbor's windows for signs of life and found none.

"Do you know what happened?" James asked Belman.

Belman was walking ten feet ahead of them, but she apparently heard the question. "Not really. Haven't heard anything from the brass in weeks. Some of the guys think the dust is messing up the atmosphere or some shit and radio signals aren't working. Last thing we heard, the whole country was fu—"

"Please don't swear around the kids," Colleen said.

"Yes, ma'am," the soldier said and chuckled. "As for why we aren't floating in space right now or burnt to a crisp, I dunno. Maybe once we can reestablish communications, we'll get some answers."

That was about what Colleen expected. The group quieted. Even when they reached the rest of the convoy, there was nothing to do but focus on walking. The road had been pelted with meteor debris, but it was easy to navigate around. A few people offered to take turns carrying Liana, including Belman. The kind gesture helped Colleen feel at ease.

Hours later, they finally made it to the high school. It

was a sprawling campus. In front of the school was a long plastic tent that formed a corridor almost twenty feet wide leading to the front entrance. The plastic was opaque, and Colleen couldn't make out what was inside. The group slowed as they approached it. There were soldiers flanking the flaps, more on the rooftops of the high school.

"This is a decontamination corridor. We're going to put anyone with a hazmat suit through first. Then you'll move into the high school where you'll remove your gear and go through a secondary decontamination and an exam to make sure you're in good shape," Belman said. "Doc'll take a look at your husband's leg."

Colleen took Liana from her. "Thank you for everything. We didn't…we weren't sure what we were going to do back there."

Belman reached out and squeezed Colleen's shoulder. "It's what we do. We're headed back out soon. See you later."

Colleen hugged Liana close to her and wiped away a thin layer of dust from the hazmat suit visor. She saw Liana's clear hazel eyes looking up at her.

"We're safe now, baby."

"Okay, mom," Liana answered in a flat tone that sent an unwelcome, surprising chill down Colleen's spine.

# JACK

The moment Jack saw the figures approaching the windows, he flew into motion. He pulled on his respirator a second before the glass shattered. Yellow dust rushed into the room and filled every crevice of it.

Jack dove into the back room. Lara kicked the doorstop out of the way and shut the door. She pulled a mop from against the wall and wedged it through the door handle.

"That won't hold long. We have to get out of here," Lara said.

Jack hadn't been this close to her before. She was much shorter than him, barely level with his chin. He wanted to take out his gun, but that meant unzipping his plastic suit. Lara pulled on her backpack and opened the door to the alley.

"Where do we go?"

Behind them their assailants pounded on the other door. The mop flexed and threatened to break. Through the porthole Jack saw a raider's face covered with ski goggles and a respirator. The goggles had white smiley faces painted on both lenses.

"You can't hide forever, stupid bitch!" the man screamed. "I'm gonna gut you both and fuck ya after!"

"Just run!" Lara yelled at Jack.

She set off down the alley at full speed. Jack huffed behind her, regretting all those years spent on the couch. He used to be fit. Now running made his lungs burn. His calves and shins already ached and threatened to cramp up.

He tried to keep Lara in his sight, but eventually she turned a corner and left him alone.

The alleyway was surreal. Every surface had a layer of dust at least a quarter inch thick. His white plastic suit was turning yellow as it coated him. The dust extended as far as he could see. There was no real freedom to be had. He'd have to take refuge in another place that would likely be just as bad, or even worse, than the convenience store.

"Jack, what the hell are you doing?" Lara's body was no more than a blurry smudge in the yellow haze. "Come on!"

Behind him, their pursuers broke through the door and flowed into the alley. Even though Jack had lagged behind, he and Lara had a solid head start. If they could get far enough away, the dust would help conceal them.

Jack met up with Lara, who didn't spare him a glance. She continued down the street but slowed her pace to stay by him as he began to lag again. Their surroundings shifted from apartments to individual houses on either side of the road. The homes were in bad shape. Windows were shattered, there were holes in many roofs. To their right, a meteor the size of a car sat on the crumbling skeleton of a house.

"We need to find somewhere to hide. We're sitting ducks out here without a weapon."

Jack thought of his handgun still tucked away. It didn't matter; he doubted he had enough rounds to take out the people chasing them. Even if he did, it could draw more raiders to them.

"Agreed," he said. "One of these houses?"

"No," Lara said. "Too risky. There could be people inside. There's a library up ahead. I don't think anyone would look for us there."

Still jogging, she led him across an intersection where the street curved sharply. On their right was an auto repair shop that appeared to be mostly a junkyard. The fence had sagged in spots, showing junk cars and a workshop. To the left, a library was set back behind overgrown shrubbery.

Jack had taken Katie to this library before. It was all glass and brick, a building that was out of place in the otherwise low-income area. He wasn't sure if it was a safe place to hide out; most of the building's facade had tall windows to show off the inside. It was a miracle the glass was still intact. Although small meteorites were embedded in the lawn and nearby road, none had touched the building.

"Are you sure about this? Anyone could see us in there."

Lara walked towards the entrance. "Only if they come looking."

She pulled at the glass double doors. Both were locked. Lara moved past outdoor book return slots to an employee-only service door. She pulled on it and then cursed.

Jack didn't like it. The building was a bad call. They should've kept running. Their pursuers weren't far behind. He could hear them shouting. There had to be a better place to hide.

"Let's go into the woods," he said, pointing to the nearby park. "Wait them out."

"Hello?"

Both he and Lara scanned wildly for the source of the voice. The library parking lot appeared empty, but visibility was poor. Jack considered taking out his gun. It meant risking contamination, but if they had a gun they had an advantage.

"Down here."

The book return slot rattled. Jack bent down and looked through it. Dark eyes, almost black, stared back at him from behind clear ski goggles. The person wore black garbage bags wrapped tightly around their mouth and head. The slot closed.

Lara dropped to her knees and lowered her voice. "We need help. Please let us in. We're being chased by bad people."

"What were you before?"

"What?" Jack shifted from foot to foot. They were going to be mowed down any second. No time for questions from some loony librarian.

"What was your profession? Just answer."

"I was a therapist," Lara said. "I had my own practice."

"What about you?"

Jack groaned. "This is ridiculous. Lara, we need to keep moving."

"He was a high school history teacher," Lara said. "Please, let us in."

Apparently those answers were satisfactory. "Go to the door to your right. The second I open it, come in just enough so I can close it."

Jack and Lara slipped through the door as commanded. The figure closed the door and shoved a metal chair underneath the handle in addition to locking the deadbolt.

Above them, three giant skylights cast the room in yellow light. There were bins on wheels filled with books. A light coating of dust kissed the bins closest to the door. Posters and notices about library events and employee reminders were pasted on the walls.

Outside, the voices grew louder. Jack, Lara, and the librarian were motionless. The voices were close enough that Jack could make out the conversation. They were angry. One wanted to keep looking. The others vetoed them and said they should keep checking the suburbs.

The door rattled as someone shook the handle. Jack's hand drifted to the zipper on his jacket, ready to retrieve his gun.

"Hey, dumbass, we're checking the 'burbs. Come on."

"We gotta at least check, man. It looks like there's footprints going in here."

"Nothing in there but fuckin' books man. Boss said those bitches probably went to the 'burbs, so that's where we going. You wanna make the boss mad?"

"Shi-it," the voice drawled. "I'm coming."

Their voices faded away. Jack's shoulders had ridden up towards his ears. He let them drop and tried to relax the tension that had built up between his shoulder blades since the chase started.

"We have to decontaminate before we go into the rest of the library," the librarian said. "If you want to stay, that is. Sounds like they're gone."

"We're staying. Thank you," Lara answered.

The man—Jack was pretty sure it was a man under the garbage bags—distanced himself from Lara and Jack. Dozens of containers of cleaning wipes were stacked on a desk alongside spray bottles of bleach and boxes of sterile gloves. They were silent as they watched him first wipe his entire body from head to toe. Each used wipe went into a trash bin. He sprayed himself with bleach and wiped down again. "First pass gets most of it off so you don't kick up more when you take off your gear. The spray and wipes get most of the residual."

He stripped out of his makeshift hazmat suit to reveal oversized jacket and pants. He took those off and then unwrapped his scarf and gloves. He stacked all the items neatly over the edge of an empty bin. Thankfully he wore another layer of clothing beneath.

"Stay there until I walk out of this room. We do this one at a time to reduce the chances of getting dust in the main library," he said. "Make sure this door is closed behind you when you leave. Once you're in the office area, you'll see a container of baby wipes and a pile of clothes by the employee lockers. Clean yourself off, put on the new clothes, and toss the old ones in the garbage bag. Got it?"

"Yes, we understand," Lara said.

Jack studied the man. He was older, at least in his mid-fifties, and his face and arms were blistered and red. He caught Jack staring.

"Not from the dust. Burns." He offered no further explanation. Before he left through the door opposite them, he said, "Stay away from the windows. Once you're in the main library, you'll see we have a path made to the back. Never leave it."

Lara began to head towards the designated strip corner. Jack put his hand out to stop her. "We don't know these people."

"Should I remind you I don't know *you*? And that there are crazy people outside trying to kill us?"

She clearly wanted to say more. Jack knew people well enough to feel the unspoken words waiting to burst out. Lara knew he was a murderer. He'd been waiting for her to say something. That was why she wanted to go separate ways, because he'd shot a man in the head. He didn't blame her. If he were her, he would've left himself to die in the store or the alley.

Jack's mouth felt dry. Whatever buzz he'd had from the cherry kirsch was long gone. Now he felt a headache brewing as his guilt amplified.

"You're right. It isn't my call whether you stay or go." He took a deep breath. "The question is, can I stay?"

"If you want to, you can. I won't tell them…what I know."

Lara broke away from him and went to the corner to begin the wipe-down process. Once finished, she unzipped her jacket and carefully peeled it away from her body. As the layers came away, he finally saw her.

Her hair was matted from the ski mask and hood, but was still a rich shade of brown so dark it was almost black. Although she wore a long-sleeved shirt, he saw an abundance of freckles creeping up her neck and scattered across her nose. The gas mask had left an angry red indentation around her face. Without the bulk of her gear, she was petite. Jack could scoop her up in his arms with no problem. She was…cute. He hadn't expected that.

She was real now. Not just a voice and a mask.

"I'll meet you out there," she said and left the room. The door clicked shut.

*What a mess.* He'd been focused for so long on finding Stewart, he'd forgotten how to interact with other people. Maybe if he just went through the motions a little longer, he'd figure out what to do. Jack took off his gas mask and set it over one of the bins. After following the same wiping protocol, he unzipped his plastic coveralls and stepped out of them. Without the protection of the suit, he felt naked. He proceeded through the door to the next room.

The office area had tall ceilings and skylights, too. All that soft yellow light was getting to him. Not quite dark, but not light enough to see well either. To his right, Lara was adjusting her new shirt at the second decontamination area. She smelled faintly of bleach and fake lemon from the cleaning wipes.

Neither of them spoke. Jack waited for her to finish and move to the door leading out of the office before he cleaned himself off and dressed. There were jeans and a long-sleeved shirt that fit him with room to spare.

Whoever was hiding out in the library had pushed the shelves to form a wall facing the windows in the front of the building. From the outside, the organization of the shelves would look odd, but as long as whoever was inside stayed behind them, they'd be out of sight.

The first floor was a single, giant space. Directly across from him stairs lead to an open loft-like area. Chest-high railings allowed anyone upstairs to overlook the main floor below. As Jack studied the loft, he saw a handful of people peek over the railing.

The path they were on led to a wide set of stairs that went up to the loft. A woman rushed down the steps to them. Slightly overweight, she had a merriness about her that reminded Jack of his stepmother. She'd always been cheerful in a crisis—and Jack had certainly brought enough of them to her door.

*Leanne.* Jack hoped she was okay.

The woman grinned as she neared. "I doubt Fred introduced himself. That was Fred who helped you. He mans the book return."

She reached the landing the same time as Jack and Lara.

"I'm Molly. Kind of the den mother around here." She held out her hand.

Lara didn't hesitate to shake it, but Jack had to force himself to do it. He knew Lara was good, but the rest of these people? It could be a trap. He'd seen it on the news, before the TV stations went dark. For whatever reason— their own sick amusement, maybe—people would pose as do-gooders looking to lend a helping hand. Once they'd gained a stranger's trust, they'd turn on them. At first they just took food and water. Then they started taking the people themselves to places like Hedone to use for trade.

"Thank you for letting us in," Lara said. She smiled at Molly. "Not sure what we would've done out there."

"Do you have any food?" Jack asked abruptly.

Molly threw her hands in the air and laughed. "We don't have much but we can spare a little. Let me introduce you to everybody along the way."

She led them upstairs, chattering away all the while.

The second story was where everyone slept. Bookshelves had been pushed to the walls to create a space for blankets and sleeping bags lined up side by side. The handful of survivors sat on the makeshift sleeping arrangements. Despite the close quarters, it was tidy. One bookshelf had been cleared completely for their pantry. Jack's heart sank. Molly hadn't been exaggerating when she said there wasn't much. These people were just as bad off as he and Lara.

Molly was introducing everyone, but Jack had zoned out for half of it. Now that he had a moment to breathe, he felt a twisted feeling in his gut. He needed to find Katie's real killer, and the odds of doing that were more than stacked against him. In fact, they were crushing him. The raiders and the dust made it impossible to go outside. Even if he had a name or somewhere to start, there was no Internet for him to search.

"What high school did you teach at, Jack?"

His name brought his attention to reality. The old man, Fred, was staring at him.

"Oh. I taught at an alternative high school for at-risk kids. It was a small operation," Jack lied.

Molly settled into a metal chair and placed a fleece blanket over her lap. "We always ask what people used to do, to get a feel for them. If someone hesitates or refuses to answer, we know they're up to no good. It's kind of a little initiation question."

Jack didn't think it was a very good initiation question. There had to be better ways of getting a feel for someone. After all, he had lied to their faces just now.

"How long have you been here?" Lara asked as she sat down cross-legged on the carpet.

Jack surveyed the group. They looked harmless enough, he supposed. There was a mix of older and younger people, the youngest maybe twenty. Their base was organized. He didn't see any drugs or alcohol around. His body ached from running, and he decided his need for a few minutes of rest outweighed his suspicion.

"I've been here the longest," Molly said. "About three months. My neighborhood was burned down by a group of bikers, and I had nowhere to go. I used to be the head librarian here, so I had keys. It's such a pleasant place. I figured I'd spend my last days here reading and sipping tea. Oh, tea!"

She leaned over and whispered something to the woman next to her. The woman was about forty, Jack's age, with a head of curly blond hair pulled into a ponytail. She nodded.

"Yvette will make you some tea. We have a decent amount of water stored up but not much food. The tea takes the edge off."

Yvette pulled out a single-burner camp stove and set it on the ground. From the food shelf she retrieved a gallon of water, a tea kettle, and some tea bags.

"And the rest of you?" Jack asked. "How did you all end up here?"

"Well, Rocky, Linda, and Ano over there were on their way to a FEMA camp about forty miles south of here in Renton," Molly said and pointed to a group of three people huddled together.

The girl, Linda, bumped her shoulder against one of the guys. "Rocky's the brains of our trio."

Rocky's name seemed a misnomer. He was taller than Jack and weighed so little a strong wind would knock him down. Linda looked similar to him, and Jack wondered if they were related. Ano was pudgy and had a soft kindness about him. Jack put all of them in their early or mid-twenties.

"We got chased off course by some freaks with

machetes. While we were hiding out in a health food store, Yvette showed up and said we could stay in the library," Rocky said. "The camp seemed too far away to bother with and we were doing okay here, so we stayed."

Yvette unwrapped a tea bag and set it in a pink mug with a kitten on the front. "I'm Molly's neighbor. We came here together. I used to go looking for food and supplies. That's when I found them," she said, nodding at the twenty-somethings. "I found Fred at a gas station nearby."

"We met Paul and Dio while we were in the hardware store looking for propane for the stove," Linda added.

The mood in the room shifted. Molly's perpetual smile faded.

"Where are they?" Jack asked.

"It was supposed to be the last day, you know?" Ano spoke for the first time. He had an accent. Hawaiian, maybe. "They wanted to go out and see the sky when Zabat's Comet came. They never came back."

The group was silent, the only sounds the propane stove heating the kettle. Just as it began to sing, Yvette pulled it off and poured two teas. She handed one to each of them. Jack got the kitten mug. The heat of the ceramic felt good against his hands. It was then he realized how cold and exhausted he was. The past twenty-four hours had used up every last drop of physical and mental energy he had.

He took a sip of the tea and tilted his head down. It took him a moment to identify the unfamiliar emotion making his cheeks red and his throat tight. It was embarrassment. Despite knowing what he had done to Stewart, Lara had helped him and he'd been acting like an ass. These people had taken him in and shared their meager supplies. He hadn't been shown that much kindness in years.

Lara touched the hot mug against her face and sighed. "Thank you so much. Nothing quite like a hot drink."

"Of course!" Molly leaned back in her chair. "So what's your story?"

Lara didn't answer. Jack blinked slowly and looked over at her. Their eyes locked. After a moment, she faced Molly.

"I'd drawn myself a really hot bath with lavender oil. Took forever to boil enough water and it ended up only being warm. I planned on relaxing up until impact."

A chorus of forlorn chuckles sounded off in the group.

"And your husband?" Molly asked, looking expectantly between Lara and Jack.

"Oh no," he said. "We're not...we just met."

Lara's face had paled. Jack noticed her shoulders slump. She looked at the wedding ring as though it had just shown up. Her tone was flat and left no room for questions. "My husband didn't make it."

"I'm sorry."

"Thank you." Lara continued after a long pause. "The house started shaking, and I saw all the dust outside. I was alive, and I knew if I wanted to keep on living, I needed to find food. I'd stopped eating, really, before the end. What was the point? Some raiders broke into the house, but I escaped. They chased me and then I ran into Jack in a shop. Then we found you."

Jack swallowed the lump in his throat. Lara hadn't lied, but she had omitted everything about Jack's bad attitude, his drinking, and Stewart's murder. For a second, he considered staying here, of rebuilding himself as the kind of guy who taught at-risk kids and volunteered to help the homeless. Then he set his tea, half finished, on the floor and headed down the stairs.

"Hey, where are you going?" Lara called out.

It was getting dark. There was no way to see the sun, but the ambient light that filtered through the yellow dust was dimming. Maybe that would provide cover while he found somewhere else to stay. One thing was certain: he wasn't staying with these people. He'd been there less than an hour and they were already making him soft. He couldn't afford to go soft, not when there was still another man out there he needed to kill.

# LARA

"What just happened?" Molly said aloud to no one in particular.

Lara's mouth hung open in shock. Jack's spontaneous exit had left her feeling just as confused as her new friends. One second he seemed fine, quietly sipping his tea, and the next he storming down the stairs.

"I'm not sure," Lara answered as Jack's bobbing head disappeared out of view down the staircase.

"Are you going to go talk to him, sweetie?"

"Oh." Lara set her mug down and stood. "Yes. Of course."

Part of her didn't want to. It felt so good to sit and drink that hot chamomile tea. Everyone here was incredibly nice. She wanted to soak up the good vibes and let them recharge her. Since Harry had left for Hedone, she'd been entirely alone. At first it had been nice to have alone time, to catch up on reading and just reflect quietly in her own head. It got old quickly. That isolation made her brain foggy and her heart heavy. Meeting Jack did nothing to dispel the feeling. In fact, it had made it worse.

When Fred asked them their "initiation question", Lara immediately lied on behalf of Jack for her own selfish gain. All she could think of was getting to safety. She couldn't very well get herself into the library without him.

And now…would it be so bad if she just let Jack go? Molly was still looking at her expectantly, and she felt like she had no choice but to go after him. How callous would she look if she didn't?

Lara stood on shaky legs. Everyone was watching her now or blatantly looking away.

"Jack, stop," she called out. "Please talk to me."

He'd made it half way to the office area when he stopped. His back still to her, he said, "I'm leaving. I can't stay here, Lara."

"Why not?" Her voice lowered as she stepped in front of him. She felt the other survivors' eyes on her, watching from the railings in the second story.

"You know why," he said.

His jaw was covered in days of beard growth. His deep black skin had a grayish cast. The overhead light cast dark shadows underneath his bloodshot eyes. Lara smelled the cherry kirsch on his breath even from where she stood, now mixed with chamomile.

"I don't. Not really. But I do know you're jeopardizing us being here."

"Not us. I'm leaving. You can stay," he spat.

Lara glanced back and happened to lock eyes with Molly. The older woman smiled and nodded encouragement. Whether Lara wanted to or not, the group expected her to convince Jack to stay. If she let Jack go, she could explain to the group how he'd murdered someone…then they'd probably question her for having brought him in and lied for him. Lara bolstered her resolve. She had to make sure Jack stayed.

"You made a mistake," Lara said. "You thought the world was ending and you did something you wouldn't have done otherwise. And now you regret it. Right?"

He was quiet. Lara rubbed her temples but then quickly brought her hands down. She'd been out of work too long. That kind of gesture showed her impatience with him. Even if he didn't consciously recognize it, some part of him probably did. He frowned, the wrinkles around his mouth and eyes deepening.

"I dreamed of killing him for almost ten years," Jack finally said. His voice was distant, like he wasn't really talking to Lara. "When this comet thing happened, I thought, why not? Why not finally have peace before I die?"

"And did you get that peace?"

He blinked slowly before refocusing on her. "No. And that's why I need to leave. I can't stay with these people. There's something I need to do." Jack turned to leave. He pushed her hand away when she tried to grab him.

"You're punishing yourself. I get it. But you don't have to do that, Jack." She picked up her pace and walked beside him.

They walked through the office and then entered the book return room. Jack wasted no time. He pulled the sleeves of his shirt over his hands, went to his plastic suit, and stepped inside. "You lied to those people because you wanted them to let me stay. They wouldn't have if they knew the truth."

"You're right. Maybe if they knew about the people I left behind to die in the hardware store, they'd think I was bad, too. The fact is, people have been living in a primitive fight or flight mode for months. We have not been ourselves."

"I *have* been myself. I probably would've shot him eventually, comet or not." Jack pulled up the plastic suit and zipped it. His hand slipped from the sleeve and almost made unprotected contact with the suit.

"Jack, stop. You're going to hurt yourself. That thing might still have dust on it!"

He tugged free a couple pairs of sterile gloves and donned them before grabbing his gas mask. "Get out of here so I can open the door."

Lara was losing the battle, but at least he wouldn't leave

until she left the room.

"Fine. But first tell me why you killed him."

Jack looked up at her. "It's complicated."

"Try me."

He took a deep breath, and then the words started tumbling out. "Stewart used to be a meth addict. He abducted my daughter and tortured her for days. He kept her in a cage like a fucking animal. He photographed her. He molested her. He killed her. But Stewart claimed he had only been an accomplice, that he'd never actually touched her. The DNA evidence that would convict him of murder and molestation was mishandled and couldn't be used in court." Jack's hand drifted away from the mask entirely. He stared at the ground. "Stewart went to prison for child pornography and kidnapping. Nothing else. He got out early, too."

Lara squeezed her eyes shut. She didn't have to have children to recognize the unfairness of the sentence. Parents would kill for their children. And if she'd had a daughter, she could easily imagine herself taking revenge into her own hands as Jack had.

If she was honest with herself, truly honest, Lara realized she understood Jack's reasoning. Before, when she saw acts of vigilantism on the news, she had clicked her tongue. If the person had had a higher moral framework, it would've stopped them from doing what they did. But when she added injustice to the mix, what Jack did seemed right.

"Stewart got all religious when he got out of prison," he continued. "When I walked into the apartment, he asked for forgiveness. He said he was sorry for what he did and knew he was going to hell. He said I had myself to blame for what a fuckup I've become. When I put the gun to his head, he said…." Jack clenched his teeth. "He said he forgave me for it."

"Do you believe he really forgave you?"

Jack waved away her question. "It doesn't matter. I don't regret killing Stewart. He was at least partially responsible for what happened to Katie, and what he *did* do was enough for him to deserve death. But I think Stewart was telling the truth about an accomplice. That's why I need to go."

Lara could see Jack better than he could see himself. He might not realize it now, but killing Stewart would come back to haunt him. Lara had worked with patients like him before. "Why do you believe him?"

"He had all of these articles printed, even some case files, that showed similar crimes occurring while he was in prison. I'm going to find the bastard. When I do I—"

A hard thud made both of them jump. Lara's eyes shot to the door of the book return room. A second later they heard it again. Someone was throwing themselves against the door. It was methodical. *Thump. Thump. Thump.* The sound of gunfire, distant but distinct, echoed nearby.

"Help," a weak voice called out.

Lara remembered the people in the hardware store. She would not be tricked again.

"Who's there?" she asked, her body still.

"It's Dio. We're hurt. Please open the door."

"Put your mask on and open the door," she told Jack. "We help them, and then we'll figure everything else out, okay?"

She walked back into the front office, putting herself at a safe distance from the door, and watched as Jack finished suiting up.

Two bodies collapsed inward the second he removed the chair and unlocked the door. A giant plume of yellow dust entered the room, reaching at least ten feet in before the two figures crawled out of the doorway and Jack slammed it closed.

"They got us," one called out.

"Get them away from the dust!" Lara ordered.

He put his hands under the shoulders of one of the men and dragged him away from the settling dust. The other man was bigger, and it took Jack longer to move him.

"Oh, shit."

Jack's voice made her blood run cold. Even from where Lara was, she saw the melted horror of Dio's face. Dozens of tiny blueish-green blisters peeked out from the red and yellow mess of blood and pus that was now his visage.

But that wasn't all she saw. Jack hadn't sealed his mask completely. There was an edge of exposed skin between the respirator and goggles. It was already puffy and red.

Molly and Fred approached, their expressions unreadable. Lara's heart thundered in her chest as Molly said, "They've been contaminated."

# CRAIG

Craig stood thirty feet away from the DZ, one gloved hand clenched into a fist and the other holding an infrared camera. It had to be over eighty degrees outside, the temperature in his hazmat suit even higher. His skin was already slimy with sweat.

The DZ was perfectly smooth. The edges went straight up about a hundred feet, then began tapering inward to form the top of the dome. Yellow dust filled it. It reminded him of blowing bubbles with smoke in your lungs, a trick he used to do at college parties. The smoke would be contained inside the soap bubble, swirling around until the bubble popped and it faded away.

In front of him was a narrow black pole nearly a hundred feet tall. It was bisected by the dome. Half of the pole faced the uncontaminated world, while the other was in the DZ. Twelve inches across, its surface was a seamless, shiny black save for a dent about halfway up. The grass around the pole was scorched, the ground slightly indented in a crater.

Before Craig had arrived at Castle Rock, soldiers sent out bomb disposal robots to study the pole. It didn't blow up or shoot lasers, even when the robots poked it. When soldiers investigated it in person, the results were the same. Right now it was a mystery, but at least it didn't appear to be a dangerous.

Craig asked Berg to order two teams to check for more poles. As it turned out, there were more. Every half mile they'd found another one of the strange poles along the perimeter of the dome. Their precise placement led him to believe they were involved with the force field. He just didn't know how it worked. He might *never* know how it worked.

"Dr. Peters, please proceed," Berg ordered.

"I'm going," Craig breathed, glad the mic inside his mask captured the faint words. He wasn't too proud to admit to himself he was afraid, but he didn't want these soldiers to know how much the DZ unsettled him.

Two days after he arrived, teams from the coast had showed up with more supplies in addition to the hazmat suits and radiation gear they needed. Their mission had taken longer than expected due to raider attacks. Although the world hadn't ended, there was still anarchy in the streets.

Craig felt safe in Castle Rock with the military presence. There were now at least forty soldiers—a mix of Army, Navy, and Marines with a dash of Coast Guard and even a few members of the Air Force. He'd rather have more soldiers than scientists any day. On his trip from California to the cabin in Oregon, he had seen for himself what the raiders were capable of.

Now he and a handful of soldiers were suited up for their first study of the DZ. Each was equipped with positive pressure suits and a respiratory kit.

Craig looked at the DZ through the thermal imaging camera. He anticipated a wash of dark blues and purples and hopefully the warmer tones that indicated the odd rodent might still be alive inside. Instead, the tiny screen showed nothing but red and bright orange. The mysterious pole was bright orange as well.

*Impossible.* Craig reset the camera. He swept it up and down the dome with the same results.

"Holy shit," he muttered, forgetting his mic was open.

"What is it?" Berg asked.

"Thermal video is showing me that the dust is emanating heat. I doubt it's residual heat from the comet's impact. It's been too long since it hit."

And just like that, he already felt back on his game. At least, he would until the slug of liquid courage he had before coming out wore off.

Berg insisted on looking at the camera's screen himself. Craig directed him to point it at the soldiers beside them. The soldiers appeared bright orange, which was no surprise. The Humvee and ground were primarily shades of purple, save for its engine which still glowed warm. When Berg pointed it at the DZ, the screen was flooded with almost solid orange.

"What the hell?" Berg said. "What are we looking at?"

Craig's adrenaline spiked as excitement overtook him. That *was* the question, wasn't it? "There are only two reasons for a reading like that. Either the dust is highly irradiated… or else it's alive."

Craig retrieved a Geiger counter from the Humvee and turned it on, holding it in one hand as he walked towards the dust. The readings were normal and continued to be until he was an arm's length away. The counter spiked slightly, the crackling noise increasing, but it was only a minor blip.

Mild nausea swept over him, paired with an uneasy feeling of being watched.

*Interesting.*

As he walked away, the feeling of unease disappeared. He retrieved the Electro Magnetic Field reader from his kit and turned it on. The EMF reader went crazy.

"This explains it," he muttered. "I'm getting a reading of 150 milliGauss, about two feet from the dome. High levels of EMF are known to cause feelings of paranoia and nausea."

"Is it safe to be this close? What about the radiation?" Berg asked.

"The symptoms of EMF exposure aren't lethal. As soon as you move away, you'll be fine. And I'm not seeing harmful levels of radiation. I'm going to take a sample of the dust to bring back to camp. Someone bring me my containers, please."

One of the soldiers closest to him went back to the Humvee to retrieve the selection of containers Craig had brought specifically for samples. Since he didn't know how the dust would react, he figured it was best to take a sample in glass, plastic, and metal. He was thinking of how they'd decontaminate the containers when he thought he saw the dust shift.

Despite the armed men around him, he felt frightened and small standing at the edge of the DZ. He wanted to chalk it up to the high levels of EMF, but he was out of range. He stared into the yellow abyss and tried to spot the strange movement again. Then Craig thought of the heat signature from the thermal imaging and shuddered. There was an explanation for the reading. There had to be. The dust couldn't really be alive. Could it?

"Here you go, Dr. Peters." A young soldier set down the bag of containers beside Craig's feet and then quickly stepped back.

Berg came up beside him as he unscrewed the lid from a glass vial and held out his hand. "I have direct orders to keep you out of harm's way. Let us take the sample."

Craig didn't bother fighting him. He surrendered the vial and watched as Berg handed it off to a soldier. The man crept towards the dust.

"Just scoop some out?" the soldier asked. Even over the mic Craig heard a shake in the man's voice.

"Yes," Craig said. "Remember, your suit is sealed. You'll be fine."

Moving as fast as he could, the soldier's hand grazed the surface of the dome, just enough to dip in the vial. He screwed on the top and held the tiny glass container away from his body. He set it in a large plastic bag that Craig had set out.

"Shit, Brody. Quit acting like a little baby," one soldier said.

"Yeah? You want to come do this? Be my guest."

"Shut it, you two," Berg ordered.

They repeated the process with the metal canister. Brody was clearly eager to finish the job, and moved too quickly for Craig to see if he was getting good samples.

"Slow down on this last one. I need to make sure we're getting enough," Craig told him.

Brody pushed his shoulders back, a barely perceptible gesture in the oversized hazmat suit, and took the plastic container. He ran it across the surface of the dust and capped it almost simultaneously. He showed it to Craig.

"Here you go. Is that—"

"It's empty," Craig stated flatly. He'd watched the soldier put the vial into the dust and scoop it out himself, but there was nothing in the container now.

Berg approached. "Private?"

"I don't know what happened. I did exactly what Dr. Peters said. Fuck, I feel like I'm gonna puke from this EMF shit."

Craig opened the plastic bag containing the glass sample. He put the vial close to his visor and peered into it. Empty.

His blood ran cold. He picked up a twig from the ground and marched up to the DZ, ignoring Berg's protest and the EMF sickness. He waved the twig through the dust, anticipating a trail of it to follow once the twig came out. Nothing. It remained perfectly intact, unaffected by his attempt to disturb it.

"This isn't right," he muttered. To emphasize his point, he waved the stick again. "Are you guys seeing this?"

Berg searched the ground and picked up a larger branch. He slung his rifle behind him and settled in front of the dome a few feet away from Craig. The man readied himself to swing the branch like a baseball bat. With four times as much force as Craig used on his twig, Berg swung into the dust. The branch cut through it. Yellow trailed behind as it exited.

Then, slowly, the freed dust returned to the dome.

"What the fuck?" Berg dropped the branch and took two strides back.

Craig's mind raced. A magnetic field could, hypothetically, be harnessed to create a force field. But what was drawing the dust back into the dome?

*The blue and white pod from Ralph's and NORAD's footage. It could've been anything. Does it have something to do with the force field?*

How the hell was he going to explain this to Tim? He went to rub the ache forming in the back of his neck, but his fingers bumped up against the bulky hazmat suit.

He had the distinct, unshakable feeling that the dome was toying with him. Not like he could tell that to any of the people around him.

Berg repeated his question. "What the fuck is this?"

"I don't know. I really don't," Craig answered. He paused, chewing his lip while he thought.

The previous day Craig, Tim, and Berg had discussed deploying rescue convoys, as well as general search teams, to check out the damage in Seattle. Their satellite pictures only showed them the magnitude of the DZ. They needed to get inside it. Part of Craig's research today was supposed to help them decide whether or not this was a safe course of action.

"I'm not going to ask any of you to walk in there. I can't tell you what will happen if you do. By my reasoning, the dust isn't irradiated and if I walk back out, it should come right off me. Other than the EMF sickness, I should be fine," Craig said, meaning every word.

Berg glanced at his men, then to Craig. "I can't let you in there; orders are orders."

Without further discussion, Berg walked into the dust. The yellow particles engulfed him. The radio in Craig's ear hissed and crackled as Berg entered. Two feet in and he was already fading from their vision.

"Berg?" Craig said into his mic. "Can you read me?"

Static filled the line. As Craig strained to listen, he heard a faint voice. He couldn't make out what it was saying, or if it was even a language he recognized. It was low, mechanical-sounding gibberish.

"Do you guys hear that?" Craig asked.

"Jesus, this is fucked up." One of the soldiers stepped forward towards the dome. "We can't just leave him in there."

"Hold your position," Brody said. "Not picking up on anything, Dr. Peters. Captain, do you read me?"

No response. Static flooded their earpieces again. Craig's heart hammered in his chest. The distorted voice faded in again. He looked around at the other soldiers. He wished he could see their faces to gauge whether they were hearing what he was.

*What if something was in there with Berg?*

"I said, do you hear that?" Craig asked again, more urgently. "There's some kind of voice in the background. It's like…."

Suddenly the Captain emerged from the dome. A halo of dust pulled off his hazmat suit as he exited.

"...read me? Can you read me?" Berg was saying.

The mechanical voice faded away. Craig strained to hear, but it was gone.

"Reading you loud and clear, Captain," Brody said, obviously relieved.

"Are..." Craig's mouth had gone dry. His mind was buzzing with fear. He worked up some saliva and swallowed. "Are you okay? Did you see anything?"

"I'm good," Berg said. "Are *you* okay?"

Craig wanted to write off the strange voice as his own overstressed nerves, especially since no one else seemed to have heard it. He debated again whether he should say anything and decided not to. His nerves *were* shot. And if he heard it again, he'd say something.

"I'm fine. What happened? What was it like?" Craig asked.

"I lost comm the second I went in. Visibility is poor, so no, I didn't see anything. I *feel* like shit though."

"Okay," Craig said. "That makes sense. Something in the dust interferes with radio waves. Probably the magnetism. That explains why we aren't picking up anything from inside. It's also going to make search and rescues or any other expedition in there a nightmare. Berg, we need to get you through decontamination—well, what we're passing for decontamination. Then I need you under twenty-four-hour observation."

"You got it. One more thing, Peters." Berg glanced at the DZ. "Inside, the dust doesn't seem to do anything unusual. I kicked some around, and it moved like you'd expect."

Craig chewed the inside of his lip in thought. "Noted. I don't know what to make of it yet."

"You're not the only one. Anything else?"

There were endless things to do. Craig needed more manpower. Most importantly, he needed the right equipment to start analyzing the dust. The convoy bringing him the biological safety cabinets had been attacked repeatedly by raiders, delaying the soldiers. He couldn't handle samples in an open, unsecured environment, but he hated to wait.

Craig clapped his gloved hands together and began walking to the Humvees. "Tomorrow, if everything looks good, start sending teams into the DZ. There are millions of people in there. We need to find out if they're still alive."

# DAN

Ever since Dan was a kid, he had hated being confined. Whether he was in jail or stuck in a small vehicle speeding through yellow dust, he hated it. He was trapped, and bad things were coming. Painful things. Things that would make him hurt for days and cry even longer.

No matter how often Dan reminded himself this wasn't Mama's house and he wasn't in the box, that there was no threat of getting his dick cut off, the feelings stuck with him. It was like he was a kid again, so vivid were his memories of Mama and Papa. They could be right here, sitting in the car with him. Mama with her big belly hanging over her sweatpants, her greasy skin that always smelled like sour milk, and her too many crooked teeth. Papa and his ragged beard, always shirtless in a pair of stained boxers. The burns on his chest and arms from the welding accident were ropy and thick, like the overgrown roots of a tree.

A sticky sweat broke out across Dan's body. It was a sauna in his plastic suit. He wiggled and felt moisture drip down his ass. At least his hood wasn't up. Some of the heat escaped through there. He could breathe, but if they opened the doors without warning the prisoners they'd all get killed by the dust.

He and six other people were stuffed in the back of a moving truck. Someone had taped a flashlight to the ceiling, weakly lighting the space. The men had taken their masks but hadn't done a good job searching Dan. His gun was still tucked into the back of his pants. He wanted to use it on them. Put a bullet in every last one of their heads for what they'd done.

After he had ditched the military guys, he left Hedone and started walking, sure he'd find a sweet new place to chill. He spotted what he thought was another group of soldiers walking along the road. Then he noticed the symbol painted on their jackets. It was a circle with little dashes coming from the top left. It was a gang symbol from Hedone. Not big-time gangbangers like the white cross guys, but still pretty powerful. Dan was stoked. Hoping they'd let him join their crew, he marched right up to them and introduced himself.

"You got room for one more?" he'd asked in his coolest, most indifferent voice.

The group looked at each other and one of them, the leader Dan figured, laughed. They told him yes and led him to a warehouse a few blocks north from Hedone. Inside was the U-Haul and six people lined up on their knees inside it. They took his mask, tied him up, and shoved him inside. That's where he was now, bouncing around the back of a fifteen foot U-Haul on the way to fuck knows where. His knees ached fiercely and he had to shit.

Dan was pissed off and embarrassed. He would've been a good guy to have in their gang. They had treated him like dirt, like another body to use. That wasn't okay with him. He was a user, not something to *be* used.

Dan had heard them talking about which one of them they'd eat first. They were cannies. Fucking cannies. He wasn't gonna be some faggot freak's dinner.

He began to work his right arm back through the plastic suit. The gangbangers hadn't done a good job with the zip ties. He had kept his fists clenched to make them as big as possible, and now he had a little wriggle room. Since the gloves were built into his suit, at first glance it would look like his hands were still tied. If anyone looked closer, they'd notice how deflated his right arm seemed.

He reached behind to get his gun and then held his arm at an angle in front of his body and stayed put. No one noticed what he was doing. Now it was just a matter of waiting for the right moment to strike. There was only one of the gang members with the prisoners.

They must've been driving an hour before the truck made a loud sputtering noise and came to a stop. The truck shifted as some of the guys in the cab exited. Doors slammed. The guard inside stayed put. The conversations outside were muffled, but the little Dan heard wasn't good.

"If we can't get moving, what the hell are we going to do with the livestock? Monroe is full of Mexicans, man. We're gonna get shot up."

"We'll fix it," one snapped. "Stop whining!"

They couldn't open the door, not out here in the open. The dust would get in and all their meat would get contaminated.

"Engine's fucked from all this ash," Dan heard one of them say.

Dan was in the back right corner of the truck. He leaned over to the person next to him and tried to look afraid. That wasn't too hard since he was.

"We need to get out of here. Now is our chance."

The middle-aged, balding man ignored Dan at first. He kept his face straight ahead. His eyes flickered to the guard.

"I have a gun, dude. If you distract him, he'll come over here to see what's wrong. I'll shoot him and then we'll have two guns." Dan paused and then added, "They're going to eat us if we don't escape. You want to get a chunk taken out of you?"

Finally the man spoke. "I don't have a mask. I was in the warehouse when they got me."

Dan nodded at the guard. He was hassling one of the women, telling her what he was going to do to her when they got out.

"That guy has gear. I'll shoot him, you take his stuff. We can get out of here."

"What about everyone else?"

Here was the tricky part. Dan could go two ways with the guy. First, he could promise he'd save everyone. Or, second, he could tap into that self-preservation shit his prison shrink always talked about.

"Fuck 'em. Either we all die, or you and me get outta here. You want to live, don't you?"

The man nodded. "Yes. Of course. What do I do?"

"He won't shoot you. Trust me, he won't. They want to save us to eat. Just get up and start yelling. Get his back to me. Then I'll shoot him."

His new friend took a deep breath then got to his feet. "Hey! Idiot!"

The guard's attention shifted from the woman to Dan's new buddy. In the small space of the moving van, it only took four steps to put the guard right in front of Dan.

Someone banged on the side of the truck. "Glen, what's going on in there?"

"Nothin', just someone acting up. I got it." He turned his attention to the older man, who side-stepped around him.

It was Dan's time now. Dan with the Plan. It was such a cool nickname. He had always tried to get his friends from before to go along with it, but no one ever would. Finally, Dan *did* have a plan, and it *was* working. Glen raised the butt of his rifle to smash into the yelling prisoner. Dan wriggled until he got his gun arm out of the suit. He pointed it at the Glen's back.

Glen hit the man in the forehead and sent him to the ground. Dan fired a shot into the guard's back, then another higher up. Headshot, one hundred points. Blood splattered the truck wall and the woman he'd been hassling earlier. She screamed, her eyes squeezed shut as gore trickled down her face.

"What the fuck was that?" Someone banged on the truck again. "Glen, you okay? Shit, I'm opening it up."

"No, you dickhead!" said one of the other gang members. "We can't open it. You'll infect all the meat."

"But Glen…."

The fight over whether or not they should open the door continued. Alarmed, the prisoners stood, backing away from the body. Some glared at Dan, while others were trembling in fear.

"You're going to get us killed," one of them shouted.

Another prisoner laughed darkly. "We were going to die anyway. At least we might die quick now."

That threw them into panicked arguments over what to do. While both prisoners and guards fought each other, Dan used the distraction to grab a knife off the guard and cut his bindings. He slipped his arm back into his suit and took one of the extra gas masks hanging from the guard's belt. He searched the body. There were no extra magazines on him, but his backpack was a treasure trove. Candy bars, Fritos, a couple bags of weed, a porno mag, and a bottle of gin. Gin was fucking disgusting, but it would do. Dan pulled the backpack on and swapped his handgun for the badass rifle.

"What the hell is going on in there?"

"Fuck this!" someone yelled from outside.

The truck doors flung open, casting yellow, disorienting light onto the prisoners. Dan squeezed the trigger, expecting a stream of bullets to come out like in the movies. Only one shot fired at a time, which sucked. Dan wildly pulled the trigger, hoping some of the shots would hit their marks.

The mag clicked and he dropped to his belly on the ground.

Around him the prisoners screamed in agony as dust flooded the truck. It ate at their skin, made them claw at their own flesh. Soon their hands and clothes were bloody. Pieces of their skin sloughed off. Three of them ran out of the truck only to make it five feet before collapsing on the ground.

Dan peered outside. He was in a city, one he wasn't familiar with. They were at an intersection with a wrecked yellow sports car blocking it. No sign of the men.

He spared a glance at the body closest to him. It was the woman the guard had hassled. Her skin was peeled away were she scratched it, showing muscle and hints of bone beneath. Her mouth opened and closed. Blood seeped from her tear ducts. It reminded him of a fish out of water, gulping air. He smirked.

If the other gang members weren't dead, they might be waiting for him. He needed to find somewhere to hide. He didn't hear anything but the groaning of the dying people around him. He was a sitting duck and had to make a run for it.

With no ammunition, the rifle was useless. He tossed it aside and got out his 9mm instead, then jumped from the truck and booked it down the intersection. His heel hit the ground at a bad angle and he stumbled. Gunfire sounded. Puffs of dust shot up around him as his attacker's shots missed their mark.

Dan tried to take as many turns as he could, but the blocks were long and running was hard in the damn suit. As he ran, he noticed footprints in the ash. They went off in different directions, but looked thicker going one way. He followed them. Maybe he'd find some suckers to help him. Worst case scenario, he'd lead his attackers to them and they'd fight it out while he escaped.

His lungs were on fire, and a cramp in his left side threatened to bring him down. After a few minutes the tracks split off. One set, heavily used, continued down the street. Fainter tracks led to a fancy looking building with big windows. Dan followed the tracks to a small metal door off the side of the main entrance of the building. There were drops of blood in the dust and smears of it around the door handle.

He tested the handle and found it unlocked. Quickly, he slipped inside, closed the door and surveyed the room. There was dust around the entrance. Rolling bins of books. What was this, a fucking library? Who hid out in a library during the end of the world?

No people. A metal chair was toppled over on its side beside the door. Dan found a lock on the top of the door and slid it into place, then shoved the chair underneath it. If the cannies were still on his trail, that would stop them for a few minutes.

He took off his backpack and hid it in one of the book bins along with his gun. If there were other people in there, he didn't want them taking his loot. Hiding the gun was a little risky, but if the people saw it on him they might freak out. He took a moment to be pleased with himself. He had singlehandedly escaped the cannies, gotten some good loot, and had the right mind to hide his shit.

He moved forward out of the room into an office area. It was empty. He walked into the main library. The ceiling vaulted above him. Across the library was an open second story. He saw light coming from it, and voices.

Someone had formed a wall of bookshelves blocking the view from the street. Halfway down the main room, Dan saw a woman and an old man talking.

"Hello?" he said. "I was attacked, I—"

"Jesus! Jack didn't lock the door. Get back there and

lock it, put the chair under it," an older man with wild gray hair ordered him. "For Christ's sake, you broke every decontamination procedure we have! Go back in the book return room and stay there."

Dan wanted to beat his skull into the ground. He fucking hated old people. Waste of space. "I already locked it and set the chair."

The old man grumbled, then said, "Well at least there's that."

Dan's attention went to the woman, and he was glad he had picked this place to hide. He didn't usually believe in fate. Now he was willing to reconsider.

She was exactly what he needed. She wore a tight-fitting shirt and leggings that showed a body a bit on the thin side, but who wasn't thin these days? She had a nice rack, which was a bonus. Her hair was a good length, just above the shoulders but not dyke-ish, and her skin was so pale it seemed to glow in the darkness.

More people came from the upstairs. A big cow of a lady led them.

"Where did you come from?" the cow demanded.

Dan was glad his mask hid his face. It meant he didn't have to force a normal, innocent-looking expression when he answered. He just had to focus on his tone.

"I was kidnapped by some bad people a few miles out of town. I escaped, but they're chasing me." He needed to sweeten it up. He made himself sound like he was about to cry. "My wife and daughter were with me. They killed my family."

"Molly, we do not have the resources to take another person in," the old man said to the heifer.

"We need to stick together," the hot bitch countered. "There's safety in numbers."

He liked her even more. He needed to find her

weakness. Then he'd have her wrapped around his finger—
and his cock—and he'd be on his way back to Hedone with
a nice piece of ass to trade.

"Did you come from the south?" a skinny kid asked
him.

Dan wasn't quite sure where he was so he couldn't say
where he came from. It didn't matter. "Yeah. That's right."

"Did you see a refugee camp?" the hottie asked. "The
military? Anything?"

Dan's gaze flickered to the woman. If you counted the
FEMA guys and the military dudes, yes. But they didn't
need to know that. The trick to getting people to do what
you wanted was to make sure they were afraid. When
people were afraid, they were more likely to do things they
normally wouldn't. Hope was the last thing he wanted to
give the pretty little brunette.

"No," he said, shaking his head. "I haven't seen anything.
I don't think anyone is coming to help us."

# COLLEEN

Colleen braided Liana's hair into pigtails while she watched the sea of people in the gymnasium. James was trying to nap in his cot, and Serena was sitting on the ground with a forgotten book in her hand, talking to her new friend Gabriela. Colleen put Gabriela around sixteen. She was alone and didn't say where her parents were. She'd been in the high school since FEMA took over and made it into a camp. Gabriela's cot was set up next to theirs, and she and Serena were fast friends in less than a day.

Colleen didn't mind the company. Gabriela was calm for her age and quite observant. With a head of thick black hair, soft brown eyes, and a toothy smile that shone against her deeply tanned complexion, she had a way of lifting everyone's spirits. Serena seemed to like having someone around who was a little older. Colleen remembered what it was like to be a kid. How much she had looked up to older, cooler teenagers.

It turned out Serena and James brought their backpacks underneath the hazmat suits. After they were decontaminated, some of their items were returned to them. James had brought protein bars and some medical supplies. Serena had stuffed hers with books and some of Liana's toys. It helped them pass the endless hours of nothingness.

"…you *really* saw him? Was he cute?" Colleen heard a fragment of Serena's whispered conversation.

Gabriela wiggled her eyebrows. "*Sooo* cute."

"I wish I could hear them live someday," Serena said. "They won't let me. They say I'm too young. Ugh."

"You might be a little too young. I didn't go to my first concert until I was twelve."

Colleen was thrilled to hear Gabriela defend her and James. She mentally allotted more brownie points to the teenager and then redirected her attention to Liana.

Colleen started on the second braid and looked out at the gym again. The family had taken up residence in a corner of the gym. It made her feel safer to have a wall at their backs. She couldn't imagine being in the middle of the room. All those people breathing, bumping into one another. No matter which way you faced, you'd see another person. At least here they could keep their area neat and make something habitable out of it.

The day they had arrived at the high school, the gymnasium had been nearly empty; only ten cots taken. Now, four days later, the two hundred cots in the gym— she'd counted them more than once to pass the time—were full. There were people sleeping in the spaces between cots on the hardwood floor, too. Lines to the bathrooms were always long. The soldiers had good intentions, but the fact was they were bringing in too many people.

The refugees had been given decent rations of MREs on the first day, but each day since, their food had been cut. Now they were at one meal a day. Resources were spread thin.

And others had wounds like Liana's, only far worse. Colleen figured that was why the doctor who looked at Liana dismissed her rash. One man's entire arm was covered in scaly patches of red. The next day, the patches turned gooey and purple. Those miniscule blueish-green blisters popped up. He itched at them and moaned constantly. They leaked pus. He wasn't the only infected person, just the most vocal. Enough people complained that a soldier and two FEMA workers took him away.

The soldier had addressed the entire gym. He asked all people who had dust-related injuries to separate to the west side of the gym for voluntary quarantine. The soldier's mistake was assuming anyone would do it. After he left, not a soul had followed his instructions.

"Mom, you're pulling my hair."

Colleen didn't realize how tightly she'd been braiding. She used her fingers to comb the braid out and restarted, her hands softer. Her fingertips brushed against Liana's right cheek.

Her daughter's scars felt different. She tilted Liana's head towards her to inspect them. The white, raised scars had faded slightly. Or was it just her imagination?

"Honey, are your scars still bothering you?"

Liana's face was smooth. Expressionless. "No. Not anymore. Can you finish my pigtail?"

She began braiding again. "Here, is this better?"

"Yes," Liana said, then refocused on braiding her own doll's hair. It was mostly a knotted mess, but it made Colleen smile.

Liana's scars weren't different. It was all in her head. And while Liana's uncharacteristic tone and calm worried Colleen, she figured it had to be a coping mechanism. They were, after all, in a very stressful situation. Colleen needed to be grateful Liana wasn't affected by the dust like all the other refugee's she'd seen.

"When moms braid your hair, it gets stronger, Liana," Gabriela said. Her smile was contagious. She stood up and pulled her hair out of its loose bun atop her head. Waves of glossy hair cascaded down her back. "See mine? Ten years of mom braiding it and it's as strong as rope."

Serena huffed and rolled her eyes then diverted

attention back to herself by mentioning her own skills at braiding, and how *she* could do her *own* hair. This, of course, provoked a massive tickle attack from Gabriela. The two laughed hysterically on the floor.

"Hey, can you keep it down over there? Jesus, this isn't a fucking fiesta, comprende? Some of us are trying to sleep."

The girls' laughter died instantly. Colleen stiffened, eyes locking on to the source of the comment. It came from a scrawny man sprawled across a cot three rows away. He wore a purple bandana over his eyes as a sleeping mask, which was pushed up on his forehead to reveal a set of glaring, beady eyes.

It tore apart Colleen's heart to see Gabriela's joy collapse in on itself. She opened her mouth to retort but James, now very awake, beat her to it.

"There's no need for that language," James said. "Or that tone."

"You owe them an apology," Colleen added.

Purple Bandana clenched his jaw. The energy between him and Colleen intensified, so toxic and thick she could choke on it.

Finally, he said, "I don't owe anyone anything."

"Come on, son. Can you take it easy and apologize to those girls?" This came from an older gentleman adjacent to Purple Bandana. "I'm tired too but there's no need to lash out with those words. I think we can all agree to keep it down, out of respect for everyone around us, and to try and not get on each other's nerves. Can't we?"

By now the scene had garnered the attention of most of the surrounding refugees. With more eyes on him, he opted to back down. With false sincerity that fooled no one, he grumbled, "Sorry about that."

"Thank you," James said stiffly.

Purple Bandana covered his eyes, lay on his side away

from Colleen's family, and was silent. The girls sat down once again and spoke in whispers.

James shared a look with Colleen. *That was something,* it said. Colleen's eyes flickered to Gabriela and Serena then back to him. *I know.*

This wasn't the first tiff they'd experienced or witnessed. Restlessness was in the air. People's tempers were short and they took it out on each other. This, by far, had been the most uncomfortable confrontation. Colleen prayed it would be the last. That something would give soon. Maybe transport to another camp to improve numbers.

She sighed. There were no windows in the gym and she desperately wanted to see how things were looking outside. The last time she'd seen daylight was just before she entered the decontamination corridor. The soldiers and FEMA people wouldn't let anyone leave their designated areas for "safety reasons". Colleen heard from another person, who'd come from a different part of the school, that the windows had all been taped over with black plastic so even if she did get near one, she wouldn't be able to see anything.

She tied off Liana's braid and kissed the top of her head again. She smelled like the baby wipes they'd been rationed for personal hygiene. "How are you feeling, sweetie?"

"I'm fine," Liana said. Her tiny voice was distracted. Her doll was abandoned beside her on the cot. "That lady is dead."

Colleen followed Liana's gaze to another family nearby. All of them came in sick. The mother's nose had been bleeding steadily for an hour. Her nose, lips, and chin were stained red. The rashes and blisters started on her arm but had traveled up her body to her face. The green blanket on her cot was soaked with sweat and smeared with blood. Colleen caught a glimpse of her eyes. The whites had turned florescent blue.

Now the woman was lying motionless. Colleen turned Liana away from the sight and hugged her. The woman was dead. Her husband and son sat by the body, their hands interlocked, tears streaming down their cheeks.

"She's just feeling icky today. She'll be better tomorrow." Liana looked up. "No, mom. She's dead. I can tell. She's not thinking like she should."

Colleen was speechless for a moment. Then she asked, "What do you mean?"

"I don't know," Liana admitted in that calm tone, one too grown-up for a four-year-old. "I can tell she isn't thinking."

That sensation took over again, the one she felt when they first arrived at the camp. That Liana wasn't right. Colleen couldn't fight the unease. She picked up Liana and gave her to Gabriela. "You and Serena watch her for a second, okay?"

"You got it, Miss C," Gabriela said.

Despite the noisy gym, James was asleep. Colleen shook him gently and put her mouth close to his ear so the girls wouldn't hear. "James, wake up."

"What's wrong?" He turned onto his back.

"The woman a few cots away from us? I think she's dead." Colleen considered telling James what Liana had just said, but thought better of it. It would sound insane and she had a feeling now wasn't the right time.

"Oh God," he muttered as he sat up. James blinked sleep away from his eyes.

The family surrounded the mother's dead body. Around them, the rest of the refugees backed away.

"Someone get that out of here," a man shouted from the crowd. "She's gonna make us sick."

Scattered agreements rose up. A burly man pushed his way out of the group to face the father and son. "Are you just going to leave her there? Why didn't you tell the soldiers?"

"Sh-she just died," the father stammered. "We're going to tell them. We needed a moment to say goodbye."

"Fuck that. We're getting rid of her. Lookit her eyes." The man turned and opened his arms to the group. "Right? Who's with me? Come on, let's toss the body."

The crowd surged forward and shoved the father away. Too young to know any better, the son latched onto his mother. He was too weak to hold on for long and a man tore him away from her and tossed him on the ground.

Colleen couldn't help but glance at Liana, who watched the scene impartially from Gabriela's arms.

Four men lifted the woman's body by wrists and ankles. Her head lolled to the side. Spit and blood oozed from her gaping mouth onto the ground. The leader, a blond man with a perpetual sneer on his face, led them. "Make a fucking path!"

To Colleen's disbelief and horror, the crowd obeyed and parted for them. Some were hesitant. Colleen saw it on their faces as they looked at one another for cues on what to do. Others went so far as to pull cots aside so the men could carry the body out. Where did they think they'd take it? No one could leave.

"Stop where you are and lower the body."

Standing in the double-door entrance to the gym were Belman and Thompson. They didn't have their guns pointed at the group, but the tone in Thompson's voice seemed to be enough. Behind them, a handful of the FEMA people waited with a body bag. The men carrying the body hesitated. The leader glanced back at them and scowled.

"We're doing a service here. This body was stinking up the place. When were you gonna come get it?"

The father stood. He was short and stooped, but he faced the mob and spoke up. "That's not true. She died minutes ago. They came out of nowhere and took her. I was going to tell you, I swear."

"Lower the body," Thompson said again. "You are not allowed to leave this room and you certainly aren't allowed to handle that body. Do you understand?"

The leader folded his overdeveloped arms across his chest. Colleen silently begged him to back down. The crowd was on the edge of rioting already.

"Yeah, that's another thing. Why aren't we allowed to leave? You're treating us like prisoners!"

Thompson didn't react. "What's your name?"

"Benny," he answered. "What the hell does it matter to you?"

"Well, Benny, the dust is lethal. You all know that and have witnessed what it does first hand. We cannot allow civilians to roam freely. It puts everyone's lives at risk," Thompson looked around the room and added, "More than they already are. We're asking you to be calm and to obey our orders while we sort everything out. Now I need you to set down the body and move away."

Benny sneered, but finally he dropped his arms and stepped aside. "You want the bitch? Fine. Take her. Let her go, guys."

His lackeys dropped the body. It hit the ground with a thud that echoed in the silent room. Colleen swore each person was holding their breath in anticipation for whatever was coming next.

The FEMA people came forward and lifted the woman into the body bag. The father and son were crying silently nearby.

"We understand this situation isn't ideal," Belman said. "But if you do not cooperate, you will not be permitted to stay here. If anyone has an issue with that, say so now."

No one moved. The troublemakers kept their chests

puffed out and their chins held high. There was no regret there.

"You all know we are over capacity. We've run out of room for infected individuals in quarantine and need to leave less severe cases in here."

"Infected with what?" A young woman pushed her way to the front of the crowd. "Do you have any idea what's going on?"

Belman squeezed her eyes shut and cursed under her breath. Colleen felt terrible for the soldiers. They'd only been trying to help. "We don't know what exactly *it* is. Some kind of infection or reaction caused by contact with the dust. It might be contagious, which is why those showing any signs of infection need to migrate to the west half of the gym. We ordered you to do this days ago and you did not comply. It is not up for negotiation."

"What about the comet? We were told it would destroy everything." This came from a man standing beside the first woman. "But we're still here."

"Again, we don't know what happened. We have no way of verifying anything. All our radio channels are malfunctioning. Once we get through, we'll have more answers. We just want to keep you safe."

"You're doing a piss poor job of it." The remark came from the crowd. Colleen couldn't pinpoint who said it.

"Comets don't just stop in midair," shouted another voice. "This is a fucking government conspiracy if I ever saw one!"

The crowd swelled with murmurs of agreement. Belman raised her hand and silenced them.

"You got something to say, tell us the next time we're doing rounds. Rations will be distributed shortly," she said. With that, most of the soldiers turned and marched out. One soldier Colleen didn't recognize remained behind to supervise.

Colleen took in the sight of the refugees again and knew, with complete certainty, it was only a matter of time before all hell broke loose. The soldiers and FEMA workers were outnumbered thirty to one. Many were on Benny's side already, and more would follow as conditions worsened. No one cared about right or wrong. They cared about self-preservation.

Once the soldiers left with the body, the crowd quieted down. The father wrapped his arm around his son, both their heads bowed, not meeting the prying eyes. People returned the cots they'd pushed aside to their original positions and resumed their hushed conversations. Those who were infected began dragging their cots to the west side. The majority of the group had regained some sense of civility, but beneath the surface Colleen imagined a wild animal itching to get out.

She didn't want to be there when it did.

# JACK

While Jack sipped the meager spoonful of chicken broth everyone was given for dinner, he watched Dan talk to Lara. She liked the guy. It was obvious, and it made Jack sick. Didn't anyone else pick up on Dan's creepy vibes? He was too far away to hear their conversation, but he could see the punk smiling and flirting with her.

Dan carried his wiry thin body like he'd always been that way. It reminded Jack of a weasel or a ferret. The guy's skin was pasty white, his black hair slicked back from his own natural grease. The more Jack studied him, the less he understood why Lara would give him the time of day.

Jack regretted pulling away from the main group. He had literally taken his blanket and camped away from the rest of them to be alone. It had seemed like a good idea at the time. Then, once the fury and determination clouding his mind cleared, he realized he had acted like a complete ass with a hefty dose of stupid on top.

Fact was, whether he liked it or not, survival was priority one; if he was to do that, he needed to make amends with those around him. He had no car, and even if he did, he couldn't go home or to Leanne's. A car would never make it that far in the dust. Plus the second he stepped out of the library, he'd be faced with gangs, raiders, and who knows what else. Even if he set all that aside, without access to the Internet he had no clue how he'd go about finding Stewart's accomplice.

Helping Dio and Paul had been a good start to mending

his image with the new group. If he hadn't been suited up when they came to the door, they would've stayed out there in the dust-addled air for much longer. He was the one who dragged them away from the door and helped clean them up. If only he'd remembered to lock the door, Dan wouldn't have slithered in.

Dan had sidled up to Lara the moment he arrived, claiming to be distraught over the death of his wife and daughter. Dan never mentioned them by name, just "wife" and "daughter." When Fred asked him the job question, he claimed he was a social worker. He said the sores on his face were from coming into contact with the dust, but they didn't look right. They reminded Jack of Stewart's skin during the trials.

He drank the rest of his broth and licked the inside of the mug to pick up the last drips. Everyone was hungry, but not quite starving. That would change soon. The chicken broth they'd just doled out was the last of the food. They still had huge drums of water from the break room in the library, which were rationed carefully, but they needed more with their increased numbers. They were short on propane, too. Soon the tea that provided a surprising amount of comfort would be gone.

They needed to get more supplies.

"Can we talk a second?" Fred asked as he made his slow ascent up the stairs. Jack didn't mind Fred anymore. The grumpy old man looked out for everyone, even if it meant coming off as a hardass. They hadn't spoken much, but when they did there was a camaraderie that Jack appreciated.

"Yeah. Welcome to my humble abode." Jack had been lying on his side, and now he sat up.

Fred lowered to a cross legged position. "How's the face?"

"Itches." Saying the word made Jack want to pick at his

face. "But overall, I'm surprised I'm not dead."

In addition to the inflammation and bleeding, a crop of tiny blisters had appeared across his cheek. Shiny and perfectly round, they were a shade of teal that had no business on a scab. The color was beyond worrisome. He remembered how the dust had moved so unnaturally outside the convenience store. He was afraid, but it was easy to squash that fear when he knew there was nothing he could do about his condition.

"Good to hear that. To be honest, Jack, I didn't come here to talk about your face." His gaze was fixed on the group. "What I can say is that we're almost out of food."

"I know," Jack agreed. "Food's hard to come by."

"Correct. You, Dio, and Paul need antibiotics, too."

Dio was the worst off. His entire body was wet with blood and sickly pus. Jack's handful of blisters were nothing compared to the thousands across Dio's body. There were so many they seemed to form a second skin. When they had hauled Dio and Paul from the bin room, Dio screamed in agony. They'd had to peel his clothing off—just a flimsy jacket, jeans, and t-shirt wrapped around his head to protect it—because they were soaked with fluid. The kid was hallucinating and feverish. When he did speak, it was gibberish that almost sounded like foreign language.

The group didn't have much in the way of medical supplies. Lara had tried dabbing hydrogen peroxide onto the wounds, but it had made Dio flail and scream. Paul wasn't in as bad a shape as his friend, since he'd been better covered while they were out, and accepted the treatment even though it hurt. They spent most of their time resting behind a makeshift privacy screen Lara had rigged up. Neither had the energy to discuss where they'd been or how they made it back to the library.

"We don't know exactly what's wrong with them," Jack

said. "What if antibiotics make it worse?"

Fred pursed his mouth and furrowed his brows. "It's necrosis, I know it. I've seen it before. We have to irrigate the wounds and cut out the infection."

"Are you a doctor now?" Jack pointed to his own face. "This isn't necrosis. This isn't anything I've ever seen before."

"No, I'm not a doctor. I saw a documentary on TV about rare infections. Sometimes they have unusual symptoms."

"I'm sorry, Fred. I don't think we should treat them based on what you saw on TV." Jack said it gently and, to his relief, the old man didn't take offense.

"You're right." Fred looked away from Dio and Paul. He stared at his liver-spotted hands. "Christ, I don't know. I'm grasping at straws here. I can't do *nothing*. I don't want to hurt them, either."

"Antibiotics are a good start. The problem is finding them. In the meantime, all of us—Dio and Paul included— are going to need more food."

"Before you and Lara came, we had no way of getting out. Now we have six plastic suits and four respirator masks. Seven suits and five respirators, if you count Dan's gear. We can cover a lot of ground scavenging for supplies."

"I don't count Dan," Jack said.

Fred turned and met Jack's gaze. His eyelids were droopy, but the eyes themselves sparkled. They shared an unspoken moment of agreement. "Neither do I. But the dust is settling. There's still too much in the air to go out unprotected. If we can get enough food to last us another few days, my bet is it'll be totally settled and we'll have a safer time leaving."

Jack had been inside his head too much the past few days. He'd barely looked outside. Now that he did, he saw the dust in the air had indeed thinned. It lay thick on the ground, covering everything. A thin sheen of it still hung in the air, but otherwise the midday sun shone brightly.

"And go where?" Jack asked. "We don't know what the rest of the world is like out there. All it would take is one windy day and that dust would be in the air again. There could be more groups of bad guys, too."

"Come on, son, don't you have any faith? The world *survived*. The government has to be rallying right now. I'm sure all those soldiers who went AWOL are remembering their duty now and getting things in order."

Jack was less optimistic. "I bet every store in Monroe is picked clean. I'm not sure where we could even start."

"I've thought about it. What places are the last ones you'd ever go to in a situation like this?"

"I don't know," Jack said. "Where?"

"Gyms sell protein bars, protein powder, all sorts of stuff like that. There's a middle school five blocks from here. If the cafeteria isn't raided already, there's probably vending machines. Candy and chips are better than nothing." Fred paused and then said, almost sheepishly, "The church I used to go to had a little cafe inside."

"A cafe?" Jack laughed, surprising himself.

"Make all the fun you want. It was a megachurch. I like the music."

"Whatever you say."

Jack looked at Dan and Lara again. They were still sitting too close for his liking, laughing at something in a magazine. Rocky, Ano, and Linda were huddled together. They'd been quiet since Paul and Dio returned. Everyone had licked their mugs of broth clean. Yvette and Molly still sipped at their tea, talking about cookie recipes and what they would do for a bag of dark chocolate *Dove* candies.

"I'll go," Jack said. "I'll need backup, though. I have a gun, which should help. Do you have any weapons here?"

"Rocky has a baseball bat. We have some knives and

box cutters." Fred slapped Jack on the back. "Thank you for doing this."

Jack pulled on his boots while Fred described where the nearest gym was, as well as the location of the middle school and church. After he was done, Jack went to the group. They fell silent as he stood waiting for their attention.

"I'm going out to find food. I'll need help. Any volunteers?"

Rocky's hand went up. "I'll go. I'm a fast runner."

"Thanks, Rocky. I could use one more, anyone?"

Lara got to her feet. Dan's grin faltered. He set his hand against hers and tried to tug her back to the ground. He didn't want her to go. Neither did Jack.

When Dan's skin touched Lara's, she pulled away, startled. Jack noted how fast her expression went from discomfort to a pardoning smile.

"Lara, you've done a lot already. You should stay and rest." Jack looked at Dan. "Why don't you come?"

"That's okay. I bet you and Rocky can handle it. I'll stay here in case someone tries to break in, or we have to run."

Disgusted, Jack glanced at Fred, whose expression matched his own. Jack hoped the display of cowardice would help Lara see Dan for what he was. She didn't seem to. She sat back down next to the grinning bastard.

"If you and Rocky find more supplies than you can carry, come back and more of us will go with you. If you think that's a good idea, that is," Lara said.

The passive-aggression in that comment didn't slip by him. Didn't she see what he was trying to do? He was looking out for her, for all of them. Jack vowed to talk with her alone when he got back. Dan smirked, and Jack's blood pressure rose through the roof.

"Let's go, Rocky," he said and started downstairs.

# LARA

Lara set the water barrel on the ground and wiped the sweat from her forehead. She had decided to haul the thing up to the loft to spite Jack. No one told her what to do. Not anymore. Then she quickly realized her decision was petty. It was heavy, she was hungry, and her muscles were still sore. Even though she'd been resting for days at the library, she hadn't fully recovered.

Hauling water jugs to prove how tough she was and Jack wasn't even there to see her do it. Jesus.

She closed her eyes, took a deep breath, and then let herself become aware of her body and mind. After a few minutes her pulse slowed and the tightness in her chest melted away. It was good to tune in to herself and let thoughts drift where they may. A mindful body check-in was something she taught each of her patients. The technique was soothing and helped her become grounded.

Her conversation with Jack was unfinished, and that bothered her. He was starting to open up a little, so she'd at least been getting through to him. It didn't surprise her how fast he had shut down; she'd seen that kind of behavior before with clients at her practice. Vulnerability was tricky. When someone opened up, their sensitivity to the slightest negative reaction or comment became heightened.

Up until his little tiff with Dan, she had been unsure what made him stay after Dio and Paul returned. He'd been ready to suit up and leave the library. Each attempt she'd made to reason with him failed. Then, magically, he decided to stay.

Once he called Dan out, she put it together. Although she wasn't totally sure what Jack had against Dan, it was obvious he harbored some ill feelings. Lara didn't quite understand it. Sure, at times Dan was awkward. Even skittish. But he was grieving the loss of his wife and daughter. She'd spoken to him about his life as a social worker and the children he'd helped during his career. She told him about her therapy practice. They had a lot in common.

"Hi, Lara," the very man in question said. "Do you need help with that?"

Dan had proven helpful around their camp. To everyone's surprise, he'd offered to suit up and dump the bucket they used as a toilet outside. It wasn't the most glamorous task. Whoever did it had to walk around the back of the library so no one from the street would see the evidence.

She looked at the water jug and laughed. "Yeah, I guess I do. Thanks."

"Happy to help," he said as he bent down and lifted it over his shoulder. The two headed towards the stairs, their pace slow.

"That thing with Jack was weird," Dan said. "He really hates me. Did I do something wrong?"

Lara shook her head. "You didn't do anything. I think he means well in his own way."

"I get it. I had a messed up childhood. Sticks with you. Sometimes that shows."

She frowned and nodded empathetically. "Same here. My father was…let's just say he was negligent. It's taken me years to move on."

Dan set the water jug on the step by his feet and sat down. He dropped his face into his hands. Lara had hit something. In therapy, her patients could seem absolutely fine, but after one comment they were reduced to tears or had a breakthrough.

"My dad hit me growing up. I haven't thought about it this much in a while. I wonder if he's still alive."

"What happened?" Lara asked. "Do you want to talk about it?"

She'd thought he was crying based on the tone of his voice, but when he lifted his face up it was dry. The sores he'd arrived with appeared to be healing. This close, she noticed how bloodshot his eyes were. His skin looked waxy. Ugly. Then Lara chided herself for being so judgmental.

"He wasn't there, you know? He'd leave for days. When he was angry he would knock me around and then blame me for it. Most of the time I thought I deserved it."

"It's very common for an abuse victim to think they deserved the abuse, or that they could've prevented it. The truth is, none of it was your fault." The words sounded rehearsed because they were. Lara had said them to many people before. Worried it came off as insincere, she added, "I thought the same things about my own father."

"How did you get over it?" Dan asked.

"Part of it was removing myself from the equation. Once I was old enough, I got out of the house. I went to therapy. I came to understand my dad's sickness wasn't my responsibility. I was just a child. There was nothing I could do." Lara laughed sadly. "Throughout college I tried desperately to stay away from men who seemed cold and manipulative. They reminded me too much of my dad. Next thing you know I'd be head over heels with one and I'd get into a vicious cycle where I'd do anything to please them."

"And your husband? Was he a guy like that?"

Lara looked down at her wedding ring for the second time since she'd arrived at the library. She had thought about taking it off. It was a gold band with a tiny emerald in it, with some kind of purple stones flanking it. Amethysts, maybe? To be truthful, she hated it. It was tacky. Lara slipped off the ring and set it on the staircase. Unsatisfied, she picked it up and threw it as hard as she could. It pinged off a bookshelf and disappeared.

"He was. He's gone now."

Dan was quiet. Lara didn't try to fill the space with words. Instead, she gave him time. She needed it herself, because she had just realized why she was hell bent on helping Jack. He reminded her of her dad before he got bad.

Jack was similar. So much self-hatred, so much blame. He'd hurt people, too. Even killed a man! Lara's sister said Lara's compassion was a curse. Despite what she knew about him, she genuinely saw Jack as a hurt soul that needed someone to help pull him out of the dark. Of course, that's *exactly* what she thought with every one of those college boyfriends.

"Earth to Lara," Dan said.

She surfaced from the depths of her own thoughts. "Sorry, my mind was a million miles away. What were you saying?"

"Just that I'm happy to be here. Thanks for talking to me and all. It's been hard without my wife and daughter." Dan leaned over and bumped his shoulder against hers. "I'm glad I ran into you."

The physical contact paired with the intimacy of his last comment disconcerted her. She scooted away an inch, suddenly uncomfortable.

"I appreciate that," she managed to say.

Dan frowned. "Shit, I'm sorry. I just made things weird, didn't I?"

"Don't worry about it. This whole thing is crazy, you know? One minute we're sure we're going to die—I mean, *positive* we're gone—then we survive. Something to be grateful for." Her words trailed off as she thought about what Dan just said. There was something odd about his story. "Your wife and daughter, what were their names?"

He didn't miss a beat. "It's hard to say their names. My wife's name is—was—Chrissy. A great mother. Bianca was three. Beautiful, sweet girl. We were young when Chrissy got pregnant."

"I'm sorry for your losses," she said. "What happened? Do you mind me asking?"

Dan's brow furrowed. "I don't really want to talk about it, if that's okay. It's hard."

An alarm went off deep inside her. Something was off. She couldn't pinpoint it exactly. The sensation was purely instinctual but undeniable. Dan was hiding something.

Lara stood and stretched her arms overhead. "Let's get that water up there, okay? I'm sure Molly is dying to fix some tea."

"Right," Dan said. He lifted the water barrel over his shoulder. "Tea. Can't get enough of it."

# COLLEEN

"You know what I miss?" James asked no one specifically. "Your mom's lasagna fresh out of the oven and a big salad on the side."

"No salad, dad. Mom always makes kale salad. It's gross," Serena advised.

"It's *healthy*," Colleen corrected.

The food line was at a crawl today. The boxes of MREs looked low behind the two volunteers and soldiers. As people approached, one volunteer checked their name off a list while the other distributed food.

Colleen shifted Liana to her other hip. Her back ached from the cot and was made worse from standing for so long. Holding Liana did nothing to help, but she wasn't willing to set her down. James and Colleen didn't like the idea of leaving them alone back at their cots, so the family stood together for food.

"I'm surprised you didn't say flank steak and corn on a charcoal grill," Colleen said. Her mouth watered at the thought of it. "With that corn slathered in lime butter and lots of salt and pepper."

He laughed. "That's *your* favorite dinner. But I'd go for it, too. Nice medium rare steak. And a big handful of potato chips with French onion dip. Maybe have a smoked brisket and ribs on the side too. And some coleslaw. Then cupcakes for dessert. Or ice cream."

Serena groaned and lightly swatted his forearm. "Dad, jeez! You're making me hungry."

The line moved a few feet. Colleen predicted another forty minutes before they made their way to the FEMA volunteers. The two soldiers lingered nearby.

She wondered what today's feast would be. Beef stew again? Chicken noodle?

"I like sour gummy worms," Liana said.

Colleen and James balked. She'd been so quiet recently, the normal childlike remark was out of place. James chuckled and shared a silent moment of relief with Colleen.

"Tell you what, sweetie," Colleen said as she smoothed back her daughter's hair. "When we get home, we'll buy you the biggest bag of gummy worms you've ever seen."

"Maybe they make bags with only the wormies that are half red half blue?" Liana proposed.

James patted her back. "If they don't, I'll buy a hundred bags and make you one of just half red half blues. What do you think?"

She peeled away from Colleen's shoulder to look James in the eyes. Colleen suddenly felt uncomfortable, as though her little girl was staring right into his soul.

"Okay, daddy. I know you're telling the truth."

With that she lay her head back in the crook of Colleen's neck was silent again.

"God, she is *so* weird," Serena drawled, eliciting a scolding from James.

"What about you, Gabriela?" Colleen asked, realizing she hadn't spoken in some time. "What food do you miss the most?"

She turned and found the girl staring at the crowd behind them. After following her gaze, Colleen was sure Gabriela was locked on to the man from the previous day. Purple Bandana. Colleen couldn't be sure if he was alone when he came to the camp, but regardless, he had friends now. People like that always found friends. They stood close to each other and held themselves like they were above it all.

Purple Bandana caught them staring. His lip curled into a slight sneer. He tapped his buddy's shoulder and gestured towards Colleen and her family.

Not willing to engage in their petty power struggle, Colleen gripped Liana tightly and freed one hand to nudge Gabriela around.

"Don't give them the time of day, sweetheart. Trust me."

Gabriela nodded. "I'll try, Miss C. It's scary, you know?"

"I know," she said, then said again, "Trust me."

Once again the line moved. Colleen took a breath to lighten the mood and ask Serena what food she missed when she picked up on commotion ahead.

"What is this? Crackers? How are we supposed to get by on crackers?"

The energy around the immediate area shifted. The girls seemed to condense at the sound of confrontation too, pressing into her and James as their gazes focused on the man and woman standing in front of the food line. The man's body decided to put all of his hair on his chin and eyebrows instead of much on his head. He wasn't particularly tall, but had the build of someone who used to be a weightlifter in the past. Beside him was a petite black haired woman who, based on her possessive grip on the man's arm, could've been his wife.

"Sir, we have to ration food tighter. We can only provide one MRE per person per day." The FEMA volunteer was patient and it showed in her tone and on her face.

"We're starving. What do you plan on doing about this?" the woman beside the man pushed.

By now most of the area surrounding the volunteers and soldier had gone silent, making it easy to follow their conversation.

"What do we plan on doing?" The volunteer pressed her fingertips into her temples in a show of exhaustion. "This isn't a restaurant. If you haven't checked, we aren't getting deliveries to replenish our stores. We're doing everything we can. You have to understand how challenging this situation is for us, ma'am. We're just volunteers."

"Well a handful of crackers isn't enough," the disgruntled man said. In defiance, he reached out and grabbed an extra ration of crackers.

The volunteer turned to the soldiers, who now stood by the other volunteer, and peeled off her latex gloves, tossing them to the ground. "I'm sorry, Mattie. I can't do this anymore. I just can't."

Colleen's heart went out to the volunteers. She couldn't imagine coming to the FEMA camp, eager to help, and being faced with the comet's infection or the overcrowded quarters. Whatever they prepared for, she doubted it was this.

Mattie looked to the soldiers pleadingly. They exchanged glances then one his hand out to the cracker hog. "Sir, you need to follow the rules just like everyone."

"My wife and I are hungry."

"So am I. So is everyone else. What's your point?"

"Well I pay a lot of taxes and those taxes paid for all of this. This school, your uniform and gun, this food. So if I want another package of crackers, I'm damn sure I deserve to take it."

James shook his head in disbelief. He leaned over to Colleen and whispered. "Can you believe this?"

She couldn't. How could someone stand in front of two armed soldiers and fight over a package of crackers?

"Jesus." The soldier's hand dropped. His cool was cracking. He looked at his friend then back to the cracker thief. "Option 1 is that you give me the fucking crackers willingly and get the hell out of my sight."

Cracker Thief puffed out his chest. "Oh yeah? What's option 2?"

The other soldier, a younger man with dark skin and hair, stepped forward into the cracker thief's personal bubble. He said something too low for Colleen to hear from where they stood. When he pulled back, the Cracker Thief's face turned beet red.

That was when Cracker Thief threw the first punch. Whether it was because he was tired or truly didn't expect it, the soldier took it right in the cheek. He staggered briefly before returning the punch with one of his own to Cracker Thief's kidney.

"Myers, quit it!" the soldier's friend shouted.

The entire gym pressed in towards the fight. Colleen heard outrage from those who didn't know what started the fight—as far as they were concerned the soldier started beating on one of the refugees. Those closer seemed to be of mixed opinion. Some yelled encouragement and others began cursing the soldiers.

Bodies pushed behind her as they tried to get closer to the fight. She held Liana tightly and made sure Gabriela was close by. James had Serena in front of him, protecting her from the horde.

The other soldier got ahold of Myers and dragged him backward, putting distance between them and the fight. His face was close to Myers, and Colleen could only imagine he was trying to calm the fight. Cracker Thief's wife helped him up off his knees.

"We need to get out of the way," James yelled.

Colleen glanced around. People were getting worked up and her family was caught in the middle. Moving out of the way was easier said than done. She clutched Liana tightly with one arm and used her other to push people out of the way as they abandoned what used to be the food line. James was leading the family towards the wall behind the MRE distribution area.

"Miss C!"

The second Gabriela spoke, Colleen realized the girl wasn't behind her anymore. She spun around and saw Gabriela crushed in a group of people who were so fevered and absorbed in shouting at the fight, they didn't realize the small girl was even there. Gabriela struggled to squeeze out when the woman behind her put her hand on Gabriela's shoulder in a foolish attempt at leverage. Her petite frame was crushed under the weight of the much bigger woman. Gabriela began to crumple.

"Hey, get away from her!" Colleen shouted. She maneuvered through the crowd to Gabriela and grabbed her hand in an attempt to break her free.

The woman barely registered Colleen's pleas until she released Gabriela's hand and shoved the woman with all the force she could muster. She backed off as much as the crowd allowed and shot Colleen a bewildered glare.

"What's wrong with you?" Colleen shouted.

"What's wrong with me?" she spat and shoved Colleen back. One of her hands connected with Liana's back, eliciting a pained yelp from the girl.

Unapologetic, the woman stood her ground, ready for a fight. Colleen would've risen to the occasional if she was willing to set Liana down. But she wasn't about to do that. Instead, she swallowed her pride and rage and grabbed Gabriela. Something going on with the fight drew the woman's attention and she turned away.

"Stay close," Colleen commanded Gabriela. "Don't let go of me, okay?"

Heart pounding, she clenched the girl's hand in hers and began the trek towards James and Serena who'd made it to the wall. Just as they broke through a dense throng of people, the rest of the soldiers came pouring in.

To Colleen's relief their mere presence deescalated most of the crowd quickly. Much of that was credited to their guns; instead of having them pointed at the ground like usual, they were pointing them at s the more aggressive participants to make them drop to their stomachs on the floor.

"Are you okay?" James asked. He looked Colleen and Liana over, then Gabriela.

"Yes," Colleen breathed, grateful to have everyone together again but dreading the moment this happened again. Anticipating that next time, it would be worse.

# DAN

Dan chewed at his lip while he leaned against a bookshelf. The water jug was fucking heavy, but he had to carry it. The knight in shining armor routine. Lara ate it up, though not as much as he'd like her to. The other chicks seemed to like it when he helped out too, so he did it a lot. The piss bucket, the water, hauling stuff around whenever someone pointed. Dan did it all. Dan the Man, Dan with the Plan.

His gaze lingered on Lara's ass as she bent down to straighten everyone's sleeping bags. She was probably at least eight years older than him but still hot. Women were so easy. There was a reason they were called the lesser sex. That was something people said, right? Dan was sure it was. Anyway, it was true. They might act like they're all smart and have standards, but at the end of the day there was a formula. If Dan followed it, he could wiggle his way in.

He'd done it countless times already. Be a bitch's friend. Pull her away from everyone. Make her hate herself. Grab her and run.

And Lara was good for it, more so than Chrissy or Bianca or any of those whores. She was a therapist—a fucking shrink!—which made her naturally want to help people. Dan's original cover story of a dead wife and daughter had been a spur of the moment invention, but it couldn't have worked out better. He saw the look on her face when he said it. Poor Dan lost his family, better comfort him. Poor Dan, all by himself!

But he'd almost messed it all up earlier. He moved in too fast. Lara was too smart for his standard play. He'd need to move slower, be more careful. He had to watch his mouth, too. Talk all intellectual and shit. The thousands of hours of TV he'd watched in his lifetime were put to good use. Guys he grew up with couldn't talk normal so they couldn't fit in. But Dan? Dan was smart enough to know when to play it up. He could act like a 9-5 shmuck if he had to.

He'd been working on turning Lara against Jack the past few days, too. That was one of the most important parts of his plan. When the time came, Lara would have no reason to want to stay. She needed to feel like she had no friends or allies. Dan was her savior and she was his. Dan was all she had. And so far, Dan's plan was working. Lara and Jack hadn't had a moment alone since he arrived. Jack had dug himself into a deeper hole without even realizing it when he tried to intimidate Dan. All it did was make Lara feel bad for Dan that Jack was picking on him.

A warm shudder coursed through him. Soon he'd be back in Hedone, Lara by his side, ready to bone and get fucked up.

"Thanks for bringing this up." Lara pulled the water jug to its spot by the food shelf. "I enjoyed our talk earlier."

He smiled and nodded. "Of course. Any time you want to talk, I'm here. Okay?"

"Thanks," was all she said. The heifer had demanded her attention, and Lara turned away from him.

That abuse thing. Damn, it was like she was laying herself out for him. When a woman talked about anything like that, Dan mirrored it. If they had a puppy who got hit by a car when they were a kid, Dan had a kitten who got killed on the railroad tracks by his house. Lara had an abusive dad, and so did Dan. Imagine that!

He tilted his head back against the bookshelf and stared

through the skylights, his good mood tarnished. That part about his dad. That wasn't a total lie. He did have a bad childhood. In fact, what he'd told her was a Disney movie compared to what really happened. If he told her everything, about the box, she'd look at him different. Disgusted but curious, like kids looking at roadkill and prodding at the guts with a stick.

Dan had to be careful. Yeah, Lara was a hot piece of ass. But she was also a shrink, and all shrinks wanted people to spill their secrets. He needed to keep his lies straight.

"Danny, do you want some tea?"

It took everything he had not to groan and slap Molly. That heifer was way too interested in his business. And he fucking hated it when people called him Danny. Instead, he looked over at her and smiled. "No thanks. I actually need to run to the bathroom. I'll be right back, okay?"

He'd hidden the goodies from the cannie's backpack in a paper towel dispenser. Now he pulled out a Snickers bar and sat in one of the stalls, savoring every bite while he flipped through the pages of one of the porno mags. Even the lingering scent of shit and piss didn't ruin it for him. Dan smirked as he licked his fingers. Everyone upstairs was starving, but he had snacks.

He considered how to get Lara separated from the group. They both had masks and hazmat suits, so that was solved. But to get her to go off with him alone would take a lot. Apparently she had saved Jack when the comet first hit. Heifer loved her and wouldn't let her go easily. Plus she took care of those two dying guys all the time, as if it mattered. It would take a lot for Lara to abandon everyone.

He bit off a chunk of candy bar, smacking as he chewed. Patience. He just had to wait for the right moment.

# JACK

"Well, this was a bust."

Jack kicked the vending machine. He was sweaty, tired, and defeated. Not to mention creeped out. There was something eerie about the empty hallways of the middle school. Graffiti was scrawled on every locker and wall. A few abandoned backpacks littered the ground. Jack wondered if disgruntled teenagers had come back during the last days solely to destroy the place. He would have, if he was fourteen again.

Would Katie have been the kind of teenager to do something like that? Jack squeezed his eyes shut and let himself think of her for just a moment. She had truly been the most wonderful thing he'd ever witnessed. That bubbling curiosity about the world and a generosity towards people and animals that rivaled a storybook princess. She had her mother's beautiful, rich brown complexion and a scattering of dark freckles. But those eyes…they were a bright hazel that came straight from him.

No, Katie wouldn't have done this.

The church and middle school had both been looted from top to bottom. There was a bottle of vanilla syrup left in the church, which Jack took, but other than that, nothing. Fred was right about one thing: there were plenty of vending machines at the middle school. The problem was, they were all broken and pillaged.

"Should have gone to the gym first," Rocky said. "Way better chances there."

Rocky was right, but the other locations were closer to the library than the gym, which was on the opposite side of town. The road here had been relatively clear, but there was more damage headed in the direction of the gym where the area was less residential and much more commercial. Carrying back any findings would be difficult.

"Let's go then," Jack said. "I want to get back to the library before dark."

They double checked their gear, taped any areas that seemed loose or losing their seal, and headed out of the middle school. They hadn't seen any signs of life, but there was plenty of death. Jack could come up with a story on how each of the corpses came to be based on how they looked. If their bodies were covered in dust, they'd died right in the beginning. Some were still pulpy and wet, dust soaking into rotting, putrid flesh which meant they'd died more recently.

They tried to stick to well-used paths as they walked, ones made by the raiders and other survivors. Jack hoped it would reduce the chances of pursuit. He wondered if he could brush their prints away or do something to destroy the trail when they went back to the library.

Jack would've happily moved in silence, but Rocky had other plans. "What school did you teach at?"

"No talking. Someone might hear."

Lara and her damn cover story. Jack quickened his pace to gain some distance on Rocky. Lara might have been looking out for him, but her quick thinking had put him in a bad position.

They turned a corner and Jack spotted the gym. It was a two story buildingwith an overly industrial aesthetic that didn't fit in with the small town. Its face was entirely reflective glass and metal from ground to roof. There were no cars in the expansive parking lot. The windows were intact. A good sign. There wouldn't be any dust inside.

His breath was damp and labored beneath the mask. He clutched his handgun and kept it level ahead of him. Dust was thick on the windows, making it hard to see inside. Jack used his sleeve to clear a spot to peek through. The dust smeared, but that was good enough. There was a check-in desk and some refrigerators. Those were open, already raided. Two hallways branched left and right around the reception desk. The place was huge.

Jack pushed open the door. Dust entered the new space, shimmering as it drifted in the muted light from the windows. Rocky entered behind him, a baseball bat in his hands. He walked over to the refrigerators. His footsteps were loud against the polished concrete floor.

"Shit. Someone already hit this place." He kicked an empty sports drink bottle. It skittered across the floor and landed by a plastic plant.

"We have to check everywhere. They might have a storage room or something where they keep extra inventory. Plus," Jack pointed to the wall behind the check-in desk, "check that out."

Stacked on glass shelves were black plastic containers of protein powder. Jack went around the check-in desk and pulled one down. It was heavy and cumbersome, bigger than a jug of milk. At best, he could fit two in his backpack. If he carried one under his arm, that would still leave his right hand free to hold his gun.

He began taking down the protein powder containers and set them under the check-in desk away from immediate sight. "We should hide what we can't carry, then come back for it later."

"Good idea," Rocky said and came over to help. "Used to hate this stuff, but damn, it sounds good right now. Imagine if we had some ice and a banana? We could make real shakes."

"I used to add chocolate pudding mix. Really makes it good," Jack said, thinking back when he used to care about his body.

"Chocolate pudding?" Rocky chuckled. "Man, take it easy. I can only handle so much."

They made fast work of hiding the powder. Jack searched the desk and found three candy bars, which elicited a few more lustful moans from Rocky. They exited the reception area and entered the gym. Dozens of treadmills, ellipticals, and bikes stood in rows. To their right, a set of stairs led upwards. There were men and women's locker rooms to their left.

"I'll check upstairs. You want to get the lockers?" Jack asked.

Rocky nodded and headed towards the locker rooms "Could use some new clothes, I guess."

"Don't forget to check the gym bags if there are any," Jack called out as he walked away.

Jack climbed the stairs and found himself in the weightlifting section of the gym. Before Katie was taken from him, Jack had been the kind of guy who hit the gym at least five times a week. Sometimes he did cardio in the morning and weights at night. He wasn't overweight now, but he was out of shape. His joints cracked as he ascended the stairs.

The windows upstairs weren't as caked with dust as those below. Jack wandered through the free weights and peered out over the city. The gym was on higher elevation than the rest of the town. From this vantage, he could see the larger scope of damage small meteors had inflicted on buildings. Roofs caved in, windows shattered, roads pockmarked. Directly across the street was a big box hardware store. The flat roof sported gaping holes, some as big as a school bus.

How were they going to recover from this? If people breathed the dust or got it on their skin, they got sick. They died. And there was dust *everywhere*. When it rained, the dust would seep into the ground. Wouldn't it? How would it affect their water supply? Farming, livestock, animals?

Jack stepped away from the window. It wouldn't do him any good to think that far ahead. What mattered now was finding food. Across the room was a snack and smoothie bar. A bit of hope sparked within him.

He tried to keep his hope in check as he went over to the snack kiosk, but he needn't have been so cautious. There were power bars, veggie chips, and other healthy snacks in a glass case, similar to a movie theater. Untouched. Perfect. Excited, he found the employee entrance into the stand and slid the case open. There were even more packages in the back.

"Rocky!" he shouted. "I hit the mother lode, get up here!"

There was a muffled response, then footsteps as Rocky ran up the stairs. Jack already formed a pile of bars on the counter. He removed the protein powder from his backpack.

Rocky did some kind of victory jig that made Jack laugh. He couldn't remember the last time he felt this *good*. He savored it. When Rocky offered his hand out for a fist bump, Jack returned the gesture.

At the mere prospect of food, Jack's stomach grumbled and churned. He'd been trying to ignore how hungry he was because he knew there wasn't anything to eat.

Rocky thrust his hand out, in which he clenched a roll of small plastic garbage bags. "Found these in the locker room. Figured we could quadruple bag anything we find just to be safe."

"Good thinking. We're going to need them. Look at all this."

"Yeah, man. Let's take the bars and—holy shit! I love these things. They're like gummy cubes with electrolytes or whatever. Used to eat them when I biked."

They quadruple bagged their findings and stuffed those bags into their backpacks. With each cupboard and drawer they opened, their smiles grew wider.

"This *is* the mother lode. Great idea," Rocky said.

"Wasn't me. Fred said we should come here." Jack didn't mind giving credit where it was due. "Smart guy."

There were boxes and boxes of bars and the gummy cubes Rocky was fond of. There were bottles of sport drink, water, and even coconut water. Far more than they could carry. Then Jack found something that made his spirit soar even higher.

"Check this out," he said, holding up his find. Six instant coffee packets. They'd been in a drawer of random junk, making Jack think it was an employee who left them.

"Coffee?" Rocky put his gloved hands over his head and did his victory dance again. "Hell yes! Just between us, I *hate* tea."

Jack laughed again. "Same here. We'll have to share them, but we get first dibs."

By the time they were done, they'd taken everything the stand had to offer. In addition to their own packs, they filled a tote bag they found in a drawer. Jack layered towels over the contents of the bag to reduce how much dust could get on it. The next trip would be for the drinks and protein powder. Since there were already blue plastic drums of water at the library, it wasn't worth it to carry them back now.

"Jack, look."

They were about to start down the stairs when Rocky

grabbed his shoulder. He pointed out the windows.

A block away, two Humvees were making slow progress down the street. Behind them was a troop carrier and three soldiers walking beside it.

"It's the Army. It's our lucky day, man." Rocky said. "Come on, we'll meet them down the street. We can—"

A crack of gunfire rang out, and one of the soldiers collapsed to the ground. The convoy ground to a halt as the remaining soldiers took cover. Jack's heart stopped as he watched the scene unfold.

More gunfire rained down on the troops. Now Jack could spot two people with rifles on the rooftop above the soldiers. The soldiers outside the convoy made a dash to get inside one of the Humvees, but their movement gave away their position.

Two men ran out from a coffee shop. They had white crosses painted on their backs, marking them as Hedone raiders. One of the soldiers turned and fired. The raider's body jerked back as the first round hit him and then went down when the second bore through his head. Gore splattered against the yellow dust.

The remaining raider wielded a shotgun and rapidly pumped two blasts into the soldier closest to him. Blood and loops of intestines slipped from the gaping wound, sliding down the soldier's hazmat suit. The other soldier, still running towards the Humvee, was brought to his knees by simultaneous shots from the rooftop snipers.

As he crawled for cover, the shotgun raider came upon him and unloaded three more times into the helpless soldier's back.

The Humvees started to move again, but to Jack's horror, dozens of raiders emptied from the buildings flanking the convoy like cockroaches. They swarmed the vehicles. Many of the raiders were shot as they approached. More replaced the fallen.

When it seemed as though the gunfight was over, Jack spotted a soldier crawling away from the scene. It was the one who had taken the first bullet from the snipers. Jack prayed the raiders wouldn't see him. He was covered in dust and moving slowly, barely visible in the carnage. The raiders were busy looting the Humvees.

Jack's prayers always went unanswered.

The raiders saw him and closed in, quickly disarming the dying man even as he went for his sidearm. Piece by piece they removed his gear, his hazmat suit, and even his clothes. Jack watched, horrified, as they lashed his body to the grill of a Humvee.

He was dead by the time they finished.

The bloodbath, from the first shot to the last, was over in minutes. The raiders yanked the bodies from the vehicles and tossed them on the side of the road. Half the raiders drove away. The other half made their way back into the buildings to wait. The convoy headed down the road.

Towards the gym.

"Rocky, we have to get out of here," Jack said. He spun around and headed to the stairs, his gun gripped tightly in hand. Rocky was silent as he followed Jack. They found an emergency exit behind the gym that led to an employee parking lot. They leaned against the building, waiting. The roar of the convoys grew louder, but it sounded as if they had turned away from the gym. Jack was sweating, his heart beating out of his chest while his mind raced. The harder he strained to listen, the more he heard the blood pounding in his head.

After an eternity, Rocky spoke. "I think they're gone. We should head back."

"Right," Jack answered automatically, his mind elsewhere.

Any ounce of happiness Jack had derived from their find at the gym vanished. No matter how much food they found, no matter how secure they thought they were in the library, they would never be safe. What had he expected? That all the terrible people, the raiders, the murderers, would lay down their arms and stop just because Zabat's Comet didn't destroy them?

"Jack," Rocky said. He placed his hand on Jack's shoulder. "Are you okay?"

"I'm fine. I just…God, what are we going to do? We can't defend ourselves against that."

"We'll try. It'll be okay. We'll figure it out. Come on, we need to get back now. People are hungry."

Jack readjusted his backpack. "You're right. Come on."

As they walked, Jack considered his own question. What were they going to do? In the end, there was only one answer that made sense.

They had to leave the city.

# CRAIG

The woman's skin was decaying, yet she was somehow still alive. Tendons and cartilage were visible beneath the smears of blood and rotten tissue. On the few areas of uninfected skin were blue pebble-like blisters. In one spot, the blisters were so thick that it looked almost like some strange, reptilian hide.

Her eyes fluttered open before she slipped back into darkness, showing neon blue sclera.

Craig felt sick to his stomach. The doctor standing next to him, Cora, seemed to be more composed than he was. Her arms were folded across her chest, her face neutral as she examined the patient.

"So this is the first survivor we've found?" she asked.

"Our very first," Craig answered. "There's military coverage around almost the entire circumference of the DZ. I'm sure there'll be more soon."

Even through the heavy duty layers of his hazmat suit and respirator, Craig felt unsafe. Spittle and blood seeped from the corner of the survivor's mouth as she wheezed labored breaths. The cot she lay on was stained with the yellowish green pus leaking from her wounds.

Hours earlier, the woman had stumbled out of the DZ wrapped in a makeshift hazmat suit of garbage bags and duct tape. Following the protocol Craig formed, the soldiers donned their positive pressure suits before they were able to help her. She had been unconscious for fifteen minutes before the first private reached her. The soldiers reported that the dust had drifted off her and back into the

DZ, just as it had from Berg's suit. Craig wished he had been there to witness it himself.

He had quarantined her in a tent with double layers of plastic sealed with duct tape to prevent the mysterious contagion from escaping. Sure, it *looked* like every bit of dust was recalled back to the DZ but they couldn't know for certain. And thus far they didn't know if the infection was contagious outside of the DZ. Jesus, they really didn't know much of anything at all.

It was the best they could do until Tim's promised supply drops arrived. Craig would've done anything for a positive pressure tent. If the rest of the survivors in the DZ were in this shape, he dreaded what Berg's search and rescues would bring back.

The men at the I-5 checkpoint were required to always be in full hazmat gear in preparation for encountering survivors like this. They were disciplined, or possibly just used to unpleasant conditions, and there was no complaint of the sweltering heat.

"Listen, I was an ER doctor, okay? I'm used to dealing with car accident victims, broken bones. Maybe a strange rash or a freak accident. This is…pardon my French… fucked up." Cora paused. Craig caught a glimpse of her shaking her head inside the hood of her hazmat suit. "More like a bad dream."

"A bad dream," Craig echoed. He knew the patient's condition had to be because of exposure to the dust, but how much was she exposed to? And for how long? He wasn't about to send a person in to solve these unknowns. "What kind of treatment should be administered?"

"How the hell should I know? I just told you, I've never seen anything like this before. It's a medical anomaly."

"Noted. But when you first saw her, you said it looked like a flesh-eating bacteria. How would you treat that?"

"First we'd need to run tests to identify the strain. If it is necrotizing fasciitis, we'd need huge quantities of antibiotics," she said. "We'd need to surgically remove the necrotic flesh in attempt to stop its spread. The problem here is that at least seventy percent of her body is infected. In addition to that, I believe her lungs are filled with blood. We can release some of it, and that would help her breathe, but without more supplies and better equipment, the only thing I can do now is make her more comfortable."

Craig sighed. "Do you at least have what you need to remove the fluid?"

"Yes. But I also need to do a comprehensive metabolic panel, a tox screen, and an ultrasound would be nice."

"You got it. I'll have Berg send a group to scavenge what you need. No promises; most hospitals have been turned over. Make her as comfortable as you can. Get me a list of antibiotics and equipment, and I'll get those, too."

Before he exited the tent, Cora touched his shoulder. The rubber glove squeaked against the plastic of his suit. Her bright green eyes were wide, startlingly bright against her tanned skin. "What is that thing out there? Why is it here?"

"That's what we're trying to find out. Anything you can tell me about that woman's condition, anything at all, is one step closer to an answer."

Cora offered a short nod of understanding and let him go. He navigated the folds of the tent and their makeshift decontamination corridor. While they didn't know for certain if the disease was contagious, obviously they couldn't risk spreading it. Berg's men had found an abandoned fire truck, which they positioned outside of the tunnel, one deck gun modified and aimed through the plastic.

Craig positioned himself under it. "Go for decontamination!"

Outside, someone turned on the water. Craig spun around and let the hard stream beat against him. Thirty seconds later he moved into yet another tent where he stripped out of the suit and stayed under the portable shower until the water ran out. He scrubbed his skin and hair with soap and then dressed in new clothes.

He emerged into the bright sun. The entrance to the quarantine tent faced the DZ. Over the last few days, the dust had thinned. A thick layer had settled on the ground, increasing visibility into the DZ. He spotted trees, shaggy and coated with yellow, and an abandoned tractor.

Coffee was on his mind. Well, not just coffee. During the drive to Castle Rock he nearly tossed his bourbon out the window. Still drunk and increasingly high on adrenaline at the prospect of the DZ, he was sure he didn't need the stuff. Just because he fell off the wagon at the cabin didn't mean he couldn't return to sobriety when he wanted to. Craig Peters reporting for duty, sober and ready to science.

But he didn't toss that bottle. In fact, it was already halfway gone. He rationed it as best as he could, but the truth was that he would shake if he didn't have a finger of it in the morning with his coffee. Or at lunch. Or dinner.

The soldiers bringing his biological safety cabinets and other equipment were arriving soon. When they did, Craig needed to be on his game. Being on his game meant taking the edge off so he could focus.

Plus, sleep had been hard to come by. When he closed his eyes, he saw the DZ and heard the strange voice beneath the static over the radio. No matter how exhausted he was, it was hard to dispel the sense of unease. Powernaps during the day were the best he could do.

He entered his tent and lay down on his cot, pulling out the photo of Betty and the kids. He'd folded it so many times it threatened to break into two each time he looked at it. In it, Brandon and Sharon were dressed as Dr. Seuss's Thing1 and Thing2. Betty was Cat in the Hat. She and the kids had spent weeks making the costumes for the kids' school Halloween party. Betty's arms were around the kids, pulling them tightly to her sides with a beaming smile. The kids were making silly faces, Sharon with her tongue stuck out and Brandon with his eyes crossed.

Craig had been too busy with work to help during the nightly costume-making sessions. As it turned out, the kids and Betty had secretly made him a Grinch costume. The barbed humor wasn't lost on him. Still, he had worn it with pride.

Tears trailed down Craig's cheeks. He used his thumb to brush them away, eyes still fixed on the photo as he remembered the little details of that Halloween.

At least the kids were safe. Berg had made good on his promise and somehow convinced his higher-ups to send a team out to check on them. Craig had even spoken with them briefly on the radio and told them as much as he was allowed to with Captain Berg hovering right behind him. If and when this was over, he was flying out and seeing them whether they liked it or not.

He folded the photo gently and returned it to his wallet. His body was fatigued, but his mind was alert. Sleep was out of the question, so he put his shoes back on and headed out into the sun for a walk. Halfway to the communications tent, Private Brody jogged over to intercept him.

"Captain needs you at the freeway checkpoint. We've got survivors. Lots of them."

Craig followed Brody as he asked, "Are they infected? What can you tell me about the dust's behavior?"

"When they walked out of the DZ, the dust went back in as expected, sir. They've got gear on and don't appear to be sick. Not that we can see, anyway."

Brody led him to a waiting Humvee. Jeff, Cora's EMT friend who had shown up with her at camp, was already inside in full hazmat gear. He had his medical kit beside him.

"Hey, Dr. Peters," Jeff said. "I've got another suit for you in the back. Sorry, I know you just got out of one."

"Don't worry about it. This is more important, right? These survivors could tell us a lot."

They drove out of camp to the I-5 checkpoint, passing thick forest and the occasional abandoned home along the way. As they ascended the on-ramp and neared the checkpoint, Craig spotted a dozen people dressed in painting overalls, respirators, and duct-taped plastic suits, their backs to the DZ.

The Humvee slowed to a halt. Captain Berg opened Craig's door and didn't waste a second before giving them orders. "Get suited up. My men are on decontamination duty. Jeff, check them for signs of infection. Dr. Peters can interview the survivors."

Craig got out of the Humvee and retrieved his new hazmat suit from the back. Berg followed.

He handed Craig an earpiece and mic, which Craig secured before putting on his hood. "We'll follow decontamination procedures as you outlined, then they're moving to the refugee camp father south on I-5. Civilians are not permitted to stay on our primary base."

"Certainly, I can interview them further later?" Craig pressed, and was met with a slight nod from Berg. Craig wondered where the hesitance came from but was too eager to talk to the survivors to think much more on it.

"Your mic is recording everything. Try to get as much as you can now."

Craig and Jeff walked down the freeway toward the refugees, escorted by three soldiers. The I-5 checkpoint guards had pushed abandoned cars aside to form a chokepoint in the middle of the blacktop.

He and Jeff exited the choke point and approached one survivor standing farther apart from the rest. From the body language, Craig pegged him as the leader. The man was tall, at least six-four with a bulky upper body. He wore white painter's overalls, the hood up, with a full-face respirator. The edges around the respirator, his neck, wrists, and ankles were sealed with leopard-print duct tape.

Craig spoke loudly enough to be heard through the survivor's getup. "Hello, my name is Dr. Craig Peters. I just wanted to ask you a few questions before we move you through decontamination procedures. Is that okay?"

"Corey Straus. Make it quick," he said, his voice booming even through the respirator. "We want to get as far away from that…that thing…as we can."

"Of course. Have you or anyone you're with come in contact with the dust?"

Corey glared at him, his head titling slightly. "That a serious question?"

"I mean, did any dust come in contact with your skin? Did you inhale any of it?"

He shifted from foot to foot. "No. But we've seen what it does."

"Can you describe what happened?"

"You get too much on you, or you breathe it in, you die. Fucks you up. Eats your skin, makes you puke blood. I saw someone run outside when the dust first came. Thirty seconds before he dropped dead."

"What if you only come in contact with a small amount? Have you seen anything like that?"

"Sure. One of our guys got a tear in his suit on the first day. Just got a little on his skin. Couple hours later, the infection started where the dust touched him. Weird fucking blisters all over his body."

"Where is he now?"

The man hesitated. "We left him behind."

"Why? Did the infection worsen?"

"Seemed like it stayed about the same, but we were worried we might catch it if we hung around him." Corey's sentence trailed off, hesitant. "He was acting weird, too. Something wasn't right about him. Like a zombie. I can't explain it. He was in so much pain, then it was like he stopped caring."

He coughed and glanced back at his group. "Anyway, raiders are everywhere up north, and you'd better believe the dust isn't stopping them. Where there's a will there's a way. Figured we'd keep going south until we hit eastern Oregon." The man crossed his beefy arms. "Then we walk out of the dust and poof—just like that, we're in the clear. Except for you for guys."

A gentle gust of wind swept down the freeway. The DZ quivered slightly. Craig stared into the yellow haze. For the second time, he thought he saw something shift. This time he recognized a shape. It was brief, a split second at best, but he swore he saw a face hovering in the dust.

Watching him.

"Listen; it's real simple. You don't let the dust touch you or you die. We don't know anything else." Corey's voice shifted, anger sharpening the edges of his words. "Unless you have answers for us, that's all I have to tell you. It's all any of us have to tell you."

Craig brought his attention back to the man. "I'm sorry, I don't know. We're just as much in the dark as you. We're going to decontaminate you, and then you'll be on your way. If you or your people need any other medical assistance, I'm sure we can help."

As Craig examined each reluctant survivor for dust

residue, his mind was elsewhere. The dust was deadly. Whatever it was made of, it killed people. Millions were likely dead inside the DZ. At least the intensity of contact made a difference in level of infection; if the same lethal results could be achieved from even a particle of the dust coming in contact with the body, they'd be doomed.

What if the DZ moved? The thought had itched at him since day one, and now that they knew how deadly it was, he was even more afraid. If the black poles were creating a force field as he imagined, there had to be someone—something—controlling them. The question was, why did the poles exist? Were they protecting the dust, or everything outside of it?

Craig finished inspecting the survivors. He gave the go-ahead to Berg, who led them through the decontamination corridor. Craig went through himself and then stripped out of his suit. Jeff stayed behind to do preliminary physicals on each of the survivors, but Craig headed back to camp.

Tim didn't want him to use the word *alien*, and Craig had gone to great lengths to avoid it in his reports. He couldn't avoid it any longer. The truth was right in front of them. They needed to embrace it.

When he got back to the camp, he was surprised to see two helicopters in the vacant field beside it and a convoy of Humvees, troop carriers, and moving trucks. A slew of people he'd never seen before were bustling about. Many were in the process of erecting new tents, while others unloaded equipment from the trucks.

Craig walked over to the communication tent, excited to find out what was going on, and ducked to enter just as a woman stepped out. They nearly collided.

Her black hair was pulled into a tight bun on top of her head, her pale skin void of any makeup. Two neon purple streaks near her temple were grown out about an inch. Two sets of wedding rings hung on a silver chain around her neck, just above the collar of her lab coat.

*She's gorgeous,* Craig thought as she reached out to shake his hand. "Dr. Peters? My name is Dr. Siyang Shen. I'm your biology and virology specialist. General Williams sent me along with the equipment you requested. We're here to help you figure out what the hell is going on."

"Nice to meet you," Craig said. "I'm glad he finally made good on his word, although you look young enough to still be deciding on a major."

Siyang raised a delicate brow. "Are you being ageist? Or is it because I'm Asian? And female?"

Craig was at a loss for words. The grave expression on her face melted away. She winked at him. "Just kidding. I might be young but I have a PhD same as any other crusty scientist."

"She's got a sense of humor. Excellent," Craig said, genuinely pleased. Nothing was worse than working with somber, lifeless old men. "Now, Dr. Shen, tell me something. How do you feel about aliens?"

# COLLEEN

"What do you mean?" James asked.

"I mean exactly what I said. Her scars are gone."

Colleen glanced at the girls to make sure they were still fast asleep. This was not a conversation any of them should hear. James reached out and gently brushed Liana's hair aside. Her complexion was a rich, unblemished brown.

He sat back and slowly exhaled. He pulled off his glasses and rubbed the bridge of his nose. "Jesus."

"And you've noticed how she's been acting, haven't you?" Colleen asked.

He kept his eyes closed and merely nodded. "I figured it was because of everything she's been through. Who knows what she heard and saw back home when the gang came. Then seeing the house destroyed. And now being here? The fight the other day? That would upset anyone."

Colleen had been thinking about Liana's condition nonstop for days. She hadn't brought it up with James for the very reason he'd just mentioned. It was easy to wave away the monotone attitude. Her scars, on the other hand, couldn't be ignored. Now that the conversation started, the floodgates were open.

"I think…"

"What, Colleen?"

"I think it was the dust."

James slipped his glasses back on and looked around to see if anyone was listening. Tentatively, he whispered, "I'm supposed to be the conspiracy theorist here."

"I know, trust me. But when I look back, this all started right after she touched that rock. What if it did make her sick?"

"If it was the dust, it would've killed her by now."

Colleen bit the inside of her cheek and shook her head. "We have *no idea* what it is or how it works. Most of the people in here were covered in it. Liana just got a smudge."

They sat in silence for a few moments. Colleen's gaze drifted to the West side of the gym. The sight of the Infected made her sick, curious, and hopeless all in one. She was positive at least a dozen people were dead on their cots. Their bodies were swollen, skin covered in patches of rotten flesh and cracked, dried pus. The opposite of her pristine daughter. Many sported the unusual blisters. Eyes were crusted shut, mouths gaped open. Under the harsh fluorescent light of the gym, the image was something out of a war movie.

James broke her from her thoughts. "What do we do? The soldiers and FEMA people haven't been that helpful so far. That doctor said she was fine when we first came in."

"I think we—"

James expression morphed into one of total repulsion. He was no longer paying attention to Colleen. "Wake up the girls."

Colleen followed his eyes to the group of troublemakers led by the man named Benny from the incident a few days earlier. They went from group to group talking. They were two cots away from Colleen's family.

One of them was the Purple Bandana man. Colleen woke up the girls and gathered them closer to her. A cold tendril of dread started to form in the pit of her stomach.

Purple Bandana went ahead to Colleen and James. He carried his angular, bony body as though he owned the world now that he had a cohort with him. His lips curved into a vicious sneer directed towards Gabriela. She tilted her head and stared at the ground.

"Look what we have here," he mused.

"Leave us alone," James said, his voice level.

Suddenly Purple Bandana reached out and grabbed Gabriela's wrist, yanking her off the cot. The movement was so sudden and forceful, it made Colleen jump. She tried to grab Gabriela but her fingertips caught nothing but air. In one fluid motion, the man brought his other hand up to Gabriela's throat.

James had sprung up to take action, but when the man's grip tightened and Gabriela whimpered, James paused.

"None of you have the right to tell me what to do," Purple Bandana spat. "Things are going to change around here now. The right kind of people are coming into power now."

Colleen's stomach churned as fear and disgust coursed through her body.

"Stop it, dammit!" Colleen shouted, surprised by her own voice.

"Let her go, Glen," a voice growled. "That's not what we're here for."

Benny and his other goon had arrived. Glen released Gabriela instantly. The girl stumbled away then quickly made her way behind James and Colleen. Despite the curtain of thick hair covering her face, Colleen still saw the sheen of tears.

Glen's gaze locked with Colleen's. "You don't tell me what to do, bitch."

With an aw-shucks grin, Benny clapped Glen on the shoulder.

"Sorry about Glen there. He just gets excited. I'm Benny. I'm going around talking to people, gettin' a feel for how we're all doing. Someone has to, am I right?" He sneered.

"No one else will."

The attempt at camaraderie fell flat. "Are you kidding me? Your friend here has it out for us. So no, we aren't doing that great," Colleen said.

Benny didn't acknowledge her. He waited for James's response.

"We *were* fine until your friend here," James rephrased.

The group hovered over Colleen and her family, well beyond invading personal space. There was something about sitting when they were standing that shifted the power balance in the goons' favor. Colleen stood beside James and made sure all the girls were safely behind her. She realized with this group of people, there was no winning. No standing up for themselves. It pained her to admit, but placating them so they'd leave was the best solution.

"We don't have any problems," James said.

"You sure you don't need anything? More food? Pretty sure I spotted a bunch of rice and bean MREs." This came from Glen whose gaze was locked onto Gabriela.

Colleen's stomach was a ball of ice that was slowly melting from the fiery rage building inside of her.

"Glen, you shut the fuck up with that bullshit. You'll regret it if I have to tell you again," Benny said. His tone shifted as he addressed Colleen and James again. "I'm not like my friend there. I'm fair and I think everyone should have a say in how this place is run. What about some intel on what's going on outside? Don't you think we should know what's going on?"

"No one knows what's going on outside." Colleen folded her arms across her chest and held her ground. "And you don't have any more food than the rest of us. We're all at the camp's mercy."

Benny grinned. Colleen's heart raced. That was the grin of a predator. "We got someone who sneaks outside to check every so often. He said the wind is picking up and the dust is bad. We're going to be in here a long time. In these conditions, with no food? Shi-it. No good."

She'd walked into his trap. Benny wanted a soapbox and she'd given him one. Colleen was ready to end the conversation, but a small, calm voice spoke from behind her.

"You're lying."

"Liana, sweetie, shh," Colleen shushed.

Benny laughed. "Ah yeah, little girl? What do you know? Step aside, mom, let your kid talk. I like to know exactly why someone is accusing me of being a liar."

"She has an active imagination," Colleen insisted. Liana tried to slide off the cot, but Colleen stopped her. "She's only four. Don't listen."

Benny lifted the hem of his shirt and revealed the butt of a handgun. "I said let her talk."

Colleen glanced at James, who looked as helpless as she felt. How in the world did Benny get that gun?

She let Liana stand, but kept her hand on her shoulder. The longer they argued with Benny and his men, the worse the situation could get.

"You think I'm lying?"

"Yes," Liana said, unafraid of the man and unfazed by what happened to Gabriela.

Glen snorted and nudged his buddy. "Fuckin' kids. Come on, Benny. Let's—"

Benny lifted his hand to silence Glen. He crouched down to Liana's level, his eyes locked onto her.

"Yeah?"

"You sent him, but he didn't come back. You don't know if he's dead or if the soldiers took him."

Colleen didn't know how it was possible, but based off of the look on Benny's face, Liana somehow knew. He stood. His eyes flickered from Liana to his side where his cohorts looked confused. In that moment, Colleen realized not only was Liana telling the truth, but Benny's lackeys didn't know it.

"I don't know how she comes up with these things," Colleen stammered, detecting a way to get the group away from her family. "She always sounds so convincing."

Benny stared hard at Liana. Suddenly the girl stepped back and a frown found its way to her passive face. "I don't want to do that," she said quietly.

"The kid is a retard," Benny announced, a smug expression on his face. "She won't be telling anymore lies, right, Mom and Dad?"

Colleen and James both nodded. Benny took a deep breath, perhaps about to launch into another speech or a threat, when Glen swore.

Everyone's attention locked on to the sick woman standing on the edge of the line between the infected and healthy. A steady trickle of blood leaked from deep scratches on her cheeks and arms where she'd tried to claw off her own skin. Colleen hadn't seen anyone with as many blisters as her. Her skin was more blue and red than white. Her shoulders heaved up as she turned her face to the ceiling and wailed.

A surge of people backed away from her. The gym went quiet. All eyes were on the woman.

"Help," she cried. She moved forward past the gap dividing the two groups. The people nearest to her scrambled away. "I hurt. I hurt so much. No one will do anything. Please help me."

"Get away from us!"

"Stop!"

The few pleas from the crowd went unheard. The woman's hands flexed into claws. "You can't keep me over there anymore. I won't stay! I'm a human being!"

The woman's chest heaved. Her hands flew to her stomach. A second later she spewed blood. It splashed onto some of the onlookers. She went into a panicked frenzy. She lunged forward and grabbed a teenage boy.

"God, please help me! Help me!"

Colleen watched in horror as the woman's pus-covered skin sloughed off onto the boy. Her skin shed from her arms where they brushed against him. As much as he struggled against her, her grip was iron tight.

No one moved. The woman wasn't hurting him, not really. She was crying and begging for help. Colleen wanted to help. Surely others did, too. But the woman was dangerous. The boy she had grabbed could be infected now. Couldn't he?

Colleen and her family forgotten, Benny pushed through the group. In a flash, he withdrew a hunting knife from somewhere in his jacket. He came up behind the woman and stabbed her in the neck, the blade buried in the spot between her neck and shoulder.

She dropped to her knees. Blood spurted from the wound, flowing through her fingers as she frantically tried to stop it. Then she relaxed. She was dead.

Benny knelt and wiped his blade on her clothes. When he stood, Colleen could tell he was trying to suppress a smile. The edges of his lips twitched.

"This is going to happen again." He brandished the knife at the rest of the infected. "They can't stay in here with us. We have to do something. We're healthy. We're alive. But if they stay in here, we won't be healthy much longer."

Liana tugged at Colleen's hand. "He's going to do bad things."

"Don't look, sweetie," was all Colleen could manage to say. She collapsed onto the cot and hugged Liana close to her. She had no idea what her daughter had become—how she could possibly know what she did—but she was still her daughter. She still needed to be protected from all this.

Serena watched the scene unfold with captivated attention while she held James's hand. Tears streamed down her face. James ran his hand over her hair, an act that normally soothed her, with no success.

"He doesn't want to wait anymore. He's going to kill the next person who tells him no," Liana's small voice noted. She tried to tilt her head. Colleen kept it firmly in the crook of her neck.

The group started to shout in agreement with Benny. On the West side, the infected were drawing farther back. Some had flipped their cots over to form a better barrier between the two groups.

There was fear on both sides. No good could come of this. Colleen stared at the entrance to the gym and prayed the soldiers would come in soon to put an end to the uprising.

"Mom?"

Liana pulled back and looked up at Colleen's face. A thin layer of sweat plastered her overgrown bangs to her forehead. Colleen kissed her and held her close.

"It's going to be okay. I promise."

Her hazel eyes were big and clear. Calm. "No. It isn't."

"We're gonna get these infected people out," Benny promised. He raised his arms in the air. "We're gonna—"

The doors finally burst open. Belman and three other soldiers came in. This time the crowd didn't quiet. They surged towards the guards.

Then the gunfire began.

# LARA

The second Lara heard the knocking on the book return room door, she rushed from Dan's side downstairs to let Rocky and Jack inside. She slipped into her plastic suit and mask before opening the door. They rushed past her, and she slammed the door shut, locked it, and put the chair under the door handle. Less dust forced its way into the room than when they left in the morning. It was a good sign.

"Did you find anything?" she asked.

"Yeah, we did," Rocky said.

Lara sensed something was wrong right away. Rocky's tone was flat, very unlike his usual vibrant, joking attitude. "What's wrong? Did something happen?"

Jack walked to the corner of the room where he began decontamination procedures. "Guys, protocol first. Frank'll go ballistic if we don't."

He was stalling. Lara waited patiently as they each followed the steps. It took longer than normal since Jack and Rocky had to carefully decontaminate their bags as well as their clothes. Eventually they all met in the main library.

Jack's mouth was set in a grim line. He dropped handfuls of white garbage bags down on the ground. At least his rash looked better.

"We saw raiders. At least thirty." Jack sighed. "They took out a military convoy. Drove off with the vehicles and whatever they had inside them."

Lara leaned forward as he opened the bags. Inside were power bars. Her stomach flipped and groaned at the sight of food.

"This is great, though," she said as she pulled out a bar. Power bars weren't healthy to eat every day for every meal, but considering the circumstances, they were the difference between life and death. Lara inspected one. It was the brand Harry had always bought. They weren't bad. The carrot cake and cookies and cream flavors were almost enjoyable.

Rocky came up beside her dropped his bags. "Lara, you gotta understand. There were a *lot* of raiders. They came out of nowhere and butchered those soldiers."

"It isn't safe to stay here," Jack said. "We're trapped in this building, in this city. It's only a matter of time before we're found. My gun won't make a difference, not against that many."

Lara glanced up. Molly and Fred were making their slow descent down the stairs. She was about to speak when Jack tugged at her arm and led her towards the back windows.

"I need to talk to you," he whispered. He looked to Fred and Molly and called out, "Rocky will give you an update!"

Lara jerked her arm away. "What do you want?"

"Please, just give me a second, okay?"

Both Jack and Rocky were obviously shaken. Lara hadn't known Jack for long, but she knew him well enough to know if he had something important to say, he'd say it to her alone. At least that's what she told herself as she followed him farther into the stacks. She spotted Dan watching them from the upper balcony.

"Well, what is it?"

"We need to get everyone out of here as soon as possible," he said. "Those men had Hedone gang symbols on their jackets. They're raiding Monroe for fresh meat.

They will check every room of every building in this town looking for people."

Lara squeezed her eyes shut. "We can't leave. Dio and Paul aren't mobile, and we don't have enough suits for everyone."

Jack was quiet. When he didn't offer a rebuttal, Lara knew exactly why he pulled her aside.

"You want me to convince them to leave people behind."

"If we stay, we'll die here or get taken by the raiders. If we leave, we have a chance of surviving."

She glanced back at the balcony and saw Dan was still watching. A prickly sensation crawled up the back of her neck. She waved at him.

Dan waved back then and disappeared from view. When she looked at Jack, he was scowling.

"I bet your friend Dan wouldn't think twice about leaving."

"Jack, this isn't about him," she stated.

Arguing on a nearly empty stomach was a bad idea. She tore open the power bar and took a bite. It was too chewy, but the flavor of chocolate and peanut butter made her mouth water.

"You're wrong about him."

She took another bite and chewed it thoroughly. Jack wanted to abandon the helpless and move on. She wanted to show kindness to him, but he made it extremely hard. And she hadn't forgotten the body in the apartment. Lara understood why he'd done it, but that didn't mean she'd gotten over it. Jack was a murderer, and now he wanted to betray the people who'd taken them in.

Jack stared at his boots. After a minute, he looked up at her. "When Rocky and I found the food, I was so happy. He doesn't know me or my past. He let me in on his joy. For a moment, I was my old self. It made me want to look after him. I wanted to come back and look after all of you. Even if it meant making a hard call."

"You can help us without leaving anyone behind, Jack."

He smiled weakly. "I don't think so."

With that he turned and approached Molly and the rest of the crew, who had transferred the bars to new bags and were carrying them to the stairs. Lara remained where she was, unsure of what Jack was going to do. He took the bags Molly was carrying and followed them.

Lara trailed after the group. As she neared the top of the stairs, the scent of Paul and Dio made her gag. Their skin was *sloughing*. There was no better word to describe it. Although she tried to tend to their wounds, nothing she did made a difference.

For a split second she wondered if leaving them behind was the best thing to do. After all, they couldn't last much longer anyway. The thought was so dark it startled her.

"You doing okay?"

Dan came down the stairs and stood next to her. His breath smelled sweet, like chocolate. She wondered what power bar flavor smelled like real chocolate.

"Yeah, I think so."

"Those guys find a lot of food?"

Lara raised a brow. "Yeah. Didn't you just eat a bar? Your breath sure smells like it."

"Right, yeah." Dan turned his face away from her. He was about to say something else when Jack spoke up.

"I know I don't talk much, but I have something to say. The raiders Rocky and I saw were looking for people to take to Hedone. I could tell by the marks on their clothes. It's only a matter of time before they find us." Jack looked at each person in turn as he spoke. "I know this is going to be hard, but we need to leave."

The group was quiet, looking everywhere else but at

each other. Especially not towards the bookshelf where Paul and Dio were.

Lara cleared her throat. "We're short one suit and three masks. And that's if Paul and Dio didn't come with us."

Yvette, who was typically quiet, gasped. "No! We can't leave anyone behind."

No one spoke in agreement. Yvette looked at Molly and then Lara, begging with her eyes for support.

"I'll stay behind." All eyes were on Fred now. He shrugged. "Old people usually volunteer for something like this, right?"

He was trying to make light of the situation. It didn't work. Lara felt tears welling in her eyes.

"Guys, hello? Where would we even go?" Ano asked. "This dust could be covering the whole world. What will we eat or drink? Where will we stay to be safe? Jack, do you have *any* plan beyond saying we need to leave?"

"No," Jack admitted. "I guess we'd stick to the back roads and move to somewhere more remote. Find a new place to set up base like you did here."

"We saw soldiers. The one convoy got hit, but there must be more of them out there," said Rocky. "If we can keep hanging on, the world will get itself back together. It has to, right?"

A murmur of agreement went through the group.

"At the cost of other people's lives?" Lara stood, commanding the attention of the room. "Can't we try to come up with a solution where no one has to be left behind?"

"We could try looking for more masks and suits," Yvette offered.

Linda raised her hand like a child in a classroom. "We could fortify the library and stay out of sight."

"This place is literally a glass house." Jack shook his

head. "The longer we wait, the more danger we're in."

"You can leave us. It's okay."

All eyes turned to Paul, who'd crawled from his spot. His shoulder leaned against a bookshelf. Coagulated blood smeared against it. His face was covered in seeping sores, the bags under his fluorescent blue eyes laden with liquid and pulling the skin away from the sockets. He hadn't spoken much since he and Dio had returned. His body was hot to the touch from a fever, and when Paul did speak he rambled. Now he was lucid, but the effort of talking seemed to cost him. Lara felt awkward standing while Paul used all his energy to stay sitting upright. She sat down and made an effort not to cover her nose at the smell.

"You can leave us," he said again. His voice was all phlegm. "Don't feel bad. We're dead weight."

Molly made a noise between a whimper and a yelp. "Don't say that! I'm sure there's something we can do."

Paul's head lolled to the left. He closed his eyes. After a moment of rest, he inhaled a wet breath. His hand went to his neck where he scratched. The skin came off, showing what Lara guessed, with surreal morbidity, had to be muscle underneath. Paul seemed not to notice.

"After the comet hit, we hid inside a gas station for days. Then we saw people from FEMA. We were too weak to get to them, but they had this megaphone. They were telling people to go to their refugee camp in Renton."

"Do you think it's still there?" Ano asked hopefully.

"I don't know, Ano. If you're leaving, why not try there?"

Lara shuddered as she saw where this was going. The mood in the room was in favor of leaving. It was now just a matter of who else was going to be left behind.

Although she'd never voiced the thought out loud, Lara had been glad the comet would wipe everyone out. If they had to go, better to be quick. One big explosion and then nothing. But now that they'd survived, humanity would have to endure starvation, illness, and the depravity of a few lawless, amoral people.

Lara didn't want to decide who lived and who died. She didn't want to go to sleep every night fearing the Hedone raiders or watch good people like Paul and Dio succumb to a horrifying infection. This world, this post-apocalyptic hell, was worse than anything she could have imagined.

"I'll stay, too," Molly said, breaking the silence. "Now we're just short one mask."

"You can't," Lara choked. The older woman leaned over and patted Lara's leg.

"Don't worry, honey. I've had a good life. I don't have many years left in me anyway. Besides, maybe the raiders won't find us. You never know."

"There are dust masks in the janitor's room," Lara said, grasping at anything she could. "What if one of us doubled up on those? Tape as much as we can to create a good seal. Would that work?"

"It could work," Fred offered. He didn't sound confident.

Lara couldn't take it anymore. "One of you use my mask. I'll try the other ones."

Dan, who'd been silent the entire conversation, grabbed her wrist. "No, Lara."

"I appreciate your concern, but I'm doing it." Lara turned to Yvette, who sat next to the trio of younger people. "Yvette, you can have my respirator. Now everyone will have some kind of protection."

Suddenly Jack groaned and said, his voice raised, "You're fucking kidding me."

Lara's head snapped around and saw Dan pulling a gas mask out of his pack. It wasn't a flimsy respirator, either. It was a real gas mask—just like the one he'd shown up with. Where the hell had he gotten ahold of two military-grade gas masks? Her hair stood on end.

Then Fred said what everyone was thinking. "Did you have that this whole time?"

# DAN

Dan had fucked himself over. He knew it. If that bitch Lara hadn't tried to play the hero, he wouldn't have pulled his second gas mask out. But she was going to kill herself, and he couldn't let that happen. No fucking way. At first he thought the others would try and stop her, volunteer to wear the stupid fucking dust masks, but no one did. What else could he have done?

The losers were staring at him, mouths open like fish dying on dry land. This time it wasn't funny. He was pissed off. Dan searched his memory for the right kind of expression to use to charm them, and came up with nothing. His face remained slack, his eyes hard.

"Yeah, Dan," Jack said. He puffed his chest up and walked closer. "Did you have that this whole time?"

He hated Jack. What an asshat.

"Dan?" Lara's doe eyes were on him, too.

Shit. He had to come up with something. Why did he take it out? What had he been thinking? Well, he knew what he'd been thinking. He'd been thinking that if Lara died, he'd never get to fuck her, let alone trade her out for drugs, food, and ass in Hedone. He could've gone outside and claimed he found it. Fucking fuck!

He couldn't let them think he'd had two gas masks all along. That much he knew. A plan started to form. Dan made himself relax.

"This is my mask," he said, holding it up. It was a bluff—one they could easily call him out on. "I...I know we're supposed to keep this stuff in the bin room, but I was afraid if something bad happened I wouldn't be able to get to it. So I carry it with me."

His actual mask was stowed in the bin room with the rest of the gear. He wasn't an idiot. He wasn't gonna carry that stuff around, not if it had dust on it. Of course, he kept the mask stored *under* one of the bins in case one of them tried to steal his shit.

No one else had said anything. Dan licked his lips and cleared his throat. "This one is mine. I don't want you to use the dust masks, Lara. I'll do it, or we can trade off. Okay?"

All he had to do was wear the shitty mask until he had a chance to get Lara away from the group. It wouldn't be that bad, right? He wouldn't get sick. Or maybe he'd "find" a mask while they were on the road, and then there wouldn't be an issue at all.

Dan was beginning to wonder if Lara was worth it. She was hot, but Dan's life was also on the line now. What good was a bitch if his skin was melting off?

Lara was here, she had a tight little body, and she was easy. What if he didn't find another girl that good? He couldn't go back to Hedone with some mediocre pussy. It had to be top shelf. Otherwise he wasn't going back at all.

"Thanks, Dan," Lara said.

He tried to read her. Face ruddy, a tiny bit of snot in her right nostril. She'd started tearing up earlier when Fred said he'd stay behind. No glare, no frown. She wasn't on to him.

"Just don't want you to get hurt," he said and threw in what he hoped was a puppy dog grin.

At that she smiled a little.

The problem was Jack. Of course. It was always Jack. He eyed Dan like he wanted to punch him in the face. Dan kept quiet. He could snap Jack's neck if he wanted to. Fucking kill him right there with his bare hands. But right then he didn't need a fight, no matter how bad he wanted one.

"It's settled, then," the old fart said. "Molly and I will stay here with Dio and Paul. The rest of you should leave as soon as you can. There's still plenty of daylight left. You'll make it out of Monroe before night if you keep a good pace."

Dan zoned out as they discussed how much food they'd take and who would carry it. There was some more crying as they hugged and said goodbye. No hugs for Dan, though. He wasn't choked up about it; he didn't like touching old people and fatties anyway.

*Just a little longer*, he reminded himself. Just until he could get Lara alone, then he'd be on his way to Hedone.

While everyone sorted the food up on the second story, Dan grabbed his actual gas mask from the bin room, wiped it off, and stored it in his pack. Then he wandered off to the bathroom to scarf his last candy bar and take a piss. He took his time, and when he was done, the rest of them were finally ready to go. He gave the women a once-over. Lara was definitely the prize bitch. Yvette was too old to be worth anything, but Linda might be okay if the lights were off. Should he try to take her too? As soon as he thought it, he reconsidered. Her face was too plain and she had the body of an eleven-year-old boy. Wouldn't go for much in Hedone, when you actually *could* get an eleven-year-old boy if you wanted.

Everyone—Dan included, he admitted it—looked funny with their backpacks under the big plastic suits. Made them look like hunchbacks. The suits were too bright. With his neon yellow and their blinding white, they'd make great targets out there. Even more reason to split as soon as possible.

Lara had plastic work goggles for Dan. The problem was, even with the goggles, dust masks, and his plastic suit, parts of his face were uncovered. Lara gave him her ski mask, too. He used tape to try and make a better seal around everything, but it was a piss poor setup.

For the first time in a long while, he felt fear. It was ice cold in his chest, wicked coils shooting into his throat and down his fingertips. He could die out there. Dio and Paul were so fucked up they looked like zombies from a horror movie. That could be him if he wasn't careful.

"Is everyone ready?" Jack asked.

*What a jackass.*

Dan couldn't suppress his giggle. Jack, jackass. Why hadn't he thought of that before?

"Give me a second," Yvette said. She was having problems zipping her suit.

Lara walked up to him, her body hidden underneath the plastic suit. "Thanks for offering me the mask. It's a big thing to do."

"No problem. I'm sorry I scared everyone like that. I can't believe Jack thought I had two masks the whole time. That I was, I don't know, *keeping it secret.*"

Lara nodded. Dan wished he could see her face, but she already had her mask on. "Jack is a good guy. Just a little misguided sometimes."

"Okay, I'm ready!" Yvette called out.

Jackass led the group, naturally. He looked like a complete fag with a purse slung over his shoulder. He claimed it was so he could have easy access to his gun and knife.

They exited the bin room quickly and then shut the door behind them, leaving the old man, the fattie, and the zombies behind. Good riddance.

Dan had been outside many times since he arrived at the library to dump the shit buckets. Today the dust was more settled than ever. The buildings were still coated, but it didn't hang in the air like it used to. When his foot hit the ground, a puff of it went up into the air. It hovered, then sank.

His Mama always used to tell him stories about some mountain in Washington that blew up when she was a kid. Mount St. Helens, that was it. He imagined this is what it looked like. He'd liked that story because it let him imagine what the outside was like. In his box, the world was tiny. It was hard to imagine a space open enough to house a volcano.

He shuddered. The box. The fucking box. Fifteen years later and he still hadn't gotten over it or, what was that fancy word the shrink used? Suppressed? Repressed? Still hadn't whatevered it. It was the smell of the dust mask that made him remember it for some reason. Maybe because it smelled just like the attic where Mama took him to take picture sometimes. Dan tried to focus on the city instead, before he got too worked up.

The city was fucked. There were craters in the ground, some the size of a pothole, others the size of a car. They passed a big one that went so deep into the ground Dan could see all the way down into the pipes and then the blackness below.

He grinned. Good place to dump bodies.

He didn't know a whole lot about Zabat's Comet, but what he did know was that it was supposed to have destroyed the earth. No survivors. No nothing. He'd seen it hanging in the sky and then breaking apart into the dust. The dust with a mind of its own. He'd blamed the scene on the meth pumping in his system. After hearing the sick guy's story, he realized that it had really happened.

Dan shuddered. He convinced himself it was nothing more than some weird science shit he'd never be able to understand. Somewhere, some space guy was figuring it out with math and physics in a super sick, shiny lab. If and when the world went back to normal—and he hoped it wouldn't, but with his luck it probably would—there would be answers. In the meantime, he had to do what he'd been doing his whole life: keep watching out for himself.

They passed a lot of dead bodies. Most of them were covered so deep in dust they looked like mounds. It wasn't until he stumbled over one or stepped right on it that the soft squish let him know what it was. Their skin was rotten and looked like meat left out to spoil. Pocketed with mold, brown and red beneath. Most of them had those shiny blue blisters. Some had so many their skin was nearly all blueish-green.

As the hours went by, eventually the city became more of a suburb. Seas of same-looking houses with matchbox-sized yards. This was the kind of place he used to scope out during holidays. Good houses, but not good enough that people had alarm systems. He could score a lot of sweet electronics and jewelry around here if he wanted. Not that there was anywhere to fence them, or any electricity.

Lara walked so close to Dan she bumped up against him.

"Sorry." Her voice sounded faint with the mask on. "I lived around here. It's where some raiders almost kidnapped me."

"Don't worry, with all of us together we'll be fine," he assured her.

Silence again. He knew he needed to keep her talking so he could build up the relationship, but he was at a loss for words. The usual stuff he got ladies with wouldn't work. The wife and daughter card was tricky since he could corner himself with a lie. There were no sports, no movies, no weather to make small talk about. He didn't read books. He couldn't endlessly compliment her looks; Lara was too smart for that tactic.

Better to say nothing.

The group cleared the suburbs and headed down the highway that bisected the town. The road stretched through fields of paper trees and a few farms. Dan stopped worrying about not talking to Lara because no one in the group appeared to be talking beyond pointing out holes in the ground or a particularly bad car wreck. There were no footprints on the highway. That was good; they wouldn't encounter anyone on the way there. It was also bad since they could easily be followed.

By the time Lara spoke again, they'd been walking side by side for at least two hours. They were on the outskirts of a town called Maltby. The exit's overpass arched over the highway. A semi had tipped over, its hitch hanging off the road. It looked like a gust of wind would send it tumbling down.

"How are you doing?" Lara asked, breaking the silence.

"I'm fine," he said honestly. The double layer of dust masks was working so far. He didn't feel any different. The smell was bothering him, that was all. His chest was a bit stiff, but that could have been anything. "Don't worry about switching."

Jackass led them up the exit and across the overpass. The road sloped down into a valley where the town was. They crossed a bridge, and then Jackass held up his hand and forced the group to stop. Underneath them, the water had turned florescent yellow from the dust. It frothed at the edges. Dan was captivated by it. Everything had been so quiet, so still, since the comet. No street noise, no animals. No TV. The churning water was the most exciting thing he'd seen in a long time.

"Pretty, isn't it?" Lara said. "Scary to think all the water on the planet is likely contaminated now."

Dan frowned. Way to ruin the moment. He took his gaze away from the water. "I wonder why we stopped?"

On cue, Jackass gathered everyone up. "It's getting dark. We need to split up and find safe places to make camp for the night."

Finally the douche had a good plan. They hadn't been able to eat while they were walking, and Dan was starving. He looked around, hoping to spot a good place to crash right away. Unfortunately, they were in a shitty low-class part of Maltby where he lived in for a few years after his first run in prison.

The two tallest structures in town were the steeple on the church that used to give out free food on Saturdays and the tower the firefighters used for practice. To their right was a strip mall that had two teriyaki places, a nail salon, and two empty spaces. The nail salon was a front for whores. Dan knew that place real good.

After another few minutes of walking, the group came upon the church. At least fifteen signs were stuck in the big overgrown lawn about how the end was nigh, people deserved what was coming, and all that religious bullshit. Farther up the street was a boarded-up restaurant, and some apartments.

"Shouldn't we stop in a nicer neighborhood?" This was from the old bag Yvette.

Jackass shook his head. "There's nowhere else. After this, it's highway until the FEMA camp. I don't know what kind of shelter we could find."

It was just when the old bag was about to complain again that a bullet whizzed through the air and hit her in the leg. She cried out as her body smashed into ground, sending a cloud of dust swirling around her.

# COLLEEN

A dense stillness hung in the gym as the soldiers hauled away the dead bodies. Prior to that moment, loyalty to refugees or soldiers had been unclear. People had been unsure who to side with—Benny or the military. Now it was decided. The soldiers were the enemy. Each refugee openly wore expressions of resentment or downright hatred. They held themselves stiffly, ready for a fight.

There were six soldiers, and four of them had their rifles pointed at the refugees while the other two worked. Both the infected people who'd been dead a while, and those who fell in the riot, were dragged from the gym one by one.

The two soldiers reached the body of the woman who'd started the riot. Either they didn't realize she'd been murdered or they didn't care. They put her on a stretcher and carried her out. There was a sprawling pool of red where she'd bled out, smeared from the soldier's boots.

Liana was quiet in Colleen's arms. The entire family sat on one cot pressed against the wall, James with his arm around Serena. Gabriela was next to Colleen. She kept moving to bite her nails, and then stopping herself. Colleen had told her putting her hands to her mouth was a sure way to get sick.

The gym was dirty and humid. The smell was unbearable, worsened by the soldiers disturbing the bodies. Colleen couldn't stay here. She couldn't let her family stay here.

She shifted and leaned over to James. "As soon as you

can, ask Belman if we can have our suits and leave. She was kind to us. She might help."

"I will." James's face was grim. His skin was ashen and his shoulders were slumped. "I'm sorry we came here. We should've left."

"We had no idea this would happen."

The soldiers began filing out. Two stayed, flanking the doors. They had their full gear on, gas masks included, and Colleen couldn't tell if one of them was Belman.

"I'll head over now," James said. "I'll be right back, okay girls?"

Neither responded. When James stood, Serena closed the space between her and Colleen and leaned against her. Colleen wrapped her free arm around Serena, glad to feel her stepdaughter's closeness.

Colleen reached out with her other arm. She didn't need to say anything. Gabriela leaned against her. Colleen held all three girls close to her, praying to God for the strength to keep each of them safe.

"I'm scared," Gabriela whispered. "Will you take me with you when you leave?"

They didn't have another suit. Colleen chewed the inside of her lip as she thought of Glen's sneer. "We'll find a way. Of course."

James made his way through the unorganized cots. Others were moving, too, visiting people or talking in small groups. Each person glanced at the infected side, as though they were making sure the quarantined refugees hadn't tried to cross into their territory.

An awful sensation of total helplessness caused an ache inside her. She was strong and had always endured, like she had in her childhood and early adult years. That strength she prided herself in was running thin. Her family's life was in jeopardy. Her home was destroyed, her child sick, and there was no clear plan of action before her. What if they couldn't get a suit for Gabriela? Colleen felt the girl was her responsibility now. Responsibility had a way of finding her even in the direst of circumstance.

"Miss C?"

Surely one of the soldiers could spare a suit and mask. They were giving them to people they saved, so they must have a ton on hand.

"Miss C! Colleen!"

Colleen's attention snapped to Gabriela who pointed to the front of the gym.

Benny and at least a dozen other men walked with purpose to the entrance. They had weapons. Colleen realized they'd dismantled the cots and fashioned shivs out of the metal frames. Those who noticed followed with their eyes or a slight turn of the head, but seemed to be in shock or afraid to speak up.

Colleen drew a breath to scream a warning, but it was too late. Wild and angry, their sheer numbers overtook the soldiers.

One soldier fired, the staccato rounds of an automatic rifle echoing in the gym. Then he was buried under a mound of bodies. The men kicked and punched, stabbed the soldier with their shivs. The other refugees closed in around it all and the scene vanished from Colleen's sight.

*Where was James?*

Colleen unceremoniously set Liana in Gabriela's arms. She stood on her cot, the uneven surface making it hard to keep her balance.

"Mom, I can't hear dad," Liana said, her voice just loud enough for Colleen to hear.

Liana's remark made Colleen's heart stop. Still, she yelled for her husband. "James!?"

He'd been wearing a forest green t-shirt. She looked for

the color and found nothing. Everyone blurred together.

Colleen jumped off the cot and circled the outer edge of the crowd. With each passing moment, the panic inside her doubled, tripled. She reached the wall by the entrance to the gym, uncomfortably close to Benny and his men.

They'd stripped the two soldiers. Both were naked, their arms wrapped around their torsos for protection as people took turns kicking them. One of the soldiers was Belman. Benny grabbed her by the ankle and dragged her towards him. She fought, but her right arm hung from its socket, obviously broken. Her face was mashed into red and purple pulp.

The onlookers began to chant. Colleen didn't hear specific words but a guttural *rah rah* that struck fear deep inside her. When another series of shots sounded off somewhere else in the gym, the volume swelled to a deafening level. The people around her pressed forward, trying to get closer to the action. Colleen was a pinball, bouncing against others as they shoved her away, then was finally pushed out of the crowd.

The refugees were packed together so tightly it left the outer ring of the gym empty all the way to the bleachers. Colleen looked around helplessly for a way back to the front of the room. Then she saw him. His body bent backward over a cot. His forest green shirt saturated dark with blood. His right eye obliterated by the exit wound of a bullet, glasses nowhere to be found. Body left behind like trash.

Colleen stumbled to him. As she neared, she saw the details of his wound; the liquid of his destroyed eye, shards of bone exposed. His mouth gaping open, two teeth shattered and bloody.

She dropped to her knees beside him, ignoring the blood seeping through her jeans, and took his limp hand in hers. James had helped pull her out of the darkest times in her life. He had been there for the brightest, happiest moments, too.

And in a split second, he was gone.

Colleen rested her head on the edge of the cot and traced James' fingers gently. The rest of the world slipped away into darkness.

*Rah rah rah!*

Startled by the ferocity of the chanting, she looked up. There was somewhere else she had to be. She'd left her daughters and Gabriela. Alone. Vulnerable. Waiting for her to come back.

"I love you," Colleen told James. "I'm sorry. I'm so sorry."

She gently set his hand down on his chest then ran over to the girls, breathless. She didn't bother hiding the stream of tears flowing down her cheeks as she pulled the blanket off her cot.

"C'mon, girls. We're going to hide in the bleachers."

"No!" Gabriela yelped. "Those guys hang out back there. We can't."

"Where's my dad?" Serena asked.

Liana stood on the cot, arms hanging limply by her sides. "Dad is dead. Someone shot him in the face."

"Shut up," Serena yelled. "Shut up you freak!"

Serena was furious. She ran over to her half-sister and pushed her off the cot. Liana fell backward and crashed to the floor. Colleen scrambled around the cot and picked up Liana while Gabriela rushed to Serena's side and tried to calm her down.

Desperate, Colleen looked around. The emergency exit was on the opposite end of the gym. Even if they broke the lock, they couldn't leave without protection. The main entrance was where Benny was. Leaving was not an option. They had to hide.

"Where's dad!" Serena said again, her voice rising to a scream.

Colleen set Liana down and grabbed the preteen by the shoulders and squeezed. Her nerves were raw, her heart aching. She wanted to shake Serena and yell at her, to tell her she needed to be quiet and to please, *please* listen to her for once.

Then Colleen's gaze fell on the cot. It wasn't much of a hiding spot, but it was all they had. She took a strained breath and fought the growing urge to panic.

"Girls, get under the bed."

To her surprise, they obeyed. Gabriela got in first and was flush against the back wall. Serena went next. Colleen pushed her own cot against it lengthwise. She tossed the blanket over the cot and climbed under with Liana. She tugged the blanket over the edge to block her body from view. It was a tight fit.

Colleen held Liana against her. She tried to focus on her daughter's breathing, on stroking her hair. It was more for herself than Liana, who was silent and motionless. This only made Colleen more distressed. The image of James's body was burned into her vision. She saw it if her eyes were open or closed. Her husband, the man who meant everything to her, dead. A brutal casualty no one noticed.

She couldn't do this without him. She couldn't.

Minutes passed, then an hour. The gunshots and screams around them continued. Her hip and lower back ached fiercely from the hard floor. Liana told her three times she had to pee but Colleen kept telling her to hold it. Eventually Liana couldn't any longer, and Colleen whispered reassurances that it was okay, it wasn't her fault, as the girl released her bladder.

Finally the crowd quieted. Her body jerked in reaction to Benny's booming voice.

"This is our place now! Those fucking FEMA pansies and wannabe soldiers are done." A chorus of yells answered his statement. "Some of you might be afraid right now, worried we won't be good to you. We will. We will. Unlike them, we'll make sure you get food and anything else you need."

Colleen's heart sank.

"First order of business, we're getting rid of these rotting motherfuckers over here!"

There was a single scream before the sound of gunfire tore through the gym again. In seconds, it was over. Her ears rang. The smell of smoke hung in the air. Colleen imagined the bodies, the blood.

"That's better, right? We're going be civil from here on out. No one is gettin' shot unless you cause a problem. Agreed?"

Mingled with the eager affirmations was a grumble of dissatisfaction. That was good, but it meant nothing unless those people were willing to act on their doubts.

It took her a moment to realize the racket she was hearing were cots being flipped. In an instant her cover was torn away. Three figures towered over her.

"Just who I was looking for," Benny said. His lips curled back into a feral sneer. "Take the kid."

All she could think to do was wrap her arms around Liana as tightly as she could. Liana cried out in pain by the force of it, and more when Glen reached down to pry her out of Colleen's arms. The struggle only lasted for seconds. Colleen was weak from lack of food and beyond exhausted. Fresh hot tears flowed from her face. A sob caught in her throat as Glen freed Liana from her arms.

Then his boot connected with her head and there was nothing but darkness.

# JACK

The crack of gunfire seemed to come from everywhere all at once. Jack's stomach dropped and his head snapped back and forth wildly as he searched for the shooter. He didn't know where to take cover.

Then Yvette hit the ground, and he was spurred into action. He hauled her to her feet. The plastic suits were slippery and made it hard to keep his grip on her. Another bullet hit the ground an inch away from his foot.

A narrow driveway curved behind the church. Jack dragged Yvette to the meager cover the building provided and waited for another shot. The rest of the group had scattered. Lara and Dan had followed him, but Rocky and his friends were behind an overturned bus in the strip mall parking lot.

A bullet ricocheted off the bus, then it was quiet. Jack pulled frantic breaths through the respirator. His face itched fiercely, and a resonating pain was coursing through his cheek into his skull. The copious amounts of adrenaline surging in his system seemed to worsen it. He did his best to ignore the pain and focus.

If the bullet hit that side of the bus, it must have been coming from farther down the street. When they first arrived, he'd noticed a firefighter training tower a few blocks down. It would be the perfect place for a lookout.

"Are you okay, Yvette?" Lara took Yvette's other arm and helped her upright.

"My leg. Oh God, my leg is bleeding." Yvette sagged

against them, but Jack kept his grip firm.

Blood gushed from a hole in her plastic suit. It splattered onto the dust-coated ground. Jack didn't know much about first aid, but at the rate it was flowing, even he knew Yvette was in serious danger.

"We need to get her somewhere safe," Lara said. "We need to get this suit off her and stop the bleeding!"

Jack scanned the immediate area. His gaze fell on an SUV parked farther down the driveway.

"Dan, help Lara with Yvette," he ordered.

Dan, to Jack's surprise, took Yvette. Jack went to the car first and jerked open the door, feeling a surge of relief and surprise that it was unlocked. The interior was pristine, untouched by the dust. A dream catcher and a cross hung off the rear view mirror alongside a graduation tassel. He reached into his bag and pulled out his pocketknife. He used it to saw off a long piece of seatbelt. When he returned to Yvette, he tied it around her upper thigh as tight as he could. The blood still seeped from her suit, but was slower now.

"We can escape that way," Dan said. He pointed to the back of the church. There was a parking lot and a fence, and on the other side, a road.

"What? We're not leaving without everyone. Not again." Lara sounded genuinely shocked.

"Jack! Over here, man!"

He turned and saw Rocky waving at him. He went as close to the edge of the church as he could without exposing himself to the street.

"Are you guys okay?" he shouted.

"We're fine. Is Yvette hurt?"

Jack swallowed a hard lump in his throat. He glanced behind him at the blood, now mixed into the dust to form a sickly orange mud. "Yeah, she is."

Jack caught something in his peripheral vision. He thought it was just his goggles, which made it hard to see. Sometimes the growing sheen of dust on the edges tricked him. But as he looked down the street in the direction he came from, he spotted something. Two figures moving slowly. They were covered in dust so thickly they were almost perfectly camouflaged.

His body felt numb. If it was a trap, they'd lose. Jack had the only gun. They'd come this far just to get killed by a bunch of raiders.

The sniper fired another round. This one splintered the wall of the church beside him. He jumped back and drew his gun. He'd convinced everyone to abandon the library and their friends in pursuit of safety, so he was going to make damned sure they were safe.

When he looked for the two figures again, they were gone. They could've slipped down any one of the side roads.

Hoping the sniper, wherever he was, couldn't hear him, Jack spoke as loud as he dared. "I'm going to fire a shot down the street. When I do, run over here. They might be distracted. Go fast, okay?"

Rocky gave him a thumbs up. Jack adjusted the grip on his gun and prepared himself to dart around the corner.

That's when Lara screamed and he figured out where the two figures had gone.

They were holding Lara, Dan, and Yvette at gunpoint. One had a sawed-off shotgun, the other some kind of submachine gun. The two figures were covered in layers of cloth caked with dust. Their goggles were black and shiny, clean compared to the rest of them. Their respirators had crude shapes drawn on them. Teeth, Jack realized. They were meant to look like monster teeth.

"Hey, man," one said. The voice was high pitched, but masculine. A teenager. "Put down your piece and come over here."

Jack gripped his gun tighter. The raiders hadn't bothered to take cover behind their hostages. If Jack was fast enough, he could shoot the one on the right. That was if he could get his hands to stop shaking.

He sprang into motion, brought the gun up, aimed and fired. For a split second Jack believed there had to be a God because the bullet went straight through the SMG-wielding raider's eye. The left goggle lens shattered and gore misted behind his head. He dropped to his knees.

Dan spun around and grabbed the tip of the sawed-off, pushing it upward. The raider pulled the trigger and fired. Jack lost his hearing in one ear. Without Dan supporting Yvette, she and Lara dropped to the ground.

Jack couldn't get a good shot. He closed the distance between him and the fight, and rushed the raider, knocking him to the ground. The shotgun flew out of his hands and landed somewhere near the women.

The boy felt frail beneath Jack's gloved fists, but he didn't stop. He pummeled the raider's chest then realized the fastest way to eliminate the threat was to pull off the respirator.

Jack saw a narrow chin with a few scraggly traces of facial hair. He still had braces. *Braces.* Jack had pegged him for a teenager, but he was even younger than he expected. Sick to his stomach, he snatched the respirator back up and shoved it on the raider's face.

It was too late. Their fight had kicked up too must dust, and the kid had sucked it down by the lungful. His limbs flailed and the mask slid off. Jack let him go and stood back as the kid convulsed. A fountain of blood bubbled up from his mouth, cascading down his cheeks. Then finally he lay still.

His skin was already mottled where the dust had

touched it. Three people. Jack had killed three people now. Something told him that number would keep going up.

"There's more of them!"

Jack spun around. Coming from the same direction the first pair came from were four—he counted again—no, *six* more raiders.

He grabbed the SMG from the other fallen raider. When he turned, he saw Dan holding the sawed-off. He was the last person Jack would have trusted with a gun, but there wasn't time to have a fight over it now.

Rocky and his friends darted from their cover and ran across the street. Two bullets sent giant plumes of dust and shards of asphalt into the air as they struck the ground at his companion's feet.

The trio made it. Rocky, Linda, and Ano, all unhurt.

The raiders were a block away. Jack heard them hollering. It was a primal sound that shook him to his core. No words. Just wild, guttural screams. Some struck cars or street poles like battle drums as they came.

Rocky got an arm under Yvette and helped Lara haul her up. Ano took Lara's place.

"Can we fight them?" Ano asked.

"We can try," Jack said. He surveyed the group. Yvette wasn't going to make it far. They couldn't outrun the raiders. "If you go now, you can get through the parking lot. I'll hold them off. Maybe they'll get scared and run."

Jack dropped to his knees and searched the dead raiders for more ammo. There were a few shells and another mag for the submachine gun.

"Leave me," Yvette moaned. "I'm going to die anyway."

"We're not leaving anyone, dammit!" Lara said. "Not again!"

"Dan, give me that gun," Jack said. "I'm staying."

Rocky and Ano kicked it into high gear and lifted Yvette

off her feet as they jogged down the driveway to the back of the church. Lara hesitated, but when Dan handed over his gun to Jack, she followed him to the others.

Jack took cover behind the SUV. He'd use up the submachine gun first, then the shotgun. He hoped the rapid fire would intimidate them. Otherwise he'd have to try to take them down before they got him. He studied the submachine gun, finding the mag release and practicing once quickly. Knowing how to reload could be the different between life and death.

His people crossed the parking lot and disappeared out of sight just as the first of the raiders entered the church's front yard. The pursuers ran right past the SUV.

Jack took a deep breath and squeezed the trigger. He'd never handled a gun like this before, but he knew enough to fire short, controlled bursts.

The raider closest to him, a hulking behemoth of a man that was slower than the rest, took a spray of bullets across his lower back. His legs gave out and he crumpled.

A stray round hit the man next to the fallen giant but only grazed his shoulder. The raider spun around, spotted Jack instantly, and ran for him with a machete raised over his head. Jack squeezed the trigger again. The rounds started at the man's stomach and climbed upward, the last bullet shattering his mask and exiting out the back of his skull and throat. Jack held the trigger too long and a few extra rounds sailed into the air, wasted. He quickly corrected his aim and mowed down a third raider.

The remaining enemies realized they were being attacked. As they turned to face Jack, his gun clicked dry. Jack ejected the mag and slammed the second home. Bullets pinged off the SUV as the raiders began to fire on him. The back and left windows shattered, glass raining down.

He scrambled to the side of the vehicle for more cover.

He leaned around the corner and squeezed the trigger, intending to spray the oncoming raiders in a sweeping motion.

Nothing happened.

He took cover again, moving towards the front of the car to buy more time, and tried to clear the jam by racking the cocking handle. It was stuck. He could barely see through his dusty goggles. He didn't have the time or ability to investigate the problem. Dropping the weapon, he switched to the shotgun.

"We got you surrounded, chicken shit!" A woman's voice, shrill and close. Right side of the car.

Something crunched on the left side. The broken glass. They were flanking him. A male voice, even closer than the woman, shouted, "We're gonna bleed you dry for what you did!"

There were three raiders left. Either the third was with one of the others or was keeping their distance. One thing was certain: he couldn't wait for them. He had to take action.

Jack pulled in a ragged breath through the respirator and gathered every ounce of courage he had. With a burst of speed and strength he didn't know he was capable of, he darted around the right side of the SUV and fired at the first thing that moved.

# LARA

Lara couldn't get enough air. Her respirator made it difficult to breathe. As they ran down the street looking for somewhere to hide, adrenaline surged through her body to keep her moving but it begged her for more oxygen all the while.

The neighborhood contained numerous apartment buildings, none over four stories tall, with shops on their first levels. Windows were shattered, front doors long gone. They needed somewhere safe they could take off their suits. So far, they'd found nothing.

Behind her, the sound of automatic gunfire was muted and distant. Despite Ano and Rocky having to carry Yvette, they'd run quite a ways. When Lara glanced over her shoulder, she could barely see the tip of the church steeple.

Jack was back there. They'd left him behind.

She'd left him.

"We can't keep going," Rocky said.

"I know!" she snapped.

The group paused, and Lara took the opportunity to draw in some slow breaths. She surveyed the street. Apartments were dangerous. Too many rooms, too many places for bad people to hide. Up ahead there was a T-shaped intersection. On the left was an old movie theater, on the right a pharmacy. The title of the film on the marquee was from eight years ago, meaning it went out of business long before the comet.

Lara noticed a defined trail in the dust on the road.

It was so deep that the dark asphalt beneath was peeking through in some spots. The trail led to the apartments and the pharmacy. But not the theater. Lara gathered herself and pointed ahead. "Follow me. We can hide in the movie theater."

It seemed no one was going to question her, but then she noticed Dan hanging back as the others moved forward.

"Is something wrong?"

He hesitated. "No. Nothing. I mean, I was just wondering, why should we hide there instead of somewhere else? How come you get to decide?"

While his comment was valid, she knew that tone and was surprised to hear it. She'd heard that defensive, slightly condescending lilt between couples during group counseling. It wasn't that Dan cared about where Lara picked to hide. It was just that Lara had made the call. For some reason, that upset him.

Mindful of keeping her own tone neutral, Lara asked, "Does anyone have a different suggestion?"

Their fear and nervousness was tangible. There hadn't been any gunshots in over a minute. That meant one of two things. Either Jack was dead and the raiders were coming, or else he won and would find them soon.

Except that if he found them, it meant Lara's hiding place wasn't very good.

"I think we're all cool with the theater," Rocky announced. "Let's go."

Dan strode ahead. "Fine. Theater it is."

The front of the building was intact. Lara stuck to the outer walls in an attempt to make her footprints less noticeable in case someone decided to follow them. She gave the door a pull. Locked. She tried each of the other doors, but none of them opened.

"Lara, we're sitting ducks out here," Linda moaned.

Between the pressure from the group and her own unease, Lara was getting dizzy. "I'm trying to figure out how to get in."

Dan came up beside her. "There are exits all around the building. We can pry one open."

An odd mixture of hope and doubt flooded her. He sounded sincere enough—and he was right. They *could* pry open a door if they found the right tool. So why was her intuition telling her not to follow Dan into the alley?

Squashing her doubts in hopes of finding safety, she nodded and led the group around the side of the theater. The raiders had left a faint trail around the building, but it looked infrequently used and stopped at a pile of building debris about thirty feet in. Lara wished she hadn't stepped to the front doors. The footprints would indicate someone was there, if the raiders were smart enough to look for them.

The alley between the theater and the apartment building beside it was narrow, no more than ten feet wide. It ran the length of the theater. The building to their left had a gaping hole in the second story where a meteor had barreled through. From where she stood, Lara saw the remains of a kitchen. She guessed that was where the debris littering the alley came from.

Her heart fluttered when she spotted the tip of a meteor sticking out of the kitchen. There was something unusual about it. It wasn't rock like the debris she'd seen before. It appeared metallic and was as smooth as glass. Grooves wove around the surface. The pattern reminded her of some kind of circuit board, with black nodes that looked like obsidian popping up at even intervals. The side curved like it could've been a piece of a larger spherical shape.

Part of a complex symbol printed on the chunk of meteor peeked out, but the rest was hidden behind the crumbling apartment wall. It was unlike anything she'd ever seen before. A series of swirls, dots, and dashes might have been purely decorative, but something about it made her think it was more than that. Maybe even…a language?

"Jesus, the fuck is that?"

Lara jumped at the sound of Dan's voice. He too had been quietly taking in the sight of the unusual object.

"I-I don't know," she said honestly, though in the back of her head the word *alien* echoed.

"What the hell are you guys doing?" Rocky and Ano came up beside them. Rocky's gaze followed Lara and Dan's to the object. "Holy shit, what is that?"

Ano spluttered, paused to regain his composure, and then finally said, "I knew it. I knew it from the very beginning."

"Not this again." Linda groaned. "Ano thought the comet was sent by aliens."

"Can you look at that and tell me it isn't alien?" Ano said. He used his free arm to gesture at it, emphasizing each word with a point of his finger.

"Keep your voice down," Lara said.

In the alley, they were fish in a barrel. As captivated as she was by the glassy black thing, their lives were at risk. She pressed on and the group followed. Rocky and Ano had to haul Linda over the debris from the apartment, which took longer than she liked.

As Lara climbed, she felt something tug her leg. She looked down and froze. Her suit had caught on an exposed nail. She hadn't yet pulled hard enough to tear the material. Carefully, slowly, she twisted her ankle until she was free.

"Watch out for nails," she told the others. Lara spared one last glance at the object now that they were on the other side. While the front was smooth and obviously engineered, by human or otherwise, the back looked like any other piece of meteor she'd seen. Jagged, pockmarked, and gray.

"I told you guys. Look, the rock is like a casing or something for the ship inside. I swear, Linda, I told you like eight million times it was aliens and you—"

"Ano," Linda gritted out. "I swear, if you don't shut up right now…."

Lara heard the fear in Linda's quivering voice. "Guys, please."

They approached the doors to the theater. Dan took the lead. There were two green doors with the words EMPLOYEES ONLY painted in white. He tugged at the handles but neither opened. Lara started to walk past him to see if they could find another door farther down when he grabbed her arm.

"I can get it open."

"How?"

He said nothing and instead went to the dumpster near the exits. He flipped it open. The dust slid off it like a fresh sheet of snow, sending up a cloud of powder as it landed. Lara expected him to rifle through it—for what, she didn't know—but instead he ran his fingers along the inner lip of the lid. Then he withdrew a skinny, flat piece of metal.

Dan returned to the door. He wedged the metal strip between the doors and ran it up and down quickly. He pushed, and the door swung open, revealing a pitch black hallway.

A lot of the little things she's noticed about Dan started to add up. He, like the rest of them, had gone through a lot, and she'd tried to give him the benefit of the doubt. But this meant Dan was familiar with the neighborhood. He should have mentioned that before. The burglary tool was even more troubling. Why had he known exactly where it was and how to use it? Had he robbed this place before?

She was curious what his explanation would be, but their safety was first priority. And even though she knew it was silly, she wanted to get away from the alien object. She didn't like having it at their backs where she couldn't see it. Rocky and Ano dragged Yvette into the hallway. The rest of the group followed. Lara was about to pull the door shut when she realized it would plunge them into complete darkness.

"Do any of you have a flashlight?"

"I've got a lighter," Ano said.

Lara was sure she heard shouting nearby. Then the door clunked shut, cutting off the sound. A razor-thin slice of light was visible beneath the door. She hoped, once her eyes adjusted, it would light more of the hallway.

"Yvette, how are you doing?" The woman didn't respond. Lara's heart skipped a beat. "Yvette?"

"Yes," she said with a small gasp. "Sorry. Just kind of dozing. What were you guys freaking out about?"

"Stay awake, okay?"

It felt odd talking into the darkness. Lara pictured where Yvette was. Rocky and Ano had propped her up against the wall and were sitting on either side of her. Big lumpy mounts of plastic suits. Linda had been opposite them. Dan was somewhere beside the exit next to Lara.

"I'll try," Yvette said.

For a moment, Lara wasn't sure what to do. She was hungry and needed to pee badly. Without better lighting, they couldn't tell if it was safe to take off their suits. If Jack *was* alive, how would they find him? And then there was Yvette. None of them was a doctor. Really, there wasn't much they could do for her.

"How long are we going to stay here?" Rocky's disembodied voice asked.

"I vote as long as we need to. We need to eat, we need to

rest. This area is crawling with raiders and this is probably the best hiding spot we've got," Ano said.

Linda objected. "What if they come looking for us? We're sitting ducks."

"Christ, Linda. You already said that like two minutes ago," Ano rebutted.

"You guys, please calm down," Rocky said. "We can't be at each other's throats at a time like this. Lara, what do you think?"

"We're all hungry and we all need a break. The raiders will expect us to keep running. I doubt they'll look here," Lara said.

If anyone objected, they didn't voice it. After a moment, Rocky spoke. "Do you think Jack made it?"

"I hope so," Lara said at the same time Ano offered, "Probably not."

Lara mustered up more energy and straightened. Her eyes were better adjusted to the hallway. She made out the forms of her group and knelt by Ano. "Is your lighter in your backpack? I want to check out the building to see if it's safe."

"Yeah. I'll get it out. I'm not staying in this suit another minute longer than I have to."

Lara understood. When they'd first donned the suits earlier that day, they didn't seem too bad. After hours of walking and sweating, they became humid and confining. You couldn't use the bathroom, you couldn't eat or take a drink of water. Nothing. It was a mobile prison.

"We can't take them off until we decontaminate somehow," Lara said despite her own wish to take off the suit.

"Shit, fine. Just so you know, I'm not done talking about that obviously alien thing we saw back there," Ano said. His suit rustled as he got to his feet. A moment later he flicked on his lighter.

It was a big Zippo that provided a decent amount of light. A couple cardboard cutouts leaned against the walls, including Neo from *The Matrix*, obscured by cobwebs and a thick coating of normal dust. Two metal shelves were full of old cleaning products. On the bottom shelves were cardboard boxes. Lara bent down and read the faint lettering.

"Thank God. Paper towels and bleach," Lara said. "Let's try to clean our suits first."

She and Tim walked about five feet away from the doors where dust from outside still hovered in the air. The library had been perfect for decontaminating. One room for each phase. Here they'd need to use the length of the hallway to separate phases of decontamination.

Ano held his Zippo high above his head while Lara sprayed him thoroughly with bleach. The dust grew darker as it got wet and began sliding down the suit. Lara kept spraying him until every bit of him was glistening, then wiped him down.

"Whoa, Lara," Ano joked as her hands went over his backside, "I know I'm handsome, but you're getting a little handsy."

She meant to be serious, but ended up laughing. "Very funny."

Finished, she stuffed the used towels back into the empty box they came in. Ano did the same to her. By the time they were done, Lara felt more confident about taking off their suits once they found the right spot for the second stage of decontamination.

"Hey, Lara. I'll come with you."

Lara turned around and found Dan a step behind her. She pointed at the group. "You stay here and help everyone clean off, okay? I'd really appreciate it. Help them, and then tell everyone to wait for Ano and me to make sure the rest of the theater is safe."

"Fine," Dan replied after a moment's hesitation. He snatched up a bottle of bleach before he shuffled away.

Lara and Ano moved farther down the hall until they found another set of double doors. Beyond was a hallway twice the size of the one they were in with numbered theaters on either side. At the far end, the hallway opened up into a concession area which was well lit by a bank of windows. That was the front of the theater where they originally tried to get in.

Most importantly, there was no dust inside.

They walked into the hallway and stripped out of their suits, laying them out neatly on the ground. When the cool air hit her skin, she shuddered in pleasure. It felt good to be free. She grabbed a power bar from her backpack and scarfed it down.

Ano flicked his lighter closed and wandered into the big hallway to a janitor cart. "Lara, check it out."

He plucked something hanging from a hook on the side.

"Yes!" Lara exclaimed as he showed her the flashlight. Ano turned it on, and a beam of light cut through the dark hallway. "But turn it off for now. Let's look around the corner up there, see if there's anyone outside."

They hadn't heard anything outside, no gunshots or voices, but Lara wanted to double check. What if Jack was wandering around out there looking for them?

She and Ano crept down the hallway. When they got to the archway that led into the lobby, she pressed herself against the wall and leaned slowly around.

The dust was thick on the glass doors, but she could still make out the street. There wasn't anyone there.

"What is that stuff?" Ano asked.

Lara looked around the lobby. There were card tables set up with empty pitchers and plastic cups. In the center of the lobby was a pile of purses and wallets. Lara spotted a few toys, too. The hair on her arms stood up as a chill ran over her.

"Let's search the theaters," Lara said. She had no explanation for the scene, but it unsettled her. "Then we can move everyone out here where it's more comfortable."

Across the lobby was another set of screens, but Lara didn't want to cross the wide-open space unless they needed to. They went to the first auditorium on their left and entered. Lara followed behind Ano as they looked around. It was deserted. They searched the next two auditoriums, both equally empty. The seats were dusty and torn and litter was strewn about. The place looked like vagrants might have been squatting here for years.

When they went to the second to last theater, Lara froze. There was a sign on the door written in beautiful cursive.

Ano read it out loud. "Psalm 118:6. 'The Lord is on my side; I will not fear. What can man do to me?'"

Lara pushed past him. She needed to see what was inside.

It smelled like dirt and, faintly, of fecal matter. His flashlight skittered across the first row of bodies, and Lara's fears were confirmed.

Each seat in the theater was occupied by a well-dressed, papery corpse. They must've committed suicide months ago, perhaps when the comet's new trajectory was announced. Their bodies were drying out, nearly husks.

"Jesus," Lara breathed. "I heard about this kind of thing. If only they'd waited…."

"When the president made the announcement, my aunt turned off the TV, got my granddad's old service pistol, and shot herself in the head," Ano said. "Me and my cousins were just sitting there on the couch. Heard the gunshot upstairs and knew exactly what she'd done. I think it was something she'd wanted to do for a while and this was just the straw that broke the camel's back."

Lara set her hand on his shoulder and gave it a quick squeeze. "I'm sorry," she said.

"Yeah," he said. "Me too."

They didn't take a step further into the tomb, but even after the doors swung shut on the theater, the images lingered in Lara's mind. She had the feeling they'd be burned there forever.

# DAN

Dan scratched his face and got grime under his fingernails. He folded his power bar wrapper into a triangle and used the stiff tip to clean out the gunk. His face itched like hell and kind of smelled. He needed a baby wipe or something.

Worst of all—and he knew this was impossible since he hadn't had a hit since he was with Bianca—he felt bugs crawling under his skin. It was as though insects no bigger than a grain of sand were burrowing paths through his body. He shivered at the thought and bit off a chunk of power bar.

The blueberry brick tasted like absolute shit, but he was starving and ate the whole thing anyway. Now his stomach was grumbling. He bet the others were hoarding the good flavors for themselves.

The idiots finished their debate on whether they should stay in the big hallway or a theater. The theater won because they could lay across the seats if they put up the armrests. Someone had to keep watch in the hallway near the entrance, and Dan elected to do it first. Not that he actually watched. He just sat and thought, not looking at the street once.

Dan's mind drifted. It had been four years, almost to the day, since his first stint in prison. The bitch's name was Celeste, and she was a meth head like him. At first, when he saw her working by Raymond's Bar, he'd wanted to screw her. Then he had found out she liked a little of the sweet stuff, so they got some and rolled for a while. Fucked, got high, the usual.

At the time, he was squatting in an abandoned house. It had been full of junk: rotten furniture, big piles of books, and a giant freezer in the basement. He would take Celeste there, and for a while they'd had fun. Then he realized how much she looked like a younger, pretty version of Mama. One thing lead to another, and the next thing he knew, he'd tied up Celeste and put her in the broken freezer. He kept her there four days, wallowing in her own shit and piss, crying for help. He'd never been so hard in his life listening to her struggle.

Anyway, eventually someone heard it, called the cops, and that was the end of that.

The fucking country shrink ate the whole thing up. Wanted to write a fucking movie about Dan.

"Why did you hold her hostage in the freezer, Dan?"

"What were you going to do to her?"

"Have you done this before?"

That last question made him smirk. He had, not like anyone knew about it.

The shrink thought he'd found the next Hannibal, and he tricked Dan into telling him about the box. Told him how Celeste looked like the picture of his mama on her wedding day, the one right above the mantel by the jars of pig's feet. How when Celeste sucked his dick, he'd started thinking about how Mama always said she'd cut off his prick if he touched himself.

The shrink said Dan could plead insanity, blah blah blah. It was all bullshit because Dan didn't plan on staying in prison long.

He called in a favor to his buddy Hector, who went and roughed up Celeste. Told her she needed to retell her story and back off or they'd slit her throat. Turned out she had kids, so his buddy said he'd kill them too. In the end, the bitch had caved and backed off her claim that he'd kidnapped her. Said she'd gone with him willingly, that she'd lied because she wanted attention. All the screaming people had heard was them fucking.

Dan had walked.

He'd ended up in this shitty town with Hector for a while. They'd been peddling in the alley by the theater when a bunch of teenagers came, got the makeshift slim jim out of the trash can, and broke in. Dan thought that was a good idea and started doing it too. Saw a lot of flicks for free that way.

Maybe that's what he'd tell Lara. He grew up in this town, and kids had always snuck in the back. The tool had been used for decades or some shit, like a local legend.

Dan sighed and leaned against the wall. He was losing ground with Lara and he knew it. With Jack out of the picture and him screwing up every second, he needed to act fast. Explain the slim jim, make it sound like some happy memory, and go from there.

"You okay out here?"

Dan jumped. Lara had come from the theater and was standing right beside him. It was nearly dark outside, and the hallway was dimly lit. He could make out her figure but not much else.

"I'm fine, just watching."

She wandered past him to the end of the hall. Dan admired that ass, got to his feet, and wandered up beside her.

"Hey," he started, putting on his father-of-the-year, good-guy voice. "I wanted to talk to you about earlier. When I opened the door."

Lara didn't reply. If she was going to play tough bitch, so be it.

"It seemed kind of bad, I know. I guess it was. When I was a teenager we—"

"Oh my God, Dan. Your face."

Dan's hand went up to his face. When he pulled it back his fingers were coated in blood. His stomach clenched up. He stumbled back to the theater and grabbed the flashlight. It left the entire group in darkness, but he didn't give a fuck. Ignoring their protests, he headed for the bathroom.

"Dan, wait! Don't cross the lobby!"

He ignored Lara, too. He shoved the door open and shone the light on his face while he looked in the mirror.

Fuck. Fucking fuck. Everything from below where his goggles had been to his chin was covered in patches of red and black. Sores leaked blood and pus where he'd been scratching. He saw the long trail his fingernails had left, angry and puffy. Dozens of blue pinprick scabs dotted his face. The whites of his eyes were almost totally neon blue.

# COLLEEN

A stocky man in a plaid shirt stood in the doorway to the gym, a rifle in hand, interrupting Collen from the tenth prayer she'd said that hour. His predatory gaze swept over the group like a hawk scoping out field mice. Whatever whispered conversations there were came to a close. The room was so silent Colleen heard her breath. Her heartbeat. A chill swept over her body. She wrapped her arms around herself and squeezed her eyes shut.

"Miss C? Are they back?"

Colleen glanced down at Gabriela and Serena who sat cross-legged on the floor quietly talking. She nodded.

After a minute, satisfied there was no uprising afoot, the man left. The double doors slammed closed and the refugees were left in bleak silence. The random checkups often included patrols where Benny's men roughed up whoever they felt like that particular moment for whatever reason they came up with.

It was obvious the bigot's victims were minorities, which put even more stress on Colleen. She knew these kinds of people existed and was unsurprised they were the ones that took advantage of a situation like Zabat's Comet to show their true colors. Not only show them, but *act* upon them, too.

The physical violence thus far had been directed towards men. She hated to say it, but she was grateful no one had laid a hand on her or the girls. Instead of being hit they were forced to ration smaller quantities of food amongst themselves. Smaller than they already had been, which meant a few bites here and there. Other people around the camp shared food, but a remarkable number chose to look the other way.

Colleen was left in agony. She had no clue how to get Liana back. Her baby was out there somewhere. She had no idea if she was alive or being hurt.

Suddenly two men stumbled into the gym. The double doors snapped close behind them. Colleen recognized them as volunteers who left the previous night. Benny's men didn't say what they needed volunteers for, just that they needed to men and "it would be worth their time."

In both of their arms were sacks of MREs. Benny, she supposed, was true to his word in his own way. Both looked haggard, but one in particular sported a black eye almost swollen shut. His nose and chin were stained red. The man in better shape staggered away to his family while the other swayed and looked like he was about to faint.

No one came to his aid. Colleen tried to remember if she'd seen him with a family and couldn't bring anyone to mind. She placed the man at about her age, late thirties.

Colleen double-checked that none of Benny's men were still in the gym, then turned to the girls. "Stay down, okay? I'm just walking over there." Colleen got off her cot and crossed the filthy gym to the man who was frozen in place.

All eyes were on Colleen. She was furious at these people for watching her like she was a spectacle.

At first she was going to ask if the man was okay, but it was a stupid question. Instead, she said, "I'm Colleen. Do you need help?"

Tears welled in his eyes. He nodded. She wrapped an arm under him to support him.

"Where is your cot? Do you have any family?"

"I came with my parents. They...took them away. They were older. Infected. Easy to get rid of."

"I'm sorry to hear that. You can come over here with me, okay?"

They were halfway back to the wall when a man stormed over and put himself in Colleen's path. His nostrils were flared, eyes wild. "You're just manipulating him so you can get that extra food!"

"I'm not," Colleen said sincerely. "He needed help. No one came. I did."

He ignored her. "He needs to share that food with the rest of us. No one should get extra food!"

"He will do whatever he wants to do," Colleen snapped. "It's his food."

"I got it for the kids," the man said, putting an end to the argument. "The food is for the children."

"Jesus, are you serious?" The man threw his hands up in disbelief and stormed away. He nearly slipped and fell on a pool of old blood, and Colleen took pleasure in seeing him awkwardly catch his balance.

Once he was gone, she led the man back to the girls. He sat down and wiped a fresh trail of blood from his nose. Colleen noticed he shook slightly, so she snatched a blanket from an empty cot nearby and put it around his shoulders. It smelled sour, but was the best she could do. She sat next to him.

Gabriela and Serena were still on the floor, only now they'd scooted closer together. Serena's face was pale and Gabriela was visibly shaking. Gabriela probably had Glen on her mind.

"What's your name?" Serena asked first. Politely. Colleen was proud.

"Emerson," the man responded weakly. He managed a smile.

Gabriela asked, "What happened? What did they have you do?"

"Gabriela, please don't," Colleen scolded, though she was curious, too. "Emerson's been through a lot."

He raised his hand. "It's fine. There are…there's a lot of dead bodies out there. They had us stack them all in a room. Get them out of the way, basically. Gave us some extra MREs as a reward."

"What happened to your face, then?" Serena asked.

"I tried to steal a hazmat suit and run outside. I didn't—I couldn't imagine staying here with them in control. I'd rather die trying to get out than stay." Emerson lightly touched his black eye then changed the subject. "Hey, are you hungry?"

They looked to Colleen first for the OK, which she gave them. For the first time since Liana was taken and they lost James, the two perked up. Emerson pulled out a package of chili macaroni and gave it to Serena.

While the girls ate and Emerson rested with them for a moment, Colleen found herself staring at the metal frame of a nearby cot. If Benny and his men could fashion weapons out of it, so could she. She could find Liana and save her.

"I've got a few more MREs to give out. It was nice to meet you guys," Emerson said.

Colleen helped him to his feet and walked with him until they were out of range from the girls.

"Did you…did you happen to see a little girl somewhere when you were back there?" Colleen asked. "Her name is Liana. She's a toddler, four years old. Dark curly hair, skin a little lighter than mine."

What could only be recognition flickered in Emerson's eyes. He went silent for a moment. An instinctual shot of panic coursed through Colleen. A wave of dizziness and nausea swept over her.

"You saw her, didn't you?"

"Yes," Emerson whispered.

"Is she hurt? What are they doing to her?" Bile rose up in Colleen's throat.

The gym doors swung open. Glen stepped through with two buddies. His gaze didn't roam the crowd. It went straight to Colleen, then past her to where Gabriela and Serena sat, happily eating their chili-mac.

Colleen froze. Her fingers and toes tingled as adrenaline flooded her body. Her muscles tensed, then she sprang into action.

Surprised by her own agility, Colleen dashed around cots and debris as she closed the short distance between her and the girls. She put herself in front of them. Her fingers closed into fists.

Unafraid and oozing confidence, Glen and his men sauntered over. The gym had gone silent.

It took only moments for Glen to reach them. He had a gun tucked into the front of his pants. His buddies both had rifles.

"Lady, you've been a real fucking thorn in my side since the second I laid eyes on you. You know that?" Glen scratched his beard. His feral grin showed crooked yellow teeth. "I get it. Even your kind has Mama Bear instincts."

Colleen stood her ground. "You people are sick. Just leave us alone."

"You think you can tell me what to do?" The back of his hand lashed out with incredible speed and connected with her cheek. Colleen fought to keep back tears but the slap stung and her eyes smarted. "You mouth off one more time and I won't go easy on you. Understand?"

"I understand," she said. "What do you want?"

"Benny said your retard kid is giving him grief. Said to get her some friends so she'll cooperate."

For the first time, Colleen felt optimism. Liana was alive. "Let me go, too. A girl needs her mother."

One of Glen's buddies snorted. "You going to make a deal with a nigger?"

Glen's chest puffed up. He pulled out his gun and pressed it against Colleen's forehead. Out of the corner of her eye, Colleen saw Serena's chest heaving.

He said, "I don't. I was *going* to bring all of you, but you, Mama Bear, piss me the fuck off. I think you need to cool down and think about who is in charge here. Take the girls."

"W-what?" Colleen stammered. "Stop, please!"

She wanted to fight them, tooth and claw. She imagined herself grabbing his gun and turning on Glen, killing them all. She could imagine a thousand fantastical outcomes that resulted in her saving the girls.

But she couldn't. Right then, in that moment, she stood no chance against Glen. She could not use force against them. She could not convince them. Her only chance of doing *anything* was to bide her time.

"It's going to be okay," she said to the girls, eyes still locked with Glen. "Don't you touch them."

Glen snorted. "Really, lady? I'm not a fucking pedophile. Jesus. But I can't speak to the rest of the guys. Now, you going to be good and think about how to not be such a raging bitch anymore?"

"Yes."

"Mom?"

"Go, Serena."

Her stepdaughter started to sob. Glen pressed the gun harder against Colleen's head. "Shut up. Lay on the ground, face down."

Colleen did as he said. Her face stuck to the grimy floor. She watched as they dragged Gabriela and Serena away.

# CRAIG

Craig leaned back in his chair and did a small spin, surveying his new lab setup. The floor was made up of hard plastic, nearly a hundred squares that interlocked together to create a smooth surface. A metal frame supported the positive pressure tent, which had a thick layer of white plastic stretched taut across the sides. It almost felt like a regular lab. Much to his pleasure, it had air conditioning, too.

Siyang brought with her every piece of equipment Craig needed to analyze the dust and then some. It was driven in from the University of Portland, which had escaped the worst of the pre-comet anarchy. Craig wondered about the state of his office, classroom, and lab down at Berkeley, but maybe it was better not to know.

She and her team had been delayed multiple times by a highly organized group of raiders. For two days they had been pinned down by snipers at the college. Once that was resolved, they had contended with IEDs on the freeway going north. It was a nightmare, Siyang said, and she left it at that. He had a feeling that it had been far more harrowing than the young doctor admitted.

"Craig, are you listening to me?" Tim sighed, making the radio crackle with static. "Can we please focus?"

He refocused his attention. When the new lab was erected, he had gotten his own radio to report back to Tim more effectively. Not like that was something to be excited about.

"I'm here. Sorry, just admiring this beautiful setup I have. You really outdid yourself, old friend." Craig stared at the ceiling as he spoke. "The survivors from the DZ have all been detained at the southern camp. Haven't heard much from Dr. Shen in the way of progress."

Siyang and her people were tasked with identifying the strain of necrotizing fasciitis killing the DZ survivors. Considering it came from space, they were unlikely to have the particular strain in their databases. But if it had any commonalities with a known bacteria, that would provide them with a decent launching point for further study. She and Craig both reported daily to Tim, keeping him informed of every detail about the camp, their medical progress, and above all, the dust.

"Next time you see Shen, please remind her she's overdue for her report." Someone spoke to Tim in the background. Craig couldn't pick up what they said. A moment later, Tim said, "Oh, and the scabbing? The blue eyes?"

"What about them?"

"First, please spare me your usual sarcasm. We're trying to get an official statement ready to broadcast. Radio, then TV if we can get the towers working. We figured the rest of the world would like to know what we're discovering, too."

Craig wasn't surprised. He imagined they were already setting up the iconic backdrop and big wooden desk for the president to film an address. "Consider yourself spared. This preface is scaring me though. What's the ask here?"

"We need something from you. Can you get us some images of patients who look more, well, normal?"

"You're joking," Craig said. "You're seriously trying to de-sensationalize this? If you're going out of your way to spread the news, spread the truth for once."

"We don't want to increase panic. Just get me the photos. And...I'll owe you one."

"You know, this is everything I hate about the government, Tim. Bureaucracy and cover-ups. I don't want anything to do with it."

"Craig, I don't want to turn the request into an order, but I will if I have to. I ask you out of courtesy, not because you're the only person who can."

"Fine. Anything else?"

"We're ordering Berg to send out more search-and-rescues now that the dust is settling and visibility is better. We're starting with a few FEMA camps set up months ago. They have air filtration systems, generators, food, supplies, and so on. They seem a likely place where survivors would hide out."

Craig couldn't imagine being trapped inside the DZ. The huge dome was horrifying from the outside. On the inside, you wouldn't even be able see how far it went. It probably seemed as though the whole world was like that. You also couldn't take a step outside wherever you were taking refuge without risking painful death. Whenever he started feeling miserable, he reminded himself to be grateful he was still alive and outside the DZ.

"I want to hear your theory on the new satellite pictures NORAD gave us of Seattle."

Craig pushed aside some papers on his desk, which already sported his trademark messiness, and found the photos under a stack of stills from Sansbury's video. The shots from NORAD were grainy from dust interference, but it was the bigger picture and not the details that was important. A large ring of meteor chunks had created a loose circle around Seattle roughly the diameter of Zabat's Comet. He could see dark shards in Lake Washington and the Sound, and it looked like multiple structures throughout the city had been completely leveled.

What interested him the most was the perfect, untouched

area of clear land in the middle of the destruction at the exact center of the dome. In the clearing was the teardrop shaped pod he noticed in Sansbury's video.

"My theory was correct. The shell of the comet fell away when it released the dust. The debris caused a lot of destruction in the Seattle area." He rifled through his papers and found the shots of nearby cities. "I asked NORAD to snap some images of the outlying area. During the dismantle, some of the comet shell blasted off up to fifty miles away from the primary impact zone. NORAD found larger chunks of debris nearly all the way to the mountains."

"Damage assessment?"

Siyang entered the tent, a thick folder of papers under one arm and steaming cups of coffee in both hands. He gave her a nod before he resumed his conversation with Tim. "Most of Seattle is gone. Moderate damage in Tacoma, and by the time you get to Olympia there's virtually no damage from the comet. I'd like to mount an expedition to the center of the DZ as soon as possible to investigate this clearing."

"We'll consider it once the resources are available. What about the incinerator proposal we sent?"

A small amount of satisfaction welled up inside him. Their initial attempt to secure a sample had failed miserably. Craig wasn't sure if it was because the dust had settled more, or because they took the sample while inside the DZ, but on their second attempt they had been successful.

He'd brought a dozen tamperproof, screw-top vials to the DZ. Berg still wouldn't let him go inside the force field himself, but he remained close by while Brody carried out the task. Brody had scooped dust into each vial. This time, the sample was intact. Granted, it still tried to return to the DZ, and they had to be extremely careful handling the samples. Craig glanced at the tabletop glove box. Siyang referred to it as a "biological safety cabinet," but he'd always preferred the more whimsical name. The particular unit they used solely for observing dust was an acrylic box with two circular ports for arm-length rubber gloves. A smear of dust rested in the upper corner. It would migrate to whichever side was closest to the DZ depending on how they rotated the table. That made it difficult to observe the samples under a microscope because it was always moving out of view.

That alone was unsettling.

"It could work," Craig continued, bringing his mind back to the present. "If you want to make giant incinerators to destroy the dust, go for it. But if you're going to do it, do it soon. If the dome collapses and the dust starts to spread, we'll be in much worse shape than we are now."

"Noted."

Siyang coughed. Craig pointed to the phone and rolled his eyes. She grinned.

"Tim, I have to go. I have huge tests planned for today now that the lab is set up."

"Keep me updated."

Craig switched off the radio and then stood and stretched. Without the headset on, he could hear the hum of generators outside. It took three to power their tent alone. He walked over to Siyang's desk and pointed to the coffee.

"That for me?"

"It is. Black as night, just how you like it."

Her own coffee was laden with cream and sugar. Normally he'd pour a finger of something stiff into his, but keeping up with his habit had been somewhat difficult around her. Fortunately he'd calmed his nerves during the call with Tim and would be okay for a few hours.

They sat in comfortable silence for a moment as they

sipped, and then Craig got down to it. "You got something?" She pushed a stray hair behind her ear. "First the bad, or at least inconclusive, news. We couldn't isolate a strain of bacteria from any of the quarantine patients. We couldn't isolate anything because there's nothing there." She carefully folded her hands in her lap, a habit Craig noticed she had developed to stop herself from picking at her nails. "We found nothing in their blood or tissue."

"What about the scabs?"

She tapped the folder on her desk. "Interesting results there, though they won't give us any fast answers. Just more questions. The scabs are negative for any kind of bacteria. What we did find was unusually high levels of fibroblasts."

"That's part of the wound healing process, right? So it makes sense you'd find fibroblasts in scabs."

"Yes, but not in these quantities. Fibroblasts are responsible for producing collagen, which strengthens a wound. Normally synthesis and degradation equalize so collagen levels never change. The quantity of fibroblasts at this stage are too high for the collagenases to break the peptide bonds in the collagen." Siyang took a deep breath. "We're monitoring fibroblast levels in hopes they even out. Meanwhile, we also found a high concentration of hemocyanin in the scabs."

Craig raked through his brain, breaking apart the roots of the word. "Blue blood?"

"It's a protein found in arthropods and mollusks. The oxygen is bound differently, with copper instead of iron, which causes their blood to be blue. There's a high concentration of it in the scabs, almost as though it's a deposit."

Craig considered this information. Like Siyang had said, it raised more questions than it answered. He had no idea how to tell Tim that the disease was caused by lobsters from outer space, and he hoped that Siyang and her team would come up with a more plausible solution before he had to make that report. Then again, it might be worth it to mess with Tim.

"So we know the dust causes this infection," Craig said. "We also know the dust returns to the DZ, so my guess is it exits the body when people leave the DZ. That's why we're not finding any on them. It does its damage inside the DZ and we get the aftermath."

Siyang sipped her coffee and nodded. "Makes sense. I can tell you're not done, so what else are you thinking?"

"Maybe the hemocyanin scabs are a byproduct of the bacteria. This all brings us back to needing to know what the dust is." Craig squeezed his eyes shut. "What's your good news?"

She finished off her coffee and wiped her mouth. "We need bigger cups. Anyway, you assume the other news is good. It isn't. I'd call it interesting at best. The neuroscience might not make sense to you—"

The preamble was killing him. Craig raised his hand to stop her.

"Dumb it down for Tim. Our buddy Carl Lambert did all of his neuroscience homework in college. However, in addition to being a meteorologist, theoretical physicist, and dabbler in microbiology, I'm pretty well versed in neuroscience. Hit me."

Red flushed his cheeks when he realized what an ass he'd just made of himself, throwing Tim under the bus and trying to impress her with his academic accolades. That wasn't like him at all. Siyang smirked. Craig hid behind his coffee cup, taking a deep pull of the hot liquid.

"Right. Again, these tests aren't conclusive. Just remember that going in."

Her fingers flashed on the keyboard as she logged

into her computer. He caught a glimpse of her desktop wallpaper, which showed Siyang and a man embracing in front of a Christmas tree. Husband? Boyfriend? They hadn't spoken about their personal lives before. That small glimpse into Siyang's life before the comet threatened to dredge up memories Craig didn't want to deal with.

The background vanished when she opened a folder of videos. "For the past two days I've been testing the dust on animals, concurrent with testing the DZ patients. My hope was to discover what a lethal level of dust exposure is. That's when this happened."

She clicked on one of the videos and made it full screen. The footage was taken just near the force field border on the DZ. It showed a rat inside a plastic tub nestled in the dust.

"Watch. I'm going to expose the rat to what we estimated would be a lethal dosage of dust."

In the video Siyang, wearing a positive pressure suit, took the rat with both hands and dragged it through the dust. She dropped it into the plastic tub.

Siyang frowned. "I hate doing this kind of work, just so you know. Animal testing is cruel, but necessary. This test in particular felt pretty barbaric."

Craig thought of his love for his late dog, Galactus, and nodded. "Agreed."

Without another word, she fast forwarded through the footage. Time sped up. The rat wandered around the box, drank some water, and ate a few pellets of food. Eventually blisters popped up across its body and its fur fell away. It lay in the corner of the box, sides heaving.

"Infection took minutes. After two hours, we thought it would die. But watch." Siyang opened another video and sped through more footage of the rat lying on its side. Miraculously, on the fifth hour, it got up and wandered to its water again. The blisters had almost entirely disappeared.

"It recovered from a dose that should have killed it."

"So there's hope for us?"

Siyang leaned closer to the computer, her chin jutting forward as she browsed through more videos. The reflection of the screen flashed in her dark eyes, and her brows were knitted in concentration. "Not exactly. I ran this experiment, same dose of dust, with six more rats. Identical results. I wanted to try it on another species, so I sent the soldiers out to catch snakes."

"Snakes?" Craig laughed, imagining Berg and his men hunting for snakes in the field.

"Correct." She ignored his laughter and moved along. "I exposed four garter snakes to the dust. No infection. I then exposed two song birds. Nothing. I even tried injecting a saline-dust solution directly into them. Nothing."

She sped through footage of her snake experiment to prove it.

"Here's my theory. The dust does the most damage to mammals with a complex neocortex. The neocortex is a part of the brain that's relatively new, evolutionarily speaking." She flashed him a grin. "Even you have one, Dr. Peters. You can thank your neocortex for most of your higher mental functions. Conscious thought, language, sensory perception."

Craig scowled at the jab. "I know what it is."

"So imagine a rat. They have a neocortex, but it's small and lacks the same convolutions as say, a cat. Neither of these mammals is particularly intelligent compared to a human. The convolutions of our neocortex allows for more surface area and complexity, which essentially means a greater capacity to carry out those higher functions we were talking about.

"You expose a rat to the dust, it gets sick. But not for long. The skin necrosis, bleeding, blisters—they all go away within hours of exposure. Even when exposed to huge amounts of dust, they will survive. You expose a dog to the dust, it stays sick longer. Sometimes it dies, but unlikely."

Craig caught her clenching her fists and felt a pang of sympathy. He still got choked up when the thought about the cats he dissected in college, and those had been dead on arrival. He was glad she didn't show him any footage of the experiments with the dogs. "Go on," he said.

"If we had a primate, I'd bet you anything—because its neocortex is more complex—it would stay sick even longer and have a greater chance of dying. We know for certain humans are impacted the worst. My correlation is that it has to do with the complexity of our brains."

"What are you going to tell Tim?"

At this, she leaned back in her chair and refolded her hands. "I'm saying we are ideal hosts for reasons yet unknown, and in our bodies the infection the dust causes is more severe than in other living organisms."

"Not that the dust is an obviously intelligent creation of an alien race and it's out to get us?"

Siyang smiled. "No, Craig. I'm not telling him that because I don't necessarily believe it. Do you have anything new to report to change my mind?"

Craig felt himself growing irritated; whenever they ventured into pure speculation, Siyang always backed off just when he wanted to dive in.

Craig looked at his workstation and tried to calm his singing nerves. "This stuff is a pain. I can't get any between slides to check under a microscope. I think I prepared a good slide, but then it always seems to have moved just enough so I'm looking at nothing. Hell, I even tried to tape it down."

Suddenly, Craig stood as a thunderbolt of an idea shocked his tired brain. His chair rolled backwards. "That's because it doesn't *want* us to know what it is. Why didn't I think of this before? As long as it's alive, we can't study it. So we have to kill it."

# LARA

Lara was beginning to think Jack hadn't made it. They'd been in the theater an entire day. Someone was always on guard to look out for him, while another stayed in the dimly lit exit hallway in case they heard something out there. They called it "hanging out with Neo" because the only thing of interest to look at in the windowless hallway was the old cardboard cutout. It had become a joke—one small beacon of humor in an otherwise dismal situation.

It was now her shift watching the front and she savored the alone time, grateful to have a moment to figure things out. Outside, the ambient glow of dawn pushed away the pitch black night. Overnight the dust had finished settling and the air was completely clear for the first time since the comet hit. There were at least four inches of dust, piled high on cars and awnings like snow. Looks were deceiving; it was still a hostile environment out there.

It was hostile inside, too.

Last night went by in awkward silence between everyone in the group. After Dan had seen the terrible state of his face, his attitude had scared Lara. His gaze, when it met hers in the mirror, had been feral. In a split second, his expression had gone back to normal Dan. Or at least, what she *thought* was normal Dan. He had withdrawn and stayed by himself in one of the theaters. He said he didn't want to infect anyone else and needed to rest. He also told Lara not to feel bad, he didn't hurt that much and was sure he'd be fine.

That, of course, was cause for her to feel guilty. If he'd worn a real respirator, he wouldn't have gotten dust on his skin. Though he'd volunteered to do it, Lara shouldered the blame. She had to find a way to help him.

Dan was in bad shape, but Yvette was even worse. The bleeding had stopped sometime in the night and she was now unconscious. Someone checked her a couple times an hour, but there was no improvement. Her leg was beginning to smell. Lara knew enough to guess the wound was becoming gangrenous from being tied with the tourniquet for so long. With Dan and Yvette so ill and Jack being gone, everyone was glum and restless.

Lara had no idea what to do. These people needed a doctor, not a therapist. Her psychology degree would do no good here. Before the mess the comet caused, Lara had lived in a world where most issues were caused by problems in the mind. Repression, anxiety, trauma. Those were ailments she had a chance of healing. A bullet in someone's leg? An infection eating away at a man's face? She'd rather try to psychoanalyze the lunatics in Hedone than try to remove a bullet.

On top of everything else, there was also the strange meteor. The sight of it still haunted her. Lara's gut told her it wasn't from this world. Every ludicrous explanation she came up with—maybe it had been part of a movie set, and an explosion from the falling debris had sent it into the apartment's kitchen—fell apart.

Ano and Rocky wanted to leave the theater and take a closer look at the thing. Lara had nixed the idea with resounding support from Linda. Their curiosity would be the death of them—and the rest of the group, if a raider spotted them.

Lara opted to save her existential crisis for later. Contemplating the possibility of extraterrestrial life seemed a lot less important when her own life was in jeopardy.

She closed her eyes and took a slow breath for five seconds. She exhaled at the same length and then repeated the process until her racing heart slowed to an almost normal pace.

They had to do something other than sit around and wait.

Lara peeked out at the pharmacy on the corner. Yvette was at risk of infection, if she didn't have one already. Dan definitely needed antibiotics. The pharmacy would have them. The place had been raided—the windows and doors were shattered—but most people wouldn't take antibiotics. They'd go for painkillers and food.

She got to her feet and joined the others in the theater. Dan had returned the flashlight, though the light from it was dim. It was running out of batteries. The group slept soundly. They'd nestled into their makeshift beds as best as they could. Lara hated to wake them.

She went to Rocky and shook him gently. "Rocky?"

He kept his eyes closed. "What?"

"I think we need to go to that pharmacy and get medicine for Dan and Yvette."

"Okay," he said without hesitation. He rubbed the sleep out of his eyes. "You want to go now?"

"Yeah. If you don't mind."

Rocky sat up. The theater seats snapped shut as he moved, and the sound woke the others. Ano and Linda looked around groggily and asked what was going on.

Lara explained the plan. Ano rubbed his face and sighed. "I wish we still had a gun."

"Well, we don't. You two stay here. We'll be back as soon as we can," Lara said. "If Dan comes out, tell him where we are."

Linda scoffed and Ano was silent. They were on the

anti-Dan team. Lara had her doubts about him now, too, but he was still a person. He'd been through trauma like the rest of them, and although he didn't fit in, she thought he deserved at least a bit of compassion. Lara kept those thoughts to herself.

She and Rocky went to the exit hallway and suited up. Even though the air was clear, should anything happen like a gust of wind or a trip, they'd be in trouble. She got the tape from her bag and they sealed any gaps on their wrists, ankles, and necks. With Dan's mangled face on her mind, she took extra precaution.

The pharmacy was just across the street. It would take less than a minute to walk from the theater's exit to the front doors and slip in. There was no reason for Lara to be so nervous, she told herself, but her pulse rate spiked as if she were about to travel through a mile of scorpion-infested desert.

They were silent as they traversed the debris. Rocky and Lara took in the sight of the meteor again before they reached the end of the alley. Lara peeked around the corner to her right in the direction of the church. As far as she could see, there was nothing out there. She checked windows in apartment buildings and around abandoned cars for any movement.

"My side is clear," Rocky said. "Ready?"

Lara nodded. They darted across the street and clung to the side of the pharmacy as they went to the front doors. There had to be broken glass somewhere under all the dust, but it was so thick their footsteps were muffled. Lara was glad for that.

Inside was about what she expected. The front of the store contained aisles of hygiene products, nonperishable foods, makeup. Much of it was gone or scattered about the floor. A thin layer of dust had made its way into the first ten feet of the store. Lara studied it closely for footprints. There was one set going in, then out. No others.

Feeling more confident, she moved deeper into the pharmacy. Small signs were placed at the end of each row stating their contents. She went through the cold remedy aisle. Nearly everything was gone. She ran her hands through the shelves near the back just in case. Her hand knocked something over. She pulled the item out and saw it was a bottle of cough syrup. She found a second bottle next to it, hidden far back on the shelf. She held onto them and picked through the debris on the ground in case there were more treasures. She found a bag of cough drops, some mucus expectorant, and vapor rub.

Rocky walked up beside her with two plastic bags. One was full.

"What did you find?" she asked.

"Just random stuff I thought might be useful. Scissors, some chocolate covered raisins, more tape."

She laughed. "Chocolate covered raisins. An absolute necessity."

Together, they went to the pharmacy at the back of the building. The employee-only door was loose on its hinges and ready to fall off. Lara walked around it carefully and surveyed the pharmacy. She and Rocky began searching the shelves.

"Look for anything with 'cin' at the end," Lara told him. "C-I-N."

Minutes passed. Lara's hope took a downward turn when she found nothing but a couple packages of birth control and some nasal spray.

Their search ended at the same shelf. "This place has been picked clean," Rocky said. "It was a good idea, Lara."

Lara nodded. "At least we—"

A gunshot. Three more. They sounded close. Lara and

Rocky ducked reflexively. After a moment, Lara peered over the edge of the counter. The scene hadn't changed. Same cars, same trails in the ground. No movement.

"That sounded like it came from the theater," Rocky whispered.

They waited. No further gunshots. No people.

Then someone was standing in the doorway. It was Dan. She recognized his plastic suit, a shade of yellow brighter than the dust. He had one of the good respirators on. Lara stood and beckoned him over.

"What happened?" Lara asked. "Where is everyone?"

"Raiders showed up," Dan said. "They got the others."

Lara backed away. His voice was remarkably calm. Too calm. She noticed he stood at an angle with one of his arms behind him. Then she realized he had on a gas mask like hers. *A second gas mask.*

"How did you get out with your gear on?" Rocky asked.

Between the shadows and his mask, Lara couldn't read his face.

"We need to get out of here," Dan said, ignoring Rocky.

Behind him, the street was still clear. If there were raiders, they would be here. They would've followed him. Dan wouldn't have had time to suit up and get all the way over here.

Dan pulled his arm from behind his back.

Lara's brain was still putting together the pieces—Dan's odd behavior, his flimsy stories about the gas masks and the ease with which he'd broken into the theater—when she realized that it was already too late.

Dan raised the gun in a fluid, easy motion and shot Rocky in the head.

For a split second, she was immobilized by shock. Then Lara tried to bolt past Dan, but he pushed her and pointed the gun at her.

"Fuck, you're stupid. This is a gun. A *GUN*." He pointed it at her head and bumped the muzzle against her mask. "You try to run, I shoot you. Got it, bitch?"

She nodded.

"Right. Now, we're leaving. You don't ask questions. You keep your little fucking mouth shut unless I tell you to talk. Got it?"

She nodded again.

"I was going to be nice about this, Lara. I wanted to get you to come on your own so I didn't have to waste bullets on these asshats. You can blame yourself for this mess."

Dan grabbed her shoulder and pushed her towards the exit. While Lara walked, she felt a cold, terrible weight settle in her chest. All the signs had been there. No one else had trusted him, and it was only at her insistence that Dan had been allowed to stay.

She, of all people, should've known better.

# JACK

Katie screamed as they dragged her away. Thousands of raiders, naked with the Hedone cross painted in blood on their chests. Their mouths were set in permanent grins, wicked sharp teeth grinding and gnashing in anticipation.

Jack tried to reach out, but she was too far away. The crowd swallowed her up and he knew, with every inch of his being, that they would do terrible things to her before they finally killed her.

Then his body was in motion and he was running straight for the raiders. Their hands tore at him, ripped his flesh. It didn't matter. It didn't even hurt. Energy swelled inside of him. He tossed his head back in ecstasy. It was like every nerve had activated. He had control of his body in a way he couldn't have fathomed was possible. The raiders dropped Jack. Light as a feather, he floated to the ground. Pulsating strands of light radiated all around him.

He raised his hands and beckoned to the dust, directing it like an orchestra conductor. He sent it toward the raiders and then they were enveloped in a cloud of yellow. Blood gushed from their eyes and noses. They howled in pain and collapsed to their knees.

Jack smiled. The dust, its work done, abandoned the dead men. It returned to him. Undulating, swirling, alive and at his command.

Then he saw Katie. Alone in the sea of corpses. The dust lifted her up.

And then it tore her in half.

He woke from the dream, disoriented and breathless. It was a sauna inside the plastic suit. Sweat dripped down his back, his pits, his chest. He'd fallen asleep. It was bound to happen eventually. He was exhausted, after all. But he had to be prepared to run at any second, so he kept the gear on and suffered.

The chair he'd wedged under the door was still in place, the window unbroken. Cartoon drawings of Jesus and other biblical figures looked down at him, lying there on the ground under the teacher's desk. There was a scattering of kid's toys around the floor. Of all the places to take a break, he had to pick the church. Jack—a murderer, alcoholic, and divorcee—had picked a Sunday school classroom as the best place to hide.

Jack took a labored breath through the respirator. He slid out from under the desk, and when he sat upright, he felt all the sweat trickle down his body. It was an unpleasant feeling that embarrassed him even though no one was there to see it.

He had to go look for Lara and the others again. After the raiders were all dead, he'd tried to find a trail but there had been so many that he'd become lost. Jack reasoned if his friends came looking for him, they'd go to the church first. That was the last place they'd seen each other. So far, they hadn't.

But what if they had come? What if they had been here, seen the dead raiders, and moved on?

Jack felt bile rise up in his throat at the thought of the bodies strewn outside the church.

Looking back, he was surprised he won the gunfight. The six raiders had been dumb, cocky teenagers. That was the only reason he was still breathing and they weren't.

When it was over, he'd numbly collected their weapons. Three guns, a couple of machetes. He had taken the guns and any ammo they'd had on them and then set off to rejoin the group, carrying the weight of six more deaths with him.

Gunshots interrupted his thoughts. Jack stilled as he listened. They were nearby. A few minutes later he heard another shot.

He scrambled to his feet and grabbed a handgun with a full magazine. Light pulsed in the corners of his vision, paired with an electric buzzing in the base of his skull. Vertigo sent him stumbling, and he fell against the desk. He sucked in a sharp breath and waited for the sensation to pass. Eventually the light faded, but the buzzing remained in his skull.

"Get it together," he said out loud. "Move. Move!"

Jack kicked aside the chair blocking the door and ran through the church. The gunshots had come from somewhere up the street. He'd briefly searched the area yesterday and remembered a pharmacy and a rundown movie theater. If he had to guess, he thought the shots had been coming from near there.

His body was stiff from sleeping on the hard floor and his knees ached fiercely. He worried the infection on his face wasn't really getting better, that he was instead suffering from some kind of neurological damage. He'd have to deal with that later.

He flung open the doors to the church and ran outside.

Minutes later he came upon the theater and pharmacy. No one was there, but the front doors of the theater were open. They'd been locked before. Jack took cover behind a Jeep and waited for any sign of life. After seeing none, he risked approaching the theater.

Ano was lying on his stomach in the middle of the lobby. Blood had soaked the back of his t-shirt and pooled around his torso. Jack rushed over to check for a pulse. When he turned the body over and saw Ano's glazed, empty stare,

Jack knew he was dead.

Strange light flashed in his eyes again. Brighter now. The sensation in the base of his skull throbbed. This time when it faded, his surroundings looked…different. Part of him knew they hadn't changed, but he had the oddest sensation that he'd never been in a theater before. Like he was a tourist seeing a foreign land for the first time.

Something was wrong with him. Seriously wrong. Jack squeezed his eyes shut.

The peculiar feeling still with him, he got to his feet and walked farther into the building, his gun leading the way. The door to one of the auditoriums was propped open. He stood in the entryway listening. It was quiet. There was a faint light coming from inside.

Jack walked in and nearly threw up.

Yvette was on her back in the aisle. Linda was in a seat, shoulders slumped forward and head tilted down. Both she and Yvette had gunshots in the middle of their foreheads. A dying flashlight stood on its end pointed upward like a lamp in the drink holder next to Linda.

They hadn't just been killed. They had been executed.

But where were Lara, Rocky, and Dan?

Jack took the flashlight and searched the rest of the auditorium. He ran out of the theater and checked the other ones. There was a horrifying room full of mummified corpses but no sign of his friends. Or Dan.

He stopped in the lobby, conflicted. He didn't have time to bury the bodies. He didn't even have a shovel. But he didn't feel right about leaving them like that. Jack closed his eyes and wished them well, hoping that would be good enough.

Outside, he searched for footprints again. This time he paid close attention to the depth and clarity of them. He found one perfect set in the dust that led from the theater doors. He continued along the footprints and searched the other side of the street. There were prints going into the pharmacy that hadn't been there last night.

He followed them inside and searched the aisles.

At the back of the building, he found Rocky's body. A bullet had shattered his goggles. Blood seeped through the hole.

That left Lara and Dan. Dan had to be behind this.

Where could he have taken her? Jack ran out of the pharmacy and looked up and down the street. There were too many trails to track which way they went. He had to use logic instead. They wouldn't go back to Monroe or stay here, he was sure. There was nothing there, and it was dangerous. Their only option was to keep going south. If they kept heading that direction, they'd reach the FEMA camp eventually. Plenty more people for Dan to charm, con, and kill.

Jack took a deep breath and started jogging.

His body count was at nine. He was ready to make it an even ten.

# DAN

His face itched so fucking bad he wanted to tear off his skin. He wanted to take a spoon and dig out the rotten parts. Dan's shoulders and chest were infected now, too. The disease or infection or whatever the hell it was covered his whole upper body. He'd taken a look down his shirt and saw patches of black skin around his pecs that reminded him of that one time he'd gotten frostbite when he was a kid. Only this hurt much worse.

And his eyes? The whites were blue, like cotton candy. If he wasn't so scared he'd think it was cool.

Dan coughed. It was wet. Little chunks of his throat and lungs came up.

"Maybe we should stop?"

Lara was ahead of him, as instructed, leading the way. He made her carry the bags of junk from the pharmacy because it looked like they'd nabbed some good stuff. One of Dan's favorite drinks was purple cough syrup, red bull, and vodka. Dan pointed the gun at her. "What did I say about talking? Shut the fuck up."

She turned away and kept walking.

At least he had Lara. He finally had the whore to himself and he felt fan-fucking-tastic. Proud. Dan hadn't worked so hard for something in a long time. Maybe in his whole life. Bianca and Chrissy, those sluts were easy. They'd fuck anything. A lady like Lara, though? Work. Hard work.

Dan grinned and ran his tongue over his slimy teeth. The idiots back at the theater didn't even see it coming when he shot them up. That had felt good, too.

Another coughing fit overtook him. Blood splattered inside his respirator as he hacked. He couldn't fight the urge to rip the fucking thing off any longer, so he did.

*Fuck it. I'm sick already.*

Air. Fresh air. He sucked it in and felt a little better.

The dust had settled anyway. As far as Dan could see down the road, it was clear. The trees were full of the stuff, but it wasn't windy.

They kept walking. They'd been going at it for about an hour when the forest thinned out and they arrived at an intersection.

"You know where we're going?" he asked Lara.

"The FEMA camp?"

Dan chuckled. "Wrong. We're going to Hedone. You're gonna like it there."

Lara said nothing. Dan grinned and scratched his cheek, not minding that his glove got more dust on his face. In for a penny, in for a pound, his mama used to say.

He pushed Lara into motion, and they turned toward Hedone. It was tough, all this walking. Dan couldn't wait for the moment he could sit on his ass and not move again. They walked for another hour before Dan spotted a beat-up two story farm house on the side of the road. The building was square with huge windows and a wrap-around porch. Two dust-covered vehicles were in the driveway. A pickup truck and some kind of sedan.

He had meant to keep going until well into the night, but he was tired and needed a rest. There were many miles left before they reached their destination. Every step made his chest hurt. His skin felt squishy. Each time he moved, it rubbed against the plastic suit and a little more slid off.

They left the main road and approached the house. Dan searched the cars for keys. Sure enough, in the tire well, a magnetic box held a spare key. People were so fucking stupid. He pocketed the key. The insignificant weight of it made him feel a hell of a lot better. No more walking after a quick breather.

Dan made Lara check the place while he kept the gun on her. The last thing he needed was for her to make a run for it. He was weaker now and didn't think he could catch her if she did.

The outside of the house looked fine. Some of the windows were broken, but not all of them. The front door was locked, but the back wasn't. They entered through the kitchen, and he kept his gun on her as they checked every room. It was an old house, probably owned by old people. It had floral printed furniture and wood burning stoves.

Dan prodded Lara with the gun to make her move faster. He needed to take a piss. They climbed creaky wooden steps that he nearly tripped on more than once.

"No one home," Dan announced as they checked the last room, an office with a boxy, piece-of-shit computer.

A few spots in the house were covered in dust near the broken windows, but the house wasn't too bad. Dan made Lara sit down at the dining room table and taped her hands to one of the table legs. When he was finished, he went into the living room, unzipped his suit, and took a piss on that ugly fucking flower couch. It wasn't as enjoyable as he'd hoped since his piss was tinged red with blood.

He returned to the kitchen, set the gun on the kitchen counter, plopped down on his ass, and then took out a chocolate fudge protein bar from his pack. As he'd suspected before, the now-dead fuckers had been keeping the best ones for themselves.

It was then he realized he hadn't taken Lara out of her gear. She looked stupid and fat in the white suit, which billowed around her like a melted marshmallow. Dan set his protein bar down and approached her. He tore her mask and goggles off, unzipped her suit, and pushed it down her shoulders to show her neck and chest. He tried to adjust her tits to make them look better. Too bad she was wearing a long-sleeved shirt. A little more skin would've been nice.

Now he could see her face. It was pale, her eyes wide and red rimmed. She'd probably been crying. Dan grinned. Crying was good. He sat back down and gnawed off a piece of the protein bar and rifled through the pharmacy bags.

He pulled out a bottle of cough syrup. "You got some good stuff in here, baby. Only thing that would make it better was if it was grape."

Dan struggled with the safety cap but eventually got it free. He took a deep swig. It stung his throat, almost enough to make him gag. Drinking cough syrup reminded him of being a kid. Mama had made him take it whenever he seemed like he was getting sick. The memory made him crave something stronger. Maybe the old farts had kept a liquor cabinet around here.

"So I gotta say, you're really stupid," he told her as he searched the kitchen for booze. "I've been playing you so hard. Sob story about my wife and kid, bad childhood, yadda yadda. You ate it up. God, you're dumb."

Lara didn't respond. Dan glanced back at her. She was staring at the floor, no sign that she'd even heard him. Dan shrugged and continued his search. In one of the little cupboards above the fridge was a bottle of cheap vodka, half full.

Fuck, the day just kept getting better! If only he had the red bull to complete the cocktail. He pulled down the vodka and chugged a few shots worth. The buzz hit him hard and fast. He sat down across from Lara again. His back hit the wood stove and he cringed.

"Hate these things. Had one in the basement where

Mama kept me, then one in the kitchen. Mama put my box right by it. Got so hot in the winter I thought I was going to burn alive."

His eyes smarted. He took another swig of the vodka to make the bad feelings go away. Like always, it just made them worse.

"Your box?" It was the first thing she'd said since the intersection.

"Yeah. You deaf *and* stupid?"

Now she was looking at him. She seemed interested. Dan wasn't sure he liked that, but there was something about her brown eyes and round face that made him feel kind of peaceful. He had a thing for brunettes. Shrinks always said he "gravitated to women who reminded him of his mother." He poured the cough syrup into the bottle of vodka, gave it a shake, and took a drink. Now *that* was good shit. Fucking shrinks didn't know what they were talking about. Lara wasn't morbidly obese with a bum leg. Didn't look anything like his mother.

"Papa was a welder before his back broke, you know? He made the box."

"Sure," Lara said. "Why did they keep you in the box, Dan?"

Dan shrugged. "She caught me jacking off. Got angry. Beat me, then made me get it up again and finish. The whole time she had these scissors and was like, 'I'm gonna cut your prick off if you don't finish.' Told Papa what I did. Left out the part about her and the scissors, though. And then he used scrap from the junk yard to make a box and they put me in. First it was just a day. Then they found more reasons to put me in there. Every time, it was a little longer. I smelled bad, into the box. I didn't eat all my dinner, into the box. I was in there a lot."

"How old were you?"

"Nine. Eight? No, nine." Dan's brain was foggy. He forgot what a good buzz vodka and cold medicine gave him. His face itched less and his muscles relaxed. The memories made him feel sad, but the booze made him feel better. And talking to Lara made him feel better, too. He took another drink.

"That must've been a very confusing thing for you." She paused, then asked, "What happened after that?"

# CRAIG

Craig crossed the lab and grabbed a sealed vial of the dust along with some other equipment. He'd believed the dust was alive—*intelligent*—since the very beginning. He should've treated it that way. Every living thing would protect itself when threatened…but once it was dead, they could study the dust at their leisure.

He inserted the vial and his other items into the glove box and sealed it. He pushed his hands into the rubber gloves and unlatched the panel to the oven extension. Siyang came up beside him, watching him work.

"You're going to kill it?"

"I feel like an idiot not thinking of it sooner."

Her voice softened. "We're under a lot of pressure. What do you want the oven set to?"

"Start low. We can always apply more heat."

Siyang set the oven to 175 degrees Celsius. Craig took a deep breath and steadied his hands. He unscrewed the cap and watched as the dust slowly wafted out and headed straight for the open latch to the oven. He pulled the latch shut and then withdrew his hands.

Heat shielding and water cooling systems prevented excess heat from escaping the oven. The external temperature gauge rose quickly, the fast ramp-up of the MB-VOH-600 working perfectly. They allowed it to stay at temperature for two minutes, then shut it down. The quick cooldown went into effect immediately.

Ideally they would open the other latch of the oven and

slide the sample out. However, if the dust was still alive, it would float away back towards the DZ. And if it touched anyone along the way, they could be infected. They needed to make sure it was dead first.

"I'll open the oven from the glove box," Craig said. "Let's see if any dust fell on the sliding tray."

Siyang hovered close beside him as she watched him unlatch the oven and slide out the tray. Sure enough, a fine scattering of soot coated the far right side of the tray.

A bead of sweat trailed down his neck. He itched to wipe it away but kept his focus trained on the task before him. He picked up a scalpel and scraped a bit of the sample off the metal, gently tapping it onto the slide before sealing it with a cover slip. Once he was finished, he pressed the tray back into the oven and latched it.

He pulled his hands free from the gloves. "I'm going to take a quick look with thermal just to make sure we don't have any excess dust floating around before we open it."

Craig went back to his desk and found his thermal imaging gun. He turned it on and surveyed the glove box. A good dose of ambient heat interfered with the reading near the right side of the box, but the sample itself contained no living dust. The rest of the chamber appeared safe.

Despite the readings, he and Siyang agreed it was a good idea to suit up before opening the box. As he pulled on his positive pressure suit and set up his respirator, his excitement level rose. He and Siyang took turns inspecting each other's suits. Satisfied, they returned to the glove box. Craig had opened the hatch and moved to remove the slide when Siyang stopped him.

"When's the last time you prepared a sample for a scanning electron microscope?"

"Not for years. I'm always looking up at the stars."

Siyang had been right to stop him. A sample this

small had to be viewed through an electron microscope because light microscopes couldn't magnify close enough. The preparation was labor intensive, and while Craig remembered most of the steps, he didn't want to risk messing it up. Part of him even had to admit the shake in his hands wasn't from nerves, but from desperately needing a drink.

No. There was too much riding on this. He turned over the lead to her and assumed the role of lab assistant.

"Let's get it prepared for sputtering," she directed. "Get me a sample mount, carbon tape, scissors, compressed air, and a spatula. I'll pull out the machine."

While he retrieved the necessary items, Siyang set up the sputtering machine on one of their rolling tables. He noticed how confident she was in hooking up the argon tank. He was lucky she knew what she was doing. He hadn't prepped a sample for SEM since college.

He also couldn't help but find her skill incredibly beautiful.

They met at a worktable, where Craig spread out the items she needed. She meticulously prepared the slide with textbook perfection. Once it was done, she took it to the K550 sputter coater.

Looking at the smudge on the sample mount, Craig felt a chill run down his spine like a drip of ice water. "It's hard to believe this stuff is capable of killing people."

"Not to me. In my field of work, things invisible to the naked eye are the scariest monsters." Siyang set the prepared sample in the K500. "Is it all coming back to you yet, Doc?"

Craig appreciated her trying to lighten the mood. It worked. A little. He couldn't pass up a chance to prove his intellect. "Some of it. We'll pump argon into the vacuum chamber, and then the DC voltage between the top and bottom of the chamber will ionize the gas—"

"Between the target and substrate, you mean," she interrupted. "Sorry, I'm a stickler for proper terminology."

He rolled his eyes, but a smile was tugging at his lips. "The voltage ionizes the argon atoms and creates a plasma. The charged argon ions are accelerated to the gold. From there, the collision will eject gold atoms, which will eventually settle on the sample."

"I'm impressed. You aren't as rusty as I thought. Check the pressure on the argon, will you?"

"We're at 30psi."

"Starting the sequence," she announced.

The machine came to life as the pump worked to create a vacuum in the cylinder. The coating process began. It didn't take long. As the sputtering gas became ionized, a plasma formed. It glowed a soft, lavender shade that stretched from the top lid to the base. It was impossible to see the atoms of gold coating the dust, of course, but the plasma glow was kind of pretty. It was also thrilling. In a few minutes, they'd get their first look at the dust under the microscope.

They let the machine run. When it was finished, it automatically shut off. The purge light illuminated, and the chamber was vented. Siyang removed the sample mount and they took it to the SEM station. The microscope itself was giant, almost three feet tall, and had to be set up on a specialized table. She turned on the user console beside the microscope.

"The pressure in the chamber is equalized," she said. "Go ahead and put in the sample."

Craig pulled open the drawer on the bottom of the microscope. He set the sample in its designated spot, a small raised platform on a metal tray. After he secured it and grounded it properly, he pushed the chamber door closed. Then he had to hold the door shut while Siyang reengaged the pump. The wait was killing him. He shifted foot to foot, wishing he could get out of the sweaty hazmat suit.

Siyang set up the viewing program on the user console, adjusting accelerating voltage and centering the sample.

"Vacuum okay. Opening the column valve and starting the beam." Something clicked inside the microscope. The screen in front of her showed a grainy black and white image. Nothing but noise. Every few seconds it clarified, the noise getting sharper, but no definite image appeared. "Adjusting the working distance. I'll have a better image in a second."

It took three more minutes before Siyang found the right position and beam settings. The image clarified.

"Jesus Christ," Craig gasped. The cup of coffee he'd drunk turned to acid and tried to crawl up his throat.

When he was a kid, he'd read *War of the Worlds*, and he'd always secretly hoped that one day the aliens would arrive—and that he'd be the one to greet them.

Now, however, blinding fear coursed through his entire being.

"What is that?" Siyang said.

"Nanotech," Craig said, his voice strangled. "They're nanobots."

# COLLEEN

Colleen inspected her progress on the makeshift blade. For hours she'd been sharpening the shiv she started the second Glen took her girls away. The frames of the cots were made of metal. Disassembly was easy; she used her shoe's heel to flatten out a bullet casing, turning it into a makeshift flathead screwdriver. The bar she scavenged from the cot's frame was long, and it had taken almost an hour of bending one piece back and forth before it snapped off into a more manageable size. Then she ground it against the concrete wall. It was tedious. Yet she finally had a weapon.

Satisfied with what she'd made, Colleen navigated around the mostly empty cots to Emerson. She sat across from him and reached out to tap him on the shoulder, then thought better of it. Instead, she called his name softly.

His eyes fluttered open. They were vacant a moment before they focused on Colleen.

"What's wrong?"

"Nothing," Colleen assured him. "I wanted to ask you something."

"She's with Benny. Your daughter. Every minute I was with them, he had your daughter by his side. He wouldn't let her leave."

Colleen clenched her jaw. Her mind raced as she thought of what they'd exposed Liana to. "I know she is. Did you see them hurt her?"

"No. I never saw anyone touch her. She just stood by

him while he watched us clear out the bodies. She was quiet. She…didn't seem upset by what she was seeing."

Colleen was grateful Liana was unaffected by what was going on around her, even if it was because of the dust. Or whatever had changed her. Colleen leaned in closer and lowered her voice. "I'm going to escape. I'm getting myself and my girls out of here."

Emerson pushed himself into a sitting position. "How?"

"I'll tell you, but first I have questions."

His brows furrowed. The cuts on his lip and face had scabbed over and the skin around his eyes was deeply bruised. Colleen tried not to look at them, and instead turned her gaze to her own hands in her lap.

"Okay," he said after a pause. "What do you want to know?"

Colleen took a deep breath. "Tell me what happened after they took you through the doors. Are there more guarding the other side?"

"No one was outside. The hallway was empty." Emerson paused. "They're in the teacher lounge all the way down the hall, then left, down another hall."

"Did you see anything along the way, like a room with the personal items they took from us? Or any kind of gear, hazmat suits, masks?"

Emerson eyed her. "Maybe. Some of the classrooms had junk in them. Suitcases, piles of clothes. I don't remember exactly. They were behind me with a gun pointed at my head before they put me to work."

"Did you pass any other people on the way?" Colleen asked. "Inside other classrooms, like a quarantined area or anything?"

He shook his head. "No. Listen, if you're trying to grab gear and escape, it won't work. They have a pipe they run through the door handles on the other side to keep it closed.

You can't get out of here unless someone takes you out."

"I've…" Colleen cleared her throat. She couldn't believe what she was about to say. "I've seen women approach guards when they come out to check on us. They're offering themselves for extra rations."

Emerson frowned and placed his hand on her shoulder. "It won't work. You're hungry and tired. You have no weapons. You can't overpower him out there. You wish you could. I know. Plus, if there's a struggle, the others might hear. There's at least *fifteen* of them. You don't want to make them angry."

A trace of defensiveness flared up in Colleen. "They took my *children*. I don't care about making them angry. I don't have anything to lose. I'd rather die trying to get them back than do nothing at all."

"You're right." Emerson withdrew his hand back under the blanket. "If there's one thing I believe, it's that death is better than waiting here with them."

"I'm sorry, Emerson," Colleen said. "I didn't mean to snap at you. You were brave going back there to help them for those MREs. You helped a lot of kids."

Emerson was not convinced and dismissed the apology and gratitude. "What's your plan, then?"

"I'm going to offer myself." Colleen tried to swallow that lump in her throat again. "I took a cot apart and have a piece of the frame, like they did. I've been filing it against the concrete. I'm going to stab him with it, take his gun, find gear, get the girls, and get out of here."

"Let's say your plan works. What about us? What about everyone else?"

Colleen looked around the gym. There were families just like hers that were suffering. They were scared. Maybe some had aspirations of escaping, but with the dust outside and the enemy within, what were they to do?

"I'll do everything I can to get them out," she found herself saying. She regretted it the moment the words slipped out. How could she possibly keep that promise?

Emerson nodded. "All the MREs are piled up in the teacher's lounge. After we finished moving the bodies, they told us to go pick some. I found something else back there and took it. They would've killed me if they caught me."

Emerson glanced around. Satisfied no one was looking, he reached under his pillow and slid something shiny out. It was a pocket knife about three inches long.

Colleen's pulse quickened, this time with excitement. She closed her hand around it and slipped it into her jean pocket. The irony of her spending hours making a shiv, only to be given a pocket knife, would've been funny if the circumstances weren't so dire.

"They must've left it there. Take it." Emerson squeezed her eyes shut. "I hope you get out. I really do."

Colleen nodded. She was about to thank Emerson for everything when the doors to the gym flung open. Colleen was grateful it wasn't any of Glen's men that she'd dealt with before. That would help her plan go smoother.

She walked to the doors. She didn't look back. She couldn't or she might change her mind. When she arrived at the door, the man grinned.

"How can I help you, sweetheart?"

Colleen laid her hand on his shoulder and smiled.

# LARA

Lara watched Dan take another swig of vodka. The liquid sloshed and made a single *glug* noise before he set it back on his lap. It was hard to believe the lunatic tricked her, but in retrospect these kind of men were her kryptonite. It was obvious to everyone except her what kind of person they were. They knew how to play her, how to play everyone.

Looking back now, she could see where she went wrong with him. She was too trusting. She took in his sob story like a kitten to milk. The therapist in her had wanted to help him. The maternal side had wanted to take care of him. He'd struck a deadly chord inside of her that made her throw logic to the wind.

Lara forgave herself for it because right then, she needed to figure out how to escape. Self-loathing wouldn't do her any good. Dan was becoming drunker by the second. All she had to do was push him over the edge and then she would try to slide the scissors from the pharmacy bag over to her. She could reach if she stretched her legs out as far as possible; she was sure of it.

In her practice, she had learned the art of guiding patients to breakthroughs while being respectfully inquisitive of their limits. It required a high level of perception and many sessions. She had to ask the right questions so that the patient came to the realization themselves, even if she saw the answer miles beforehand, because that way was more powerful and meaningful to them.

But there was another way to trigger a breakthrough or

dredge up memories. In her opinion, it was manipulative and unethical, and ultimately ineffective for therapeutic healing. Negative character traits were easy to exploit. In the case of a power-hungry narcissist like Dan, Lara knew if she could keep him talking he would keep drinking. If he kept drinking, eventually he'd pass out.

"Shit, I don't know," he rambled. "They kept finding reasons to put me in the box until finally they just kept me in there all the time. Stayed there a long while. Two years. They let me out once a day to piss and shit because they didn't want to stink up the house. Dropped in scraps of their leftovers like I was some kind of dog."

Dan brought the bottle up to his face. The rim was bloody, and he looked at the red stain as though he was just noticing it for the first time. He tore his glove off and dabbed at his mouth. It took every bit of will Lara had not to gag. Dan's lips were like Play-Doh, misshapen and swollen, mottled black and red. He took a drink anyway.

*Good*, Lara thought. *Keep going.*

"How did you get out?" she asked.

"Just, like, escaped one day when they let me out. Mama was watching me but something was burning in the kitchen, so she left me for a second and I ran out the door." Dan's eyes were hooded with heavy lids. His face was slack. "You're a fucking nice piece of ass. I would tear you up. You'd like that, wouldn't you?"

Repulsed, Lara ignored him and quickly turned him back to the subject at hand. "Where did you go after that? Eleven years old, that's young to be on your own."

"I ran. Kept running until I couldn't hear Mama screaming anymore." Dan took another deep swig from the bottle. It was almost empty. His speech was slurred, his movements slowed as if under water. Between the alcohol and the cough syrup, he was on the brink of passing out.

"Weren't you afraid she'd find you again? That she'd find you and put you back in that metal box?"

A wet gurgle caught in the back of Dan's throat. His body slumped forward, veering to the left, and suddenly he was lying on his side. His bloody face left an imprint on the linoleum. Lara wasn't sure if it was pus or tears leaking from his eyes. Maybe both. The liquid made his aquamarine sclera sparkle.

"I was scared. Shit, I was so afraid. I'm still afraid they'll come and put me back in. I wanted to kill 'em you know? Fucking cut their legs off so they'd fit in the box and *then* they'd know. But I was afraid, dammit. I was so fucking afraid." Dan used his left arm to push himself upright again. He finished off the bottle and threw it against the wall behind Lara.

Lara couldn't help but jump as the bottle shattered, but she quickly schooled her face into a neutral expression.

"You must have been very brave," she said.

Dan's face shifted into a sneer. "You fucking with me? You doing your shrink mind games? I've been here before, bitch, I know what you're doing. You think you're so smart. I'm going to fuck the smart right out of you." He bared his teeth in a feral grin. "I'll put you in your place. You'll fucking like it, too. You'll beg for it."

Dan tried to stand and unbuckle his pants. The task proved too difficult, and he fell to his knees. A coughing fit overtook him. Chunky bits and blood splattered everywhere as he coughed. He wiped his face and leaned against the stove.

*Go to sleep*, Lara repeated in her head. *Just go to sleep, Dan.*

"Can't get it up anyway. But you know what I can do?" His head lolled in a circle a few times until he caught it and stared straight at her. "I can make you squirm. I can make you hate me even more so when I take you, all you can think about is how bad you fucked up."

Lara's anxiety quadrupled. He'd drunk half a bottle of vodka mixed with cough syrup. Surely that was enough. She had no chance of getting those scissors unless he passed out.

"What my folks did to me, that's nothin' compared to what I did. This older guy named Stewart took me in and helped me out when I ran away. I hung with him for a few years. He was a pedo, you know? He was so high one day, I convinced him we should snatch us a kid. Stewart had this cage." Dan tried to show her the size of the cage by opening his arms wide. "Used to keep his dog in it, but the dog ran away. So we kidnap this little brat and put her in there. Just like my folks did to me. Now *I* was the one in control. I decided when she could come out, what we'd do to her."

Lara froze, horror churning her gut. Dan killed Jack's daughter. She couldn't process the realization. Not now. Not when her own life was on the line. She filed it away and focused.

"What did you do, Dan?"

"Stewart the pedo just wanted to take pictures and shit. Like, why go to all the trouble of kidnapping the little bitch if you ain't gonna use her up? He got spooked and split. Kids aren't really my thing, but I showed her what was what. Stupid fucker took the fall because it was his trailer they found the girl in. Got out on some bullshit technicalities, but bottom line is no one caught me. I've killed lots of people, but that little girl was the best. I want you to know, when I'm giving it to you, that's what I'll be thinking about. I'm gonna be remembering what I did to her, and then I'm gonna do ten times worse to you."

Dan laughed. Then his eyes dropped and his head lolled back. In moments he was snoring.

The breath Lara had been holding finally released. She choked back a sob, thought better of trying to repress it, and let herself weep for a full minute. After a long inhale, she straightened up. Jack obviously didn't know that Dan had been Stewart's accomplice, otherwise he would've killed Dan the second he saw him. Lara typically liked the phrase "small world" because it implied a sense of interconnectivity between humanity. Now, it seemed like a sick joke. She stared at Dan's unconscious form, his face slick with pustules and blood, and wished he would choke to death on his own vomit.

The contents of the pharmacy bags were scattered around him. The scissors were in their packaging right by Dan's hip. Lara didn't have long legs, but she believed if she arched her back and kicked out, she might be able to land her heel on the scissors and pull them over.

She gathered her energy up and tried to execute the move. Her heel landed at least a foot short. Her boot hit the ground with a loud thump that made Dan shift in his sleep and mumble something incoherent. A muscle in her lower back clenched and sent searing hot pain all the way up to her neck. She sucked air between her clenched teeth and waited out the spasm.

"Okay," she whispered, trying to boost her own confidence. "I can figure this out."

She tried one more time, her heel landing a little closer but nowhere near close enough. She just didn't have the necessary reach. Lara craned her neck to assess what was behind her. There were some shards of glass nearby, but those were even more out of her reach than the scissors.

What if she moved the table? The thing was vintage hardwood. When Lara tried to scoot forward and drag the table with her, it budged an eighth of an inch at most. Her hands hurt from the duct tape, which was cutting off her circulation. No matter. An eighth of an inch was hope. It was an eighth of an inch closer to the scissors.

She flexed her muscles and bucked her entire body. The table slid forward another half an inch. Dan shifted but didn't wake up. Lara flung herself forward as hard as she could two more times and then tried kicking out again.

Her heel struck the scissors. She bent her knee and carefully dragged them toward her until her knee was up to her chest. She wiggled, fighting the duct tape as she shifted the scissors under her butt until they were at her hands. She finally managed to pick up the package of scissors. Lara tore into it, hoping she could get the right angle to cut her tape, knowing that freedom was only a few seconds away.

That was when Dan woke up.

# JACK

The first breeze Jack had seen since the comet hit rustled the trees and yellow dust fell from them, shimmering in the sunlight as it drifted to the ground. All was incredibly still and quiet. Jack knew he had to keep moving if he wanted to find Lara and Dan, but the scene made him stop.

One summer when he was a kid, his family had made it a summer project to clean out the attic. There had been so much dust floating in the air as they worked. Seven-year-old Jack had thought it was magical, the way it swirled and moved in the slightest shift of air. His sister, on the other hand, had terrible allergies and her nose ran and her eyes watered. At that age, Jack was amused by that, too. Nothing quite like a snotty, miserable older sister to lift a young boy's spirit.

When the task was done, his mother had packed a picnic with his favorite homemade potato salad, ham and Swiss sandwiches, and orange soda. They'd enjoyed the picnic on the front lawn in the warm summer evening.

That sensation of being a tourist in his own life popped up again, as though part of him were watching the memory like it was a movie and it was his first time seeing it. He hadn't thought of that summer in years. Jack hadn't thought of *any* good memories in years. It was much easier to dwell on Katie, on his failed marriage, on his miserable life. His brain had wallowed in negativity for so long, the mere taste of something pleasantly nostalgic made him dizzy.

Jack let the memory linger as he continued walking.

He'd been following the route to the FEMA camp and hadn't seen any sign of Dan or Lara. More than once, he considered backtracking but decided against it. They could have gone anywhere. His best guess was the camp, so that's where he would go.

Suddenly, light surged in his eyes, and Jack collapsed. The hard connection between his knees and the ground traveled sharply up and down his legs. More memories flooded him in rapid succession, against his will, some of the moments ones he couldn't possibly remember.

His mother nursing him, her face smiling down on him. His first step, the sensation of shaggy brown carpet beneath his baby feet.

Riding his bike, making his first best friend. The first girl he kissed.

Guilt and desperation while he stole glances off someone else's calculus test in high school.

Jack tried to gain control of the spiraling visions. He was weak in comparison to the force within him. The unseen intruder in his mind barreled forward, violating his memories.

Katie's body in the morgue.

Colleen giving him her last, pitiful goodbye.

Killing Stewart. Killing the raiders. The urge to kill Dan.

The images shifted. Jack was in a black void where three dimensional symbols flashed before him. They were complex dashes, dots, and curves. None made sense to him. After a dozen appeared, they changed. They were more familiar, perhaps Japanese characters.

Flash. Arabic.

Flash. Russian.

As soon as Jack recognized the letter A, he saw a B, then a C, then darkness.

Outlines appeared. A human figure. A smiley face. A

knife.

Jack's pulse quickened at the sight of the gun. Then the images worsened.

Handgun. Grenade. Rifle. Warhead.

Warmth spread from the base of his skull into his body. His pulse slowed to a regular beat, and the tingling in his limbs lessened to a tolerable level. The void in his head remained empty. No more symbols or images appeared.

His vision came back slowly, turning from blackness to blinding white light and then fading until the dust-covered world returned. The sensation of a visitor inside him was stronger than ever. It was like someone was watching him, but whenever he looked he couldn't spot them.

He then noticed his face no longer itched. The throbbing in his knees was gone. In fact, his body felt *good*. He wasn't tired or stressed. On an intellectual level, that disturbed Jack, but his unease couldn't dim his overall feeling of good health.

Somewhere in the distance Jack heard rumbling. It was faint at first and hard to tell what direction it came from. Eventually he realized it was coming from behind him and it was the sound of engines. *Raiders.* Now that there was less dust in the air, they were probably out looking for victims.

Jack searched for somewhere to hide. He stumbled down into a ditch beside the highway, his boots slipping on the dust, and made his way into the surrounding forest. He cursed the obvious trail he left behind. If the raiders were in vehicles, maybe they'd be going too fast to notice.

He took cover behind a wide pine tree. His heartbeat was steady, his thoughts clear. In less than a minute, the vehicles rolled by. They looked military, but Jack wasn't convinced. Not after what he'd seen. First two Humvees went by, then a troop carrier. None of the vehicles had any telltale signs of raiders—no emblems, nothing.

Another pair of Humvees rolled by. The second had a mounted gun on the roof and was manned by a soldier in full hazmat gear. What if they were headed to the FEMA camp? What if they were actual soldiers?

What if civilization was clawing itself out of the chaos?

Screeching brakes drew Jack out of his thoughts. A Humvee had stopped on the highway just across from him. It was another gun-mounted vehicle.

"Hey!" the soldier on top yelled. "Anyone back there?"

Jack stood and walked slowly from behind the tree, his arms raised.

"Set your weapons down," the soldier ordered, "Then come up here."

Jack obeyed. He threw down the sawed-off shotgun. Not that the soldier knew, but there were handguns in his pack. He set the pack down, too. He couldn't do anything about the gun under the suit.

After Jack climbed the ditch, another soldier exited the Humvee. It was dusty inside, and Jack caught a glimpse of the other troops. They all wore hazmat gear.

When the new soldier spoke, his voice sounded amplified. His gas mask had a microphone built in. "Are you injured?"

"No." In fact, he felt like he was twenty again.

"Where you headed?"

"FEMA camp," Jack said. He was aware of how loud he had to speak through his own low-tech respirator. "I'm trying to find my friends."

The soldier nodded. "We're headed there to see if there are any survivors, then going farther south. You wanna hitch a ride, you can. Stay here and the troop carrier will grab you."

"Where are you going after that?"

"About eighty miles south from here, there's no dust.

You'll understand when you see it, man. It's some weird shit." The soldier shifted from foot to foot. "We gotta get moving. Just stay here if you want to hitch a ride on the carrier."

The soldier was getting back in the Humvee when Jack asked, "Hey, do you guys know what happened?"

The soldier shrugged. "Hell if I know. All I know is that furlough is over and it's time to get back to work. Feel me?"

He pulled the door shut. Jack stepped away from the vehicle and watched it drive away. He waited until the troop carrier arrived, and before he could second-guess himself, hopped on.

# COLLEEN

The hallway was cool and quiet compared to the gym. At one end was the door leading out to the front courtyard. The doors had been covered in plastic before, but the men must've stripped them at some point. Bright sunlight shone into the hallway. It glistened where it caught on the metal handles of lockers. The last time Colleen had seen outside, the dust was so thick she could barely see ten feet in front of her. Now it was settled on the ground like an alien snowfall.

There was dried blood going up and down the checkered linoleum. The doors to the classrooms were open.

Colleen was too aware of a faint tingling in her hands and lips. Nerves. The more she focused on the feeling, the more lightheaded she became. She staved off the panic and took a slow breath through her nose.

The man had a shotgun in his right hand, the butt pressed into his shoulder and barrel pointed at the ground. He used his left hand to pick up a metal pipe beside the doors and thread it through the handles. He didn't seem concerned with her.

That bolstered her confidence. Hunger and weakness be damned, she had a mother's courage on her side. She kept her arms hanging loosely, her hands by her pockets. Her right hand itched to grab the knife and try to take him right then.

No. It had to be at the right moment, when she could do it quickly and effectively use her element of surprise.

"Hey, baby. I know things are tough these days," the

man said, drawing her attention. He wore an expression Colleen thought was meant to be attractive but ended up looking stupid. "It's easy to feel lonely, right?"

*You can do this,* she told herself. *You have to do this.*

"Definitely." She pitched her voice a little higher and tried to sound sexy. "You're doing a good job though, around the camp. I'm glad you took this place from the soldiers. They didn't know what they were doing."

He rubbed his bearded jaw with the palm of his left hand, his eyebrows raised. "Hm. Guess you're coming around. Benny said you would, but I didn't think it'd happen."

Colleen took advantage of the moment and sauntered over to the classroom. She leaned against the doorway and peeked inside. She hoped it looked casual and coy. At first glance, she didn't see any suits or respirators. It all appeared to be personal belongings.

"Hey, why don't you come here for a second, sweetheart?"

Her stomach twisted. She suppressed the urge to vomit and walked closer to him. Fluttered her lashes and pouted. "Sure. Why don't you set that big gun down? It's kind of scary."

The man looked at the shotgun hanging in his arm. He set it on the ground. His eyes were hooded as he stepped towards her. "Aw, no problem. Benny don't let us have bullets anyway. Worried we're gonna try and kill him or some shit the kid told him."

*The kid.* Colleen's heartbeat fluttered.

He reached out and fondled her chest through her shirt. His hand trailed to the hem and he lifted it. His rough touch was repulsive, but she made herself lean into it. She took his head and pulled it to her chest. The scent of greasy, unwashed hair and body odor almost made her gag.

"Mmph." The man mumbled into her cleavage, both hands now groping her.

While he was distracted, Colleen reached into her pocket for the knife. The man was pawing clumsily at her, clearly pleased with the exciting turn of events. She made herself moan to cover the soft *click* when she opened the blade.

The knife went in easier than she had anticipated. It sunk into the soft flesh of his neck just below the ear before meeting cartilage and bone. Colleen pushed harder until every inch of the blade was buried. She heard things popping and crunching beneath the skin as she wiggled the knife back and forth to make sure the job was done right.

He flung himself away from her and fell on his butt. Blood spurted from his neck when he jerked out the knife. It cascaded over his fingers and down his chest, mixing with the old blood on the ground.

"Help!" It was nothing more than a gurgle, but his cry sent Colleen into motion.

She dropped to her knees beside him and covered his mouth. She directed all her bodyweight into her hands. He fought. She held on. She felt his movements grow weaker until finally he stilled.

Her hands were drenched in blood. She tried to wipe it away on the clean bits of the man's shirt but it had stained her hands. Cleaning them was a waste of time. She stood and listened. Nothing from down the hallway.

Then the reality hit her. She had just killed a man. She dropped back to her knees and vomited what little food she had. It splattered and mixed with the muck already on the ground. The sight of it made her heave again.

Liana. Serena. Gabriela. She thought of the girls, of Emerson, of *everyone*. She had to keep fighting. Colleen got to her feet again.

There was no way to know how long the others would wait before they came looking for their missing friend, so she had to act fast. She reached underneath the dead man's shoulders and hauled him towards the classroom. He was heavy and the task was difficult. She'd only moved him a foot before she had to stop and take a breather. This, too, was a waste of time.

She checked the classrooms. The one with all the personal belongings was a mess. Suitcases were piled in stacks of ten or more against the walls. Backpacks lay in heaps. She looked around for her family's packs, but there were too many.

Colleen remembered the clear air outside. Worst-case scenario, they could layer on clothing and make a run for it. It wasn't ideal. In fact, they probably couldn't run because it would kick up dust. A fast walk. They could cover their faces, make sure their cuffs were sealed.

The farther down the hallway she went, the more anxious she became. Each step took her closer to where Emily had said the teacher's lounge was. She darted into the next open classroom. What she saw made her laugh and sob at once, choking her with joyful tears.

Hazmat suits were folded over desks. Heaps of them. Some looked brand new, while others showed minimal signs of use. They looked like the ones the soldiers gave out to people when they first rescued them.

There were enough to get every person in the gym out of the school and on their way to somewhere else. Anywhere else.

Colleen picked out four in good condition.

All she had to do was get the girls out of there. She'd tell the others the door was open and where the hazmat suits were. Beyond that, their fate was their own responsibility. She dragged four suits out of the classroom and headed back to the gym.

"Colleen?"

She froze. The voice called out to her again. It was female. Barely more than a whisper. Colleen turned slowly and looked for the source. The door to one of the classrooms was ajar. She hadn't searched the rest since she found what she was looking for.

"Colleen, please."

Nearly every part of her told her to keep going. She went to the door anyway and pressed it open.

The windows were partially uncovered. Something about the clarity of light accentuated Belman's ashen gray skin—what little of it there was left. She was naked and strapped to a desk chair. Colleen's gaze locked on to Belman's left thigh. So much skin had sloughed off there was nothing but muscle showing beneath a lattice of black rot.

"I thought they killed you."

"Wish they...wish they woulda." A thin stream of bloody drool slipped from Belman's lips. "Tossed me around in the dust after they had their way. Funny thing about it. Your kid. The little one..."

"Liana?" Colleen glanced out the door. Still, no one had come. She slipped inside and knelt in front of Belman. "What about her?"

"Shit it hurts," she gritted. Her eyes fluttered. Colleen wanted to touch her to help her stay focused, but didn't want to touch any part of the poor woman.

"Belman, please tell me, what did you see?"

"I tried to lie. Tried...tell them backup was coming. Fucking kid called me out. Then they...they knew..."

The dust. The dust had changed her little girl. Colleen took the sight of the broken soldier before her. "What can I do, Belman?"

Miniscule flecks of blood hit Colleen's face when Belman coughed. "Kill those fuckers."

"I'll try. I swear I'll try. I promise."

Belman's chin dropped to her chest. Colleen thought she was dead until she spoke again. "Lunch...49. Lunch in 49, okay?"

The soldier wheezed. She was delirious and began to ramble. "Basics, private. Remove safety clip. Grip it, pull the ring out. Pull hard. Keep your grip on it until you can throw. Couple seconds. Take cover."

"Hey, it's okay. It'll be over soon," Colleen whispered.

"Fucking camp...I swear to God..."

Belman's body jerked violently against her restraints, then she slumped. Her head lolled back. She was still.

Colleen stared at the dirty, blood streaked ground. How could she possibly think she could do this? She was one woman with a shiv. Belman, the soldiers; they were trained and had guns and still, they couldn't fight Benny and his men.

She stood and lingered in the doorway, attempting to battle the sense of defeat consuming her. Her gaze followed the winding blood trail down the hallway where her daughters might be.

*Lunch in 49.*

Colleen took a deep breath, calmed her nerves as much as she could, and looked at the lockers. Was Belman trying to tell her something? Maybe they weren't delirious dying rants.

She set the hazmat suits in the doorway and scanned for locker 49. It was close to the teacher's lounge and had a smear of bloody handprints on the handle. Colleen expected it to be locked, but as she tugged on the door, it gave freely.

Inside was a pink and white striped lunch bag with

the name *Krissy* embroidered on it. And another smear of blood. Hope swelling, she opened it.

Inside was a handgun and an extra magazine. And a grenade. Colleen looked up and down the hallway, checking again to ensure she was alone, then withdrew the grenade. It was heavier than it looked. She studied it. She'd seen one before, an inactive one that had belonged to her dad, and identified the safety clip.

*Kill those fuckers. Lunch in 49.*

"Wayne, where the fuck are you?"

Footsteps drew near. Colleen kept the grenade in her right hand and the gun in her left. It was her non-dominant hand, but she'd shot with it before. None other than Glen came around the corner.

He had a gun and he pointed it at her but didn't shoot. She kept her left hand strong as she pointed her own at him.

"What the hell? Is that a fucking *grenade*?" He looked past her. When his jaw dropped, she assumed he'd spotted the body of his buddy in the hallway.

"I know you don't have any bullets," Colleen stated. She tried to keep her voice calm. "I do. And yes, it is a grenade."

Granted, it wasn't armed yet. But Glen didn't know that. She hoped.

"Bitch," Glen spat. "Put it down before you hurt yourself."

"*You* can't tell *me* what to do. Put the gun down and slide it over here."

"It's empty."

"I don't care. Do it."

He obeyed and slid the rifle across the floor. It only made it halfway.

"How many of you are in the lounge?"

"Ten," he said. "Lost a couple to difference in opinion."

Colleen was trying to decide what to do next when Benny came around the corner and shot her.

# DAN

Fucking bitch. Dan was out one second! *One second*! Despite a kick to the fucking face, Lara's hands were still working to open the package in her hand. Dan crawled over, the vodka and cough syrup still in full force in his system, and snatched it away. Scissors. The little kind, no bigger than his middle finger.

Dan snickered. "Trying to escape?"

She said nothing.

"Well? What did you think you were going to do with these? You really think you could cut through all that tape?"

Again, no reply.

That made Dan angry. If there was one thing he couldn't stand, it was other people making a stand. He couldn't take her to Hedone all wild like this. She had to be broken. A girl like this, you had to make her think she had a chance. Make her confident. Then tear her down and show her who was boss.

Finally, he felt his dick perk up.

Dan tore open the package and held the scissors in front of her face. Lara's eyes followed them as he moved them left and right. He pressed the tip into her cheek and savored her tears and whimpering. A fat droplet of blood trailed down her cheek. Dan smiled.

"I'll make you a bet. You cut yourself free in thirty seconds, you can try to run."

He set them by her hands.

She probably thought he'd lost it. He hadn't. There was

no fucking way she could get through all those layers with the tiny scissors in thirty seconds. When she failed, she'd give up hope. She'd see there was no use in trying. *Then* he'd break her in.

"One, two, three ..."

Lara grabbed the scissors. Dan watched in amusement as she tried to get them into the right position to start cutting.

He sat back against the wood stove and closed his eyes while he scratched his face. Just for a second. He wouldn't fall asleep like last time. No way. It felt so good to scratch off the gummy, itchy shit on his skin. He kept going until he felt something hard on his cheek.

Holy shit. That was bone. His eyes fluttered open. Lara was still cutting away at the duct tape. She'd made progress. Not enough. Dan forgot where he'd been counting, so he picked up at ten again.

"You shrinks are all the same. You get off on mindfucking people, but when the tables are turned it ain't so good, is it?" Dan laughed. "Your time is up, Lara."

"No," she said. The bitch was *smiling*. "No, I'm not going to give up. You know why?"

Dan fidgeted. He didn't like the way she looked at him. "Why?"

"I'm going to cut your prick off with these."

Dan's stomach churned. His brain was fuzzy with the cough syrup and vodka. For a moment, his vision blurred. "W-what did you just say?"

"You heard me," Lara shouted. Her hands had been working furiously on the duct tape the whole time. She pulled herself free and stood, brandishing the scissors at him. "Your mother told me to cut your tiny prick off with these scissors."

Dan was in the box again, wallowing in the scent of

his own piss, shit, and fear. Hungry, afraid. Not that. He couldn't go back to that. He wouldn't. He needed to be a good boy or his mama would punish him.

"God, no. I'll be good. I swear!"

"Okay, okay. Calm down. I'll tell your mama not to put you in the box as long as you behave. You just have to stay here and be quiet. I'm going to leave to tell her now, okay, Dan?"

He began to sob. Long, shuddering sobs that tore things loose in his chest. Tears stung his bloodied face.

Then something caught in his throat and sent him into a coughing fit. He rolled onto his hands and knees, hacking like a cat with a hairball. Blood splattered on the floor. A lot of blood. Too much blood, then a big chunk of something. It looked like a piece of raw liver, but he thought it was part of his lung.

For the first time, he started to wonder if he wasn't going to make it to Hedone.

Dan looked around the kitchen and found the door to the back yard. He dragged himself to it. He'd see the sun one last time before he went. At least he could do that. He could see the sun set. Feel the fresh air. Have one last second of freedom before the box took him forever. That's all he'd ever wanted, really. People never understood. These uptight bitches, the jackasses, they didn't get it.

The world flickered. He saw faint symbols, faces, and letters. It didn't make sense. He wanted them to go away. Darkness pulsated at the edges of his vision. He took one last breath, and just as his fingers touched the doorknob, the void swallowed him whole.

# CRAIG

Craig wasn't the first to say it, but he sure as hell was the first to say it with scientific backup. Irrefutable proof.

Extraterrestrial life existed. *Aliens* existed.

The nanobots weren't exactly little green men, but they were undeniably alien.

He rubbed his face, palm rasping against overgrown beard. He tried to remember the last time he had eaten in the past twenty-four hours and didn't have an answer.

Before him an assortment of photos were spread across his desk. Each contained images of the nanobots. Their bodies, two nanometers thick, were oblong with a set of claw-like protrusions at both ends. Smaller tentacles, almost cilia-like, filled the space between the claws. Their exterior was unexpectedly smooth, with almost no bumps or cracks despite having been burned.

They were bug-like little monsters and hundreds of them were interlocked into small pods.

Siyang wanted a transmission electron microscope to conduct further study. If they could section a sample of the nanobots, they could get a look at the dust's inner workings. The TEM was higher resolution and could show morphology, crystallization, stress, and magnetic domains.

Whatever they were made of, it was resilient. He and Siyang had run three more samples, eventually cranking the oven all the way to its max temperature. Only at the highest temperature did the nanodes disintegrate, and it still took five minutes.

At least there was hope. Tim's incinerators would work if they got them hot enough.

Craig shook his head in wonder. Alien nanotechnology. It explained everything in a bewildering, harrowing sort of way. The comet had to be a ship. It had stopped itself because it didn't want to destroy the planet it was going to take over. Or study. Or whatever it was it intended to do.

Humans were decades away from creating nanobots this powerful, and that was if Craig was being optimistic. There had been small advances in the field—Craig allowed himself a chuckle at that—but none were at this level. In fact, the closest thing humans had created to a functioning nanobot so far was too big to even be *considered* a nanobot. It was a macrobot.

Most scientists thought of nanobots as machine versions of bacteria. Many practical applications were medical. They'd be inserted into the bloodstream and function on a molecular level. Destroying cancer, repairing cells, and eliminating genetic disorders were just a few uses.

Where these scientists stumbled was in creating a nanobot small enough to do what they wanted. To create a microscopic machine made entirely out of electromechanical components wasn't an easy feat. They had to have transporting mechanisms, an energy source, and some kind of internal processor. Current technology simply didn't support shrinking these components to nanoscale.

This discovery was astounding but also troubling. Nanobots were created with a purpose. Somewhere inside they had code telling them what to do. Craig couldn't fathom how to figure out what that intent was.

"Here. Eat something." Siyang set down a plate of rubbery eggs and a steaming Styrofoam cup of black tea. They'd been out of coffee for two days, putting Craig in an

even worse mood. "We can't think straight if we're hungry."
*I can't think straight if I'm sober,* Craig thought darkly.
He'd been out of booze long enough to be feeling the agony of withdrawal.

The small talk was surreal. Craig managed a bite of eggs—they were definitely powdered—and then cradled the warm cup in his hands as he thought. The scouting mission Berg sent into the DZ had returned shortly after Craig and Siyang's discovery. They'd retrieved fragments of the comet's crust from the outskirts of Seattle. The crust, at twenty-four meters deep, was built-up debris on a substrate of something else. On the outside, it looked like a comet. Pockmarked, stony. Chip away all that, however, and there was a smooth convex surface, definitely part of a bigger sphere. It looked like metal. On the concave side were complex grooves and indentations for what he guessed was wiring or mechanics of some kind.

Whatever had been in those grooves was gone. There were scorch marks, which led him to believe it might have burned up when it entered Earth's atmosphere.

Tim had promised a dozen portable containerized incinerators, which should arrive within the next two days, with more on the way as soon as he could round them up. Nonessential personnel were being evacuated to the refugee camp an hour south. Craig wasn't sure where they were putting the severely infected patients; Berg said it was a need-to-know situation.

What in the hell were these nanobots doing? Craig blinked slowly before regaining control of his spiraling thoughts.

"What were you saying?" he asked Siyang.

"All missions entering the DZ have been cancelled. We won't be retrieving any more of the comet until we get the go ahead from the Secretary of Defense."

He forced himself to take another bite of eggs. "This thing is a spaceship, not a comet. They *made* it look like a comet to screw with us."

"Do you really think this is about us?" Siyang leaned back and stared at the tent's roof. She fiddled with her necklace as she spoke. "What I mean is, this really can't be personal. The beings that sent that dust, they don't have a vendetta against us. How could they? We didn't know they existed until now. We can't take it personally."

Frustrated, Craig set down his drink, shuffled the nanobot photos and then flipped them over. How could he *not* take it personally? Human existence was on the line. If that wasn't personal, he wasn't sure what was.

"That doesn't make me feel better," he said. "How are you so calm?"

Her hands rose in defense. "This is how I handle stress, with rationality."

"Well, it doesn't work for me. It's really fucking disturbing that it works for you." He downed the rest of his tea, and his stomach gurgled in protest. Even as he spoke the next words, he regretted them. A monstrous sense of hopelessness was in control of his mouth. "Is that why you never talk about your husband? I bet he didn't make it, and you can't even pretend to care."

Siyang's hand closed around the necklace resting against her chest. "That was unnecessary."

Guilt tried to needle its way into the anger building up inside him. He squashed it and stood. "I need to go for a walk."

Siyang let him go without another word. The cool night air felt good against his face, the fresh air calming him. With the dust almost totally settled and the sky dark, he needed to get closer if he wanted a better look at the DZ.

The same thoughts he'd had when he believed the world

was going to end started popping up again. The same sense of futility, of meaninglessness. Tim's incinerators would work, but it was only a temporary fix. Whoever sent the dust would certainly be keeping tabs on it. With their technology, they'd come back to finish whatever it was they wanted to do.

Craig found himself wandering the dirt path to the DZ. The dust glowed in the moonlight. A thick carpet of it coated everything in sight. It filled him with questions that had no immediate answers. How long did it take the aliens to make it? Were there more? What was it meant to do?

Did they care about all the people they killed? Not just from the dust, but before that, when humanity had imploded in the face of doomsday?

He searched around him for something to throw at the DZ and settled for his shoe. He tossed it as hard as he could. It landed with a soft plop and sent up a cloud of dust.

"Fuck you!" The other shoe came off. He threw it and achieved another two feet into the DZ. "I hope your planet gets hit by a real comet and you go extinct, you bastards!"

Turning on his heel, he started back to the camp. He'd only gone a few steps before he heard a hundred vibrating whispers speak behind him.

"What a cruel fate to wish upon anyone, Dr. Craig Peters."

# LARA

Lara hopped over Dan's prone form and grabbed the gun from the counter. The weapon was heavy and cold in her hands. She held it in front of her, ready to pull the trigger.

Then Dan took a final ragged breath and collapsed. As far as Lara was concerned, dying on his own instead of making her kill him was the only good thing he'd done in his life. She lowered the gun and plucked the car keys out of his pocket. Blood seeped from Dan's mouth and pooled around his head. His fingers twitched twice before going limp.

Dan had offered up all his triggers—his mother, the scissors, the threats—and Lara had taken advantage of them. She pushed him to give herself extra time, hoping he'd break down, but then kept pushing him because she wanted him to suffer.

It didn't matter. He was dead now, and she was free. He didn't deserve her pity.

She became aware of how hard her heart was beating. Dizziness swept over her. There was a tightness in her chest that had become painful. Lara exited the kitchen and went all the way to the staircase, where she plopped down and tried to stabilize her breathing.

Lara used to think all people were worth saving. Everyone had a seed of goodness inside them, and sometimes all it took was the right person to nurture it into something beautiful. She didn't think that any more.

Not after Dan. Maybe he'd been an innocent victim when he was a kid, but those experiences had shaped him into a monster.

Lara gathered all the supplies she could find. She discovered a first aid kit in the downstairs bathroom and cleaned her split lip where Dan kicked her and the wound from the scissors, and then carefully put her gear back on and tightened her respirator.

She cleared dust off the pickup and got in. It roared to life on the first try and handled well as she drove. She did not look back at the farmhouse once as she began her trek to the FEMA camp.

Nearly an hour later, a faint roaring overhead caught her attention. The sun was minutes away from setting, and the sky was ablaze in deep orange and red that faded into an inky indigo. Those colors were a relief from the ashy yellow she'd grown accustomed to. The forest and fields around her, still covered in dust, reflected the fiery sky. She came to a stop in the middle of the highway and peered out the windshield.

The sky was dotted with a fleet of black helicopters heading south.

The overwhelming sense of hope that began to consume her when she saw the helicopters vanished in an instant. Lara gripped the steering wheel tightly. Angry tears slipped from her eyes. It didn't matter that she'd survived. It was all for nothing.

She stared at the tear in her suit's wrist. Felt an uncomfortable itchiness that meant only one thing; somehow, at some point, her suit had been compromised. She'd been infected.

Lara took a deep breath. She screamed.

# COLLEEN

"What the fuck, Benny!" Glen screeched. "She's got a fucking grenade!"

The grenade in question was sitting beside Colleen's leg. Her limp, bleeding leg. She used both hands to press against the bullet hole in her right thigh. Her mind raced. She'd taken cover in Belman's room after she was shot, leaning against the wall beside the door. She'd lost the element of surprise.

"I didn't know that, you cocksucker! Where'd she get it?"

"Fuck if I know."

She heard footsteps. She freed one hand to grab the gun.

"I'm armed!" she shouted. "I've got a loaded gun and yeah, a grenade. I *will* use them."

The footsteps approaching her stopped, but more came from farther down the hall. A lot more. It had to be the rest of the men from the lounge.

"Okay, okay. Calm down. We aren't coming any farther," Benny said. "What do you want?"

Colleen broke out into crazed laughter. "You have to be kidding me."

"Right. Liana. You want her back."

"And Serena and Gabriela."

"Of course."

She pulled herself to the door and peeked around the corner. Liana stood in the middle of the hallway beside

Benny. She appeared unharmed. Serena and Gabriela stood behind Glen, their wrists taped together. Tears welled in Colleen's eyes. They all appeared unharmed. Her heart was beating so fast it felt like it was going to explode. She was doing it. She was going to save them.

Colleen tried to still her shaking hands. Nothing could calm the turbulence within her. This had to be a trick.

"Send them over here right now."

"We can talk about this. Liana is a very special girl. You know that. I know it. She's real useful and—"

"You send them the fuck back or we all die!"

Even as she said the words, Colleen knew it wasn't true. Obviously she wasn't going to throw the grenade and kill her own children. She could still bargain with the grenade and see how far it got her.

Then a voice echoed in her mind, almost as though she were dreaming.

*Don't give up, mom. I'll tell him you aren't lying. These are bad people. They do bad things. They should die.*

It was Liana. She could hear Liana talking in her head. She sounded different and grown up, but it was her. And it felt right. Somehow Colleen knew it was really her little girl talking in her head. Not only that, but what Liana suggested made all the sense in the world.

Benny laughed. "Is your mommy telling the truth? She gonna kill us all?"

Liana said, "Yes. She will kill everyone. Even me and my sister and Gabriela."

"Jesus, lady." He paused. "You're fucking insane. You'd kill your own kids? For what?"

*Say yes, mom. Yes.*

"I'd rather they were dead than in your hands. Here's what I want," Colleen began. "You send them back here right now. Then I want you to free every single person in this place. Give them the hazmat suits down the hallway and let them go. Give them some food first, then let them go."

The murmured conversation in the hall was too quiet for Colleen to hear. Her pulse was thundering in her ears so loudly it was almost deafening. The pain in her leg was fiery and sharp all at once.

"Well? Are you going to do it or do I have to blow this place?"

"You can't win this," Benny said. His voice was closer now. "I know it seems like you can, but you can't. You're not going to kill your kids. You've got nothing."

*Show them you are serious. We will live. Trust me, mom.*

Liana was right. Colleen needed to prove she wasn't bluffing. She jerked out the safety clip on the grenade. Her heart skipped a beat when she tore the pin out. Belman was right; it required a hard twist and pull. They made it look so much easier in the movies.

She cracked the door open and tossed the pin into the hall.

"Shit," one of them groaned.

"What is that?"

"The grenade's live, dumbass."

Colleen would've enjoyed making them afraid, but she *did* have a live grenade in her hand. She couldn't believe what she was doing. As soon as she let go, it would only be seconds before it exploded. She kept one hand on the grenade and the other against her leg. She was lightheaded from blood loss, but she couldn't let her concentration slip for even a moment.

*Good. Good work, mom.*

"You're going to put all your guns on the ground before I come out. Do you understand? And don't you dare try to make a run for it or I'll blow you to hell."

"Whatever you want, you stupid crazy bitch," Benny yelled.

Colleen waited until she heard the last clatter of a gun hitting the ground, then managed to stand. Her leg throbbed and threatened to cave under her. She peeked around the corner of the door and saw ten men standing in the hallway, unarmed. The girls had just arrived. Liana smiled and gave Colleen a reassuring nod.

"Mom, what are you going to do?" Serena cried. "What are you doing?"

"Keep going," Liana told her out loud in that too-grown-up voice.

Some part of Colleen was pained by the worried, frightened look on Serena and Gabriela's faces. They were afraid of little Liana, weren't they? Yet, wasn't she? Somehow, wasn't Colleen a little afraid of her baby girl? Liana's presence flared again, calming Colleen.

Serena began to cry and whimper. Liana turned her delicate head, held her sister's eyes, and in moments Serena was silent, her face slack. Gabriela was ashen. She remained quiet, eyes cast down.

"You." Colleen used her grenade-clenched fist to point at the nearest goon. "Go open the gym doors. Tell everyone they're free."

He looked to Benny for permission, to which Benny gave a nod of consent.

The man scurried to carry out her order. When he was done, he came back to Benny's side like a loyal dog. A few minutes later, the first of the refugees staggered out of the gym. Two men and a woman.

"Come over here," Colleen called. "Take these guns."

They were hesitant. The two men were much younger than Colleen had first thought, and the woman looked like she could be their mother. Colleen nodded at the guns lying on the ground. "Check to see if any are loaded."

As it turned out, three were. One had been Benny's rifle, and she guessed the other two were from his first and second in command. Apparently he'd only trusted his closest allies with live ammunition.

Colleen felt the ground shift beneath her. She stumbled and caught herself against a locker. Too much blood loss. The men gasped, their eyes fixed on the grenade in her hand. Refugees were pouring into the hallway now, so she had to do something with it before she fainted.

The young man standing next to her held Benny's rifle with confidence. "What now, ma'am?"

*Tell the bad men to go outside.*

"You," she pointed at the tyrants. "Go stand outside."

They kept their guns trained on Benny's people as they filed out of the building to the front of the school.

She struggled to her feet and followed them as the last of Benny's men went outside. She waited until they were far from the building before turning to Liana.

*Throw the grenade. Kill them.*

Colleen looked at Liana. The being standing in front of her wasn't her daughter anymore. Of that, she was sure. Her sweet toddler obviously would not order her mother to slaughter eleven men. Even ones that deserved it. There was a sharpness in Liana's eyes that no child should have. A fierce, predatory intelligence that chilled Colleen through.

*End them.*

She wanted to consider it—they might be mass murderers; it didn't mean she was—but for a moment her body disobeyed her will. Colleen threw the grenade towards Benny and Glen and slammed the door shut.

The explosion shook the building and sent a giant cloud of dust and gore into the clear sky.

It was over. Colleen let herself fall to her knees. She

tried, God how she tried. But she had failed. James was dead. She'd promised to protect Gabriela and Serena and now they'd be alone. Worst of all, they'd be alone with Liana. Her own daughter was...

Colleen closed her eyes. It didn't matter how the dust changed Liana. Nothing mattered anymore.

She took one last gentle breath and let the world slip away forever, ready to embrace James once again.

# JACK

Jack heard an explosion, even over the roar of the truck's engine. It had to be close.

The idea struck him that he should be afraid. He'd seen raiders destroy groups of military convoys before. Just because there were a lot of soldiers with a lot of guns, didn't mean he was *safe*.

Yet there was a peculiar numbness within him that stopped him from feeling anything. The watcher inside his mind pumped more apathy into his system and Jack stopped thinking about fear all together.

Minutes later the convoy came to a stop. A soldier lifted the canvas flap to the back of the truck and announced, "We're at the FEMA camp. Sit tight until we clear the building."

With that, he disappeared.

There were only three other people with him now, two of which huddled together speaking what Jack guessed was Chinese in hushed voices. Jack had never learned it but, somehow, the language seemed familiar. It irritated him, picking at the edges of his consciousness. He needed to get out of the truck.

He stood and made his way to the back of the truck where he lifted the flap.

His stomach churned for just a moment before an unnatural flood of calm swept over him. There were two rows of bodies outside the high school, lying on their stomachs with their arms by their sides. The people lying in front of him had been executed. Jack had no doubt about it. There was a light coating of yellow dust on their bodies, indicating they'd been there a while.

About twenty feet from the main steps was a crater. Wisps of smoke still wafted from it. The concrete around it was blasted away. Beneath it, dark, fresh earth showed through. There were bloody chunks of what Jack guessed were human parts scattered around the impact site.

The soldiers filed into the building. Jack sat down on the bench by the open flap of the truck and watched. Troops circled the building while others investigated the bodies and the crater. After fifteen minutes, soldiers led a handful of people from inside the school. They wore hazmat suits a shade of yellow more intense than the dust. The soldiers settled the newcomers into a nearby troop carrier.

"Where do … they'll … south …"

Jack's head snapped to the Chinese couple. He'd understood some of that.

"Were you speaking English or Chinese just now?" he asked them.

The two looked at him, then at each other, uttering two words before resuming their conversation: "No English."

Insanity was looking like a more plausible answer by the minute. Jack took a deep breath and focused on the scene outside. For the next half hour the soldiers led groups from the high school to the truck.

*Hello? Can you hear me?*

Jack sat up straighter and looked for the source of the voice. It couldn't have been in the truck. It sounded like his own thought, but in a child's voice.

*Yes, I can hear you. Who are you?* Jack thought.

*I'm Liana. You're Jack.*

*Why can I hear you, Liana? How do you know who I am?*

*Why are you in my mind?*

*I don't know. Are you in that truck?*

The truck shuddered to life. Jack shifted and looked at the school again. *I'm here. Are you in that school? Do you want to come with us?*

A pause. *No. I want to stay here. There's something waiting for us here, Jack. You should stay, too. You feel it, don't you?*

Now that he heard the little girl's voice, he recognized a subtle pull on the edge of his mind. It didn't want him to go. It wanted him to stay here in the dust. The feeling had been there a while, but now Jack was strongly aware of it.

He stood and prepared to exit the vehicle at the same time a soldier pulled back the flap.

"We're moving out. Sir," he ordered Jack, "Sit back down."

"Ok," Jack said, and his body obeyed the soldier despite the protest in his mind.

*I feel it. But I can't move. Something is wrong with me. It's....you'll...back...*

The truck was moving away. Jack could do nothing. He wanted to go back to the little girl. He realized then that he wanted to stay in the dust. But his body wouldn't obey his thoughts. He felt too clam, too placid to disobey the soldier's orders.

The little girl's voice faded away.

They drove for hours. Eventually the landscape changed. It was sudden, striking even, through the narrow slit in the canvas flap Jack peered from. One moment they were watching the dusty yellow world fly by and the next they weren't. The dust on their suits quivered, slid off them, and slipped through cracks and into the air behind the truck, particle by particle until there wasn't a speck left in the truck.

A faint itching sensation crossed his skin, like insects crawling over him. In moments, it was gone.

"Jesus Christ," one of the refugees swore. "What the hell just happened?"

"Who cares? It's gone. We're gonna be okay!"

Jack pushed open the flap of the carrier. The verdant colors of southern Washington were a welcome sight. Clouds of yellow dust drifted behind the convoy, already receding into the distance. Jack realized the dust clouds were slowly returning to what he'd heard the soldiers refer to as the DZ.

The convoy passed a checkpoint of soldiers and some kind of camp off the freeway. People were being evacuated from it by the truckload. They drove another hour to a larger camp where there were hundreds of white tents set up on a vacant field. People walked freely; no hazmat suits, no respirators. There were signs posted every twenty feet directing refugees to the nearest safe zone in case of emergencies.

As Jack looked around, he wanted to feel joy. Despite everything he'd been through, he'd made it. But he couldn't feel happy. Something inside stopped him. It kept him numb. Placated.

When the truck came to a stop, the soldiers led them to a processing tent. Groups of three were admitted into a section where they removed their remaining gear. There was little need for precaution as not a particle of dust was to be seen. After Jack gave up his gear—there was a moment of tension when he explained he had a gun and forfeited it to a soldier—he moved into another section where a woman with a clipboard asked for his name, date of birth, and place of residence. She didn't look at him once, eager to process as quickly as she could.

He thought the interview was over, but then she then

asked, "Have you come in contact with the dust?"

Jack nodded and said he had. His hand went to his face where he expected to find the slick texture of his rash. To his surprise, it wasn't there. The skin was healed. "Yes. I'm okay now, though. It was red and itchy, but it seems healed now."

The woman lowered her clipboard and finally looked at Jack. Her brows were knitted together. It took him a moment to realize she wasn't looking into his eyes, but *at* them. "Have you experienced hallucinations of symbols or strange images, or seen any bright lights?"

"Yes, all of those," Jack answered. "I thought I was crazy."

She smiled. It was the fake kind of sympathy doctors gave when they had bad news. She clicked the radio on her shoulder.

"Miranda here. I have another one."

# CRAIG

Craig had never known a fear as pure and cold as when he heard the whispering. For a split second he was paralyzed. He wanted to scream for help, but his voice was caught in his throat. His heartbeat fluttered wildly.

"Turn around. Do not fear us."

His body shook, but he obeyed. His legs threatened to give out beneath him. When he faced the DZ, he saw nothing.

The dust shifted. Tendrils of it crawled up from the ground, twisting and compressing as they began to form a shape. In seconds, a humanoid figure stood before him. Its face was that of a mannequin, smooth and unremarkable. The dust quivered as the figure began to move. It walked strangely, the gait stilted. Unpracticed. When it spoke, its tone diplomatic and smooth, Craig heard the sound all around him. The thing's mouth didn't move.

"You have questions. We will answer them all in due time." The figure stopped. It looked at its hand and made a fist, then released it. "What is most critical for you to understand now is that we are here on a mission that will benefit both our species and yours. If you cooperate."

A flash of outrage and anger dimmed his fear and Craig found the courage to speak. "You're killing us. You do realize that, don't you?"

"We've studied you; you are a scientist," the entity remarked, pausing to stare directly at him. Or at least stare as much as an eyeless mannequin could. "Surely you understand the pursuit of knowledge sometimes comes with loss."

"I don't believe you. It didn't have to be this way," Craig argued, feeling bolder still. "You're smart enough to create nanotechnology. Smart enough to travel who knows how many light years through the vastness of space. And you're telling me there was no way to avoid colliding with our planet and *mass murdering us*?"

He thought of the bloodied and dying refugees he'd seen; of the massive destruction the comet caused over the Pacific Northwest. But that wasn't the only devastation the comet had caused. Not when he added the collapse of humanity before the comet hit.

When the figure didn't respond, Craig pressed forward.

"Do you have any idea what happened when your comet—or ship, or whatever the fuck it is—changed course for us? How—"

"Cease your wailing, human."

At that, Craig was reminded exactly what he was dealing with. While his fear had abated, he needed to put his usual snarky self in check. "I apologize. Please tell me what you want."

"A ship traveled here with us. Consider it a stowaway. We want you to locate and destroy it. It has defenses we cannot penetrate and it does not belong here." It paused. "Know that this stowaway interferes with our plans in a way that causes your species profound suffering. Were we not limited by this interference, the process would be much less painful. It is truly in your best interest to help."

The figure started to pace again while it spoke. It grew larger and smaller in size, altering its shape from male to female and then back to an androgynous body. Still, it remained inside the DZ, giving Craig some semblance of security.

Craig swore under his breath. Stowaway? Was it another dust entity or another species of alien? Regardless, at least it provided some kind of bargaining chip. The enemy of your enemy is your friend, according to Sun Tzu. Of course, he hadn't been talking about aliens or intelligent clouds of dust.

"Say we destroy it. Then what?"

"Then, once you destroy your pitiful incinerators, we will begin to answer whatever questions you may have. Of life beyond Earth, of our technology. Whatever you wish."

Craig glanced at the camp. Jesus, he shouldn't be doing this alone. First contact with an alien species shouldn't be up to one man. He'd already made it angry and he'd been speaking to it for only a few minutes. What would Tim say? Or Siyang?

"We see your hesitance. We knew you would not want to help us willingly. According to our current count, there are three million people still alive inside our walls."

"Please, don't…" Craig began, sensing where it was headed.

"If you disobey, we will kill every one of them. We assure you their deaths will be painful."

"You're a monster!"

"We are that and more." The figure drifted closer to the edge of the DZ. "Now, Dr. Craig Peters, do you accept?"

From their conversation thus far, it was obvious the alien had no qualms about what it had done to humans. Whatever plan it had, it wasn't win-win. The dust was a terrorist, pure and simple. Hell, it even had hostages. This was the worst case scenario: an alien species intent on a hostile takeover of their planet.

He needed more time. That left him with only one option that he could see. Agree to the entity's demands for now and reconvene with higher powers.

"Yes," Craig answered. "I think I can call off the incinerators. I'll see what I can do about the ship."

The one thing that gave Craig any hope—the force field—disappeared as the figure stepped over the precise line of the DZ and walked to Craig. With each step a ghost of its body was left behind. By the time it stood five feet in front of him, it was nearly transparent. Particles lazily drifted back to the DZ.

"Understand this. The fate of your species is in your hands," the ghostly figure said as it faded. "This is a kindness not all are given. Do not squander it."

Craig stood and watched until he was sure the thing was gone. It had been baiting him, messing with his head, but it had also been telling the truth. The future of the human race was in his hands, and he had no idea if he was up to the task. He ran, barefoot, back to the lights of the camp, while behind him the dust swirled and eddied, watching and waiting for his return.

# ACKNOWLEDGMENTS

Thank you so much for reading! Please consider taking a quick minute to leave a review. I work full time in the videogame industry and pursue writing as a passion. Seeing reviews on my books helps give me a boost to come home from work and keep on writing more, and also lets me know there is an audience for what I'm creating.

Now, for the rest of the acknowledgments!

The Dust of Dawn was one of the most challenging books I've written. I wrote the entire first draft in two months in 2015 and from there it went through more revisions and editing than I could count until it became the story I truly wanted it to be.

I would like to thank many people who were critical in helping this book become what it is. First, Jonathan Lambert and Nicholas Sansbury Smith. Thank you for reading, letting me bounce ideas off you, and helping me craft one of my best novels yet. Without your help, I don't think I could've gotten through this one.

A huge thanks to my focus group who came in and helped me put that last bit of polish on the book. Thank you for your support and encouragement.

Thank you to all my readers who waited patiently while I took forever to write another full length novel, and for your constant support and encouragement. You guys are the best!

# ABOUT THE AUTHOR

Eloise J. Knapp hails from Seattle and never complains about the rain. She works in the video game industry by day, and is a graphic designer and author by night. When not writing you'll find her hiking the Pacific Northwest or cooking something delicious.

Learn more about Eloise's writing at www.EloiseJKnapp.com.

**Other books by Eloise:**
ANAMNESIS
Pulse: Genesis
Pulse: Retaliation
The Undead Ruins
The Undead Haze
The Undead Situation

Made in the USA
Columbia, SC
21 December 2018